Bixby Timmons
And
The Snowenwood Rennen

Bixby Timmons Book III

By

Dwight D. Karkan

A Tiny Fox Press Book

ISBN: 978-1-946501-67-7
Library of Congress Control Number: 2023952232

Tiny Fox Press and the book fox logo are all registered trademarks of Tiny Fox Press LLC

Tiny Fox Press LLC
Parrish, FL

This book is for those who have disciplined the Leviathan in them to destroy fear with love.

Brave is a funny word as it only exists in the face of fear. You and I were not designed for fear. However, sometimes we have to see the darkest pits to realize that what lives inside some of us is the scariest thing on the planet: the leviathan called perfect love.

Though the scars of battle still boast a memory, they are worn as a prized possession of the places to which we will never return.

Darkness has no place in my life because of the Leviathans of faith around me. I daily thank God for my family: Amber, Selah, Delaney, Theo, Zoe and Greta.

For the men and women who stand ready for battle with me: Adam, Paul, Shane, Wes, Will, David, Jon, Zach, Dean, Kenny, Rich, Chuck, Sheldon, Brent, Emily, Heather, Barbie, Amberly, Katelyn, Liz, Sam, Kathy, Suzie, Seth Holmes, my young adult small group, and the staff at OC.

For my parents, David and Mary. And last but certainly not least is Galen and the team at Tiny Fox Press who poured so much energy into making this book pop!

Never Stop Seeking Great Adventure!

Light Voids The Darkness.

It Only Takes A Spark.

Strike True.

Chapter One
In Too Deep

The cold water rose to just past Bixby's ankle as she ripped it from the liquid's icy grips and put it up onto the next foothold. Sweat streamed down her face as she frantically searched for the next place to grasp. She had been climbing feverishly for almost twenty minutes, and the finish line was only meters away. Her eyes darted side-to-side, panicked. Her mind was split between the hypothermic water that was creeping up below her and the desperation to find the next hand hold in the rock to pull her up on. All the while she was taunted by her nemesis from above her who wanted nothing more than to see her fail. If she made it all the way to the summit, he would definitely attempt to fling her off the edge.

Think, Bixby! she screamed inside her head.

"Give up, Bixby. It's all over for you," Wesley said in his sniveling voice while a gigantic grin rippled across his face.

Bixby's heart was racing because the dark blue water had again snagged ahold of her foot and moved up past her calf. She was flustered at the banter from above and the idea of losing was clouding her focus. Her whole body started to shiver.

"Why do you keep going, Bixby? You never belonged here in the first place," his badgering continued. "Simply let go and you get your family back. You get to go home to your big house with your silly little friends, and you can live out your life. The only price you will have to pay is a little bruise to your ego, knowing that I won," Wesley said in his detestably wicked voice.

The water was up to Bixby's waist and her body was going numb. Her fingers started to tremble from the frosty chill that ran up and down her spine. She pulled herself close to the wall and began to grimace. Slowly the water reached her ribs as she clung to the handhold. Her mind was no longer there on the side of the cliff, but with her family sitting around the fireplace back at Pinnacle Manor.

Her father was on the floor wrestling with her twin brothers. He was home a lot more because Dragonthorp Inc. recognized and respected him for his genius mind. The boys were rough and tumbly, growing by leaps and bounds every day. By now they were babbling fake words and carrying pretend conversations in toddler gibberish. Her mother was stealing treats from the snack cart that she was keeping well stocked. She had taken up a new hobby of livestreaming herself trying new baking recipes and rating them on how easy the treat was to make for a beginner, the taste, and of course her baking blunders. That gave Miss Marmalade time to take her new upgrades for a spin. She had been practicing her own food combinations, as well as doing online classes for just about everything the Timmons Nation wanted to watch. The only time she stopped was to charge. With such a delectable, new adventure every night, Bixby had cut back on her turkey, cheese, and hot-sauce sandwiches to save room for the next food exploration. Hucklebee was writing his own jokes now that he had an upgraded system that allowed him to think freely for himself. His goal in life was to become a stand-up comedian and was really getting the knack for it.

Though it had been several years since Grandpa passed, it was Bixby's daydream to escape the reality of her situation. She could insert her favorite person in the whole world at the base of the Great Hall's fireplace, explaining a puzzle to her if she wanted to; so, she did. Every day that went by she thought of all of them. She wanted nothing more than to be there in the memory that she was creating of her family, as the icy water had passed her shoulders.

In the Command Center that was set up in the den at Pinnacle Manor, in real time, Bixby's team stood staring at the screen blankly.

"Should we cut the live feed?" Bixby's closest friend, Tipton, asked the room of teammates.

"The feed has quadrupled in size in the last two minutes," Pippa replied, bustling from monitor to monitor. Because she had given aide to Bixby in Level Two, the only safe place for Pippa and her grandfather was inside the walls of Pinnacle Manor. She was the queen of misfit hackers and newest ally to Bixby. Her secret society of I.T. geniuses and tech wizards, known as the Timmons Nation, log into the live feed from all over the world. Each person watching donated twenty-five cents each day they logged in to watch Bixby solve her morning puzzle. The small donation kept them personally entertained and provided the orphans of Pinnacle Manor some income for their day-to-day needs. Today's simulation was like none they had ever seen before, and the buzz was spreading fast.

Marin had settled into her role as strategist on the team after sacrificing herself in Level Two so that Bixby was guaranteed to compete in Level Three. She was leaning forward in her chair in the corner of the Command Center, because for the first time in a long time she was baffled by what Bixby was doing. Her only assessment of the simulation was to ask, "Did Bixby just... give up?"

Nobody could be sure just yet, so silence thickly hovered over the room like a dense fog.

At this point Bixby's head was tilted back and the only thing exposed was the cap of her face barely above the water as the darkness had encased itself around her like a blanket.

For a moment Bixby felt as if she was floating weightlessly in space. The voice of her agitator was gone. Her body had gone completely senseless. She could see, hear, smell, feel, taste... nothing. She had fully cleared the mechanism of her mind. She knew everyone was expecting her to shoot out of the water and make some dramatic climb to the top of the cliff and win the day...

Not today, her brain told her through the nothingness. She learned to embrace defeat. The weight of the world had finally crushed her below its tremendous thumb. She *had* finally broken.

I could get used to numb. Her thoughts continued to weigh options.

In Too Deep

It had been over a year since Bixby was duped into going to Shadow Deep for the Second Level of Cody Dragonthorp's Riddle, and nearly two since she signed a piece of paper agreeing to Cody Dragonthorp's terms. Before Pinnacle Manor she was a simple girl who was content with her life. Her parents may not have spent as much time as she wanted with her, but they were there if she needed them. It was more than she could say for some of her less fortunate friends back in Snagleyville. Many of them had parents who were driven to hollow home lives and even full-on brokenness. To make ends meet, many of her friend's parents both worked exhausting hours, money was tight, and fighting was inevitable. Somehow her family was able to circumvent those stresses. Even though her life seemed mundane, to those who were looking in, Bixby's life was something to be envied. She hadn't come to that realization of how truly spectacular her life really had been until those moments of tenderness were ripped away from her during Level Two. She was mad at everyone for the emotions she lived with day-in and day-out, but she hid them well, making her more and more bitter as each day passed.

Since moving to Pinnacle she had been an outcast in her school, despised by any sort of authority figure, betrayed, beaten up multiple times, her family was missing, seen unspeakable acts of hate, and in each level, they tried to trap her inside.

Doesn't matter, she thought, pushing everything aside.

In that moment of letting go, she felt free of all the pressure that came with signing her name and taking on the task of finding Cody Dragonthorp; the weight simply shed away from her consciousness.

Why was it so much work to do the right thing? she asked herself as she floated in void.

People who were close to her stood staring dumbfoundedly at the Holo-TV. In the past they had watched Bixby brilliantly survive riddles, dangers, and foes time and time again. The entire Timmons Nation sat speechless as they witnessed something they had never seen before; Bixby surrendered to a riddle. A coldness rang out though the world as fringed as the waters that Bixby now floated in. The Holo-Simulation that Harvey created had finally run its course. Nobody spoke a word as they looked on at Bixby hovering motionless as the water continued to rise to the ceiling.

As the simulations turned off, Bixby found herself lying in the middle of a dark Launch Room still staring at the grey ceiling. After about five minutes of motionlessness, Bixby sat up and climbed to her feet. She softly placed her hand on the latch to open the door as it let out a hiss signaling everyone who was loitering outside to hide. Nobody wanted to be the first one to engage Bixby. It was unspoken and understood that when this moment came that Bixby was going to have to figure out where she stood on her own. The onlookers hurriedly disappeared into doorways adjacent to the Great Hall as she made her way sluggishly through the grand living space. Once down the bedroom corridor and into the refuge of her private quarters, everyone regrouped in front of the towering mantle that was now crackling with a small fire. All eyes were now squarely resting on the creator of the simulation that had brought Bixby to her preverbal knees.

"She has been through more than any of us could ever imagine, and we would be stupid to think this day wouldn't come," said Harvey in a somber Scottish accented voice from the back of the room.

For a brief time after Level Two, everyone feared Harvey was gone forever. Thanks to the quick thinking of her parents, before they were taken, and Harvey himself, Bixby had the blueprints to give to Pippa and the Timmons Nation. They began to rebuild Harvey the day after Bixby finished Level Two. With the help of the Timmon's Nation and Tipton's brilliant creative mind, her team were not only able to rebuild Harvey and the H-Bots, they were also able to make them independent from Holo.

"She seemed fine when she ghosted in," Tipton replied.

Bixby could hear his comment through her earpiece. What he didn't know was she was fine, until she wasn't: it came and went.

"And her Ghost-Suit is working fine," Pippa added as she reviewed the new gear Bixby was wearing.

"Ghost is done, and Level Three hasn't started. Let's cut her some slack," Marin said to the group.

"Marin is correct. Let's see what she does," Harvey added.

Bixby put her head on her bedroom door as she latched it closed and slumped down against it. Her friends' conversation sparked a memory of Cody when he interjected himself into Shadow Deep as a little boy to let her know that everything in the virtual world of Holo had been compromised by Dragonthorp Inc. Her mind meandered over the brilliant creation of Ghosting.

When Tipton had proposed the idea to her it seemed so very complex, but Tipton had the best way of dumbing it down for her.

She could hear him explaining it to her the very first time in her mind, "You're going to put on a Holo-Riddle Suit with all the pain and pleasure sensors turned on so you can feel everything. I have also added the technology from your dad's gloves so that you can feel holograms..."

"Why do I need to feel holograms inside Holo?" Bixby asked sharply.

"Because you are going to launch from one launch room into a second launch room as a hologram, and *then* we will launch you into Holo from the second room. You will be a hologram inside a massive hologram program and will need to feel the world around you."

"I'm sure there is a point to the extra step?" Bixby replied skeptically.

"Remember when Hemsley launched into Level Two without being detected by... pretty much anyone unless they could physically see him?" Tipton asked, handing Bixby her new Ghost-Suit.

"Yeah," she replied, still following.

"Unless Dragonthorp Inc. has eyes directly on you in Holo, they can't digitally find a hologram inside of Holo," Tipton said with a smirk at his brilliance even though the original idea was Pippa's.

Bixby had to laugh thinking back to the guards of Shadow Deep trying to tackle Hemsley. Each guard outstretched their arms to catch him, and as they fell through his hologram, she spoke his snarky response out loud, "Ghost."

It was how Tipton chose the name Ghosting. Dragonthorp Inc. had no way of tracking a hologram inside of a holographic program, while everyone at Pinnacle Manor could experience all of Holo without fear of being tracked or hacked.

This kind of technology was one of a kind, with endless possibilities. But for right now it was only to be known by the people inside Pinnacle Manor. It was their only hope to help Bixby get into Level Three without Dragonthorp Inc. compromising them.

"She's never acted like this before," Tipton said, snapping Bixby back from the thoughts of how Ghosting started. The comment caught her attention because, again, he was correct.

For a brief period after her family went missing, during the development phase of the Holo-Ghost Program, Bixby was able to bury her emotions in the creation process. However, now that Holo-Ghost was alive and exceeding expectations, her mind had begun to wander back to the reality that her family was still gone, and the start of Level Three still remained a mysterious cloud of questions hovering over her head.

Ghosting had done one more peculiar thing for Pinnacle Manor. Harvey was no longer Artificial Intelligence bound to a house that he digitally controlled and paraded around in as a hologram. Pippa and the Timmons Nation had upgraded an H-bot to look identical to Harvey's projected self. They fused together the H-bot world and House Holosystem into one supercomputer that could interact with the world around him. He was now both digital house system that could shift everything around as needed at Pinnacle Manor on a whim as he was a tangible Artificial Intelligence H-bot. Dragonthorp Inc. couldn't steal a system that fluidly moved from house system to H-bot or both at the same time.

"What should we do, Harvey?" Pippa asked genuinely. Bixby listened intently to his answer over her intercom.

"Be ready. The Leviathan that she promised has just been fully awakened, and we need to be there to help her control it, or I fear it may destroy more than just her," Harvey said somberly as the sun began to break through the darkness over Worthy Lake.

"You have no idea," Bixby said to the emptiness of her room.

Chapter Two
Don't Let Them See

The clasp of Bixby's bedroom door clacked as a small rap on the wood broke the stillness. Bixby sat on the edge of her bed staring through her wall into another world. She said nothing as the slender figure of an old Scotsman slowly slipped in and closed the door behind him.

Bixby's hair, still wet from the simulation, dripped down on the blankets she had wrapped around her. Her eyes were permanently painted with the dark shadows of exhaustion. She hadn't slept a whole night without a night terror about her family since they were taken. She didn't want visitors, but she was so lost in emptiness that she didn't have the energy to tell Harvey to go away. He strolled over to her bookcases where Cody Dragonthorp's solved puzzle boxes sat on the shelves.

"Can't believe Hucklebee got these put back together," he whispered at the painstaking detail he had put into rebuilding each puzzle to their exact form. Harvey stooped down to peer at one of the puzzle boxes that looked like a small dog. The enigma was in honor of Cody's dog, Bucksberry. He rocked back and forth to marvel at the stunning ornateness of the rebuilt relic as minutes passed; neither of them wanted to breach the silence, but it needed done. "If only we didn't figure this silly little contraption out, huh?" he pondered aloud.

The thought had crossed Bixby's mind a million times as anger welled up in her, but she held her piercing stare through the wall. He was a program. He had no idea what it meant to lose his entire sense of purpose in life. He couldn't compute what it was like to hurt as bad as she did. He could never answer the question, *Why was it taking Cody so long to start the Third Level of his Riddle?* He could try to answer her with some sort of computed logic, but he would never feel the desperation and painful longing of *needing* that answer but only getting silence. Therefore, she would not engage his game of charades.

Knowing that his approach was futile, he cut straight to his point, "I want more than anything to help you solve these puzzles and bring your family home. There is not a day that goes by that I wish I could ask Cody why he was hosting this digital conundrum."

Bixby's attention was suddenly focused. This was the first time Harvey had ever called Cody Dragonthorp by any other name except the Grand Master.

"But I realized something, Bixby; these games wouldn't be so bad if it wasn't for the people inside the game with you. Every morning you wake up and effortlessly disassemble every challenge we throw at you. Which leads me to believe that the enemy is not Cody's riddles."

There it was again...

"The enemy is greed, hate, social judgement, secrets, and the power that comes by keeping those hidden truths. We know that Cody has something that he wants so desperately to tell, but for whatever reason he can't. We can speculate on whether it's Cody's autism or..." Harvey paused to think of a wild scenario. "...or maybe he had to sign some sort of nondisclosure agreement. Whatever may be, I believe he has made it clear that he has chosen you to discover whatever he is hiding," Harvey said, putting the puzzle box back on her shelf and making his way to the door. He stopped as he unlatched the door's handle.

"I didn't make these mini Holo-Simulations to hurt you. I made them to train and protect you against those who wish to hurt you while in the real riddle," he finished.

Bixby only slumped her head in response.

"Then I shall leave you to your thoughts, but please make sure you come back from them," he said somberly before he slipped out the door.

Bixby's gaze never wavered, but she knew he had good intentions. Harvey, keeping to his promise to prepare her, had pushed her to the brink of collapse more times than she could count. She had wobbled on the edge of defeat for months now, but each time she somehow found a way to overcome. Today her body finally broke, which let her mind wander into uncharted territories. Oddly enough, it felt good to give into the demands of her agitators and simply give up. Now that she had time to reflect though, giving in was so much more bruising to her morale than the times she hadn't given up: failure hurt much more mentally than physically. Bixby stood up and began to dry her hair with a towel. As she finished, she stopped, catching her reflection in the mirror. She was no longer the little girl that she was when she moved into this room. She had grown a few more inches in the few years. What struck her though was that she ceased to have the average, brittle, physique she used to. She was strong both in gaze and stature; the miles had sharpened her overall appearance. Bixby wasn't sure if it was the multiple years of growing up, or the two hours before breakfast each day spent in one of Harvey's simulations that caused the change, but she had a suspicion that both had something to do with the powerful young woman that was staring back at her.

"Every day I have to wait, the more numb I feel to the pain," she said aloud. She knew he had left the room, but because he was the house system, he still heard her.

Bixby had more than once stood alone in the hidden library, in the place she had accepted Cody's offer and screamed into the void, "I quit Cody! Do you hear me? I quit! Give me my family back!" The darkness only stared back at her without granting her wish. However, she also had moments where the thought of her dad telling her to keep going before his message was cut off stirred deep passion and desire to find out what he knew.

While brushing her hair it reminded Bixby of how much her dad loved her thick red curls as she tried untangling all the curly knots with her brush. She missed his talks about him and grandpa deeply, but she forced herself not to linger on the subject too long for fear of it turning back to a weakness. With a blink of the deep green eyes looking back at her, Bixby erased the longing of her family from her mind. She had finally felt the sting of defeat and she knew that she despised how it made her feel. She quickly slipped back into her Ghost-Suit, took a deep breath, and set off toward the kitchen in haste.

"She's coming," Bixby overheard Miss Marmalade say from the kitchen before anyone was able to see her approach.

Everyone ducked their heads into their plates of French toast that Miss Marmalade had whipped up in an attempt not to make eye contact. As good as they smelled in passing, Bixby made an abrupt turn for the Ghost-Rooms.

"School doesn't start for another thirty minutes," Tipton announced to the large group of people around the table whose gaze followed Bixby's course change.

Hastily exchanging glances, everyone dashed out of the kitchen to see what she was up to.

Even though Tipton had made little adjustment to his appearance in the last year, he was the first one out the door with a plate of French toast in hand.

"Wait for me, Bear," he heard Pippa shout from behind him. She had been officially his girlfriend for almost a year now, but he was still clumsy in etiquette when it came to girls and letting them go before him. This time she had fallen behind because she paused to put her fingerless gloves on and rewrap her suede scarf over her shoulder. She had tamed down her blend of gothic comic book nerd phase to something more modern nerd hipster—thick rimmed glasses with earth tones and crystals.

"Sorry about that," Hucklebee blurted out as he was hot on the tale of Pippa and nearly ran her over. His clumsiness had yet to improve even though Harvey tried to fix it in his H-bot programing. Somehow, Cody Dragonthorp had hidden Hucklebee's individualized personality traits so well that it was pointless to try and tamper with his creations.

"What is it with this house and all the running around?" Marin said, pushing herself slowly away from the table with a small groan. She took a more modest pace towards the launch room, walking with a bit of a limp as the pins in her leg, courtesy of Mad Maggie in Level Two, still gave her fits in the morning. After the incident, Marin was able to convince her parents that Pinnacle Manor was the safest place for her under the security of Arthur and the newly rebuilt Harvey system. It was also her only chance at helping Bixby while getting a high-level education now that the General had kicked them out of Plumberry Isle. With some hesitation, they agreed to let her go while they moved in with Marin's aging grandparents, under the stipulation that she met them in Holo every night. Marin never missed her time in the Ghost Room with them knowing what some people in the Riddle have given up moving forward.

"What is she doing?" Tipton asked as he slid into his plush chair, pulling the monitor attached to his head rest in front of him.

"She is going to climb again," Mr. Richards said from the shadowed corner of the command center.

The somewhat ghoulish voice right behind him made Tipton flinch so bad that he smacked his face on the newly positioned monitor.

"I hate when you do that!" Tipton blurted out at the old man with freakishly wild hair who was now sipping coffee in a chair. He was new to Pinnacle Manor as a plus-one, courtesy of Pippa. Nobody ever saw Max Richards unless he wanted to be seen, and normally he showed up when least expected.

"Grandpa, why do you do that to him?" Pippa asked, already knowing that he loved, more than anything, to pick on Tipton.

"Control your grandpa," Tipton insisted, trying to regain his composure.

"Oh, stop it, you big baby. He's harmless," Pippa jested playfully, swatting Tipton on the arm to try and defend her grandpa, but also playfully enough to give Tipton some attention.

Grandpa Richards needed Pippa as much as Pippa needed him in the absence of her parents. Now that Pippa was blacklisted at Dragonthorp Inc., so was he. Mr. Richards had spent nearly his whole life writing code for them, but he seemed to be having fun working with Harvey on the daily challenges. Bixby had grown up solving many of Mr. Richard's early puzzles and riddles as well as the ones in Holo-Basic created by him. To Bixby, it was like having a celebrity in the Manor, even though he only came out from time to time when things got interesting; this morning's incident was most fascinating to him.

"Good to see you, Gramps," Marin said, giving Mr. Richards a fist bump as she strolled in.

"I got him really good," Mr. Richards said in his slapstick voice that made him sound as crazy as he looked.

"Aww, sorry I missed it. Stupid bum leg," she said, taking her place.

"I'll wait for you to be in the room next time, deary," he said with a cackle. Marin didn't mind the pet name, because it was nice to have someone around who loved teasing Tipton as much as she did. Plus, he had helped convince her parents that he would look after her while at Pinnacle Manor and even faked a heart attack at the hospital Marin was stuck in so that Pippa could spring her out the service doors past the nurses and the Dragonthorp Inc. guards. He was brilliant, resourceful, and Marin loved his kookiness.

"She *is* going to climb again," Tipton blurted out, looking at his screen that showed the simulation reloading.

"Seriously, my boy. You didn't figure that out until now?" Mr. Richards asked, sipping his coffee surprised that Tipton really had any doubt as to Bixby's intentions.

As he spoke Bixby had launched the program just as Mr. Richards predicted and was quickly scaling the wall.

"Bixby, if you make it to the top, I am going to push you off!" shouted the hologram of Wesley. "You will never finish this level!"

"Harvey, I think Bixby has purposely turned off her communications," Pippa said as she did a scan of Bixby's newly developed hear-back device. The team was sure that Wesley and Greg now knew about the communication coin, and the Tako earrings that Tipton had developed for the previous two levels, and their ability to transmit. That meant that they also knew how to sever the connection. So, Tipton had to come up with a version 3.0 to keep them guessing, but he had yet to put in an override. Bixby had exploited that error and shut everyone out.

"Leviathan," Harvey said, now standing in the corner next to Mr. Richards with a bit of a smirk. Pippa realized that neither Harvey nor her grandpa were going to help them, just like nobody was going to help them in Level Three. She sat back and began slamming away at her keyboard trying to override the system. Marin was good at strategy, and so she began analyzing how Bixby could neutralize Wesley at the top.

Tipton was wiping the syrup from his hands and doing data analysis. How fast was the water rising? What was the distance to the top? What was the cave size and the volume of water it could hold? How cold was the water temperature? How long a person could survive in water that cold? Etcetera.

Bixby raced up the side of the rock wall never letting the killer liquid get anywhere close to reaching her as she neared the top of the overhang. Wesley was there to grab her arm and fling her away from the ledge into the frigid doom. Reaching down, his firm hand grabbed her wrist. Bixby had planned for this and immediately turned her grip from the side of the ledge to Wesley's wrist. She let her body go limp as she squeezed with all her might. She could see the panic wash over his face. From the ledge, she and Wesley tumbled down into the icy abyss below.

"What is she doing?" Marin asked, quietly trying to figure out her strategy.

Harvey pushed off from the wall wondering the same thing. It was rare that Bixby had even the creators of the challenge pondering her next move.

Once in the frigid waters below, Bixby wrapped her legs around Wesley's torso and held on to his neck as he flailed in order to keep them both afloat. He said nothing as he splashed around with Bixby on his back. She was certain that Harvey hadn't written a program scripted for a scenario like this one.

"Has she gone mad?" Pippa shouted as she stopped typing and was now watching what looked like Bixby trying to drown Wesley on the Holo-TV.

"I think you pushed the Leviathan too far, Harvey," Tipton interjected.

The liquid was now well above the ledge and both Bixby and Wesley's extremities were about to go numb which would most certainly lead to an unfortunate end to both of them. There were now only a few inches of air left between the ceiling and the enclosed rock ceiling above.

"Nice try, Harvey," she shouted, gasping one last gigantic breath with Wesley still in her clutches. They both disappeared under the glacial water.

"I can't watch," Hucklebee squeaked from the corner where he cowered in fright.

"Did she just...!?" Tipton shouted as he looked back at Harvey and Mr. Richards.

Neither one of them moved from their position.

"Turn it off, Arthur!" Pippa shouted at the Bulldog who stood fast in his place in the corner. He was the only one who could override the system in case of an emergency.

Confused, even Marin sat back in her chair to figure out what had just happened. Everyone in a Command Center chair was afraid to say it, but it just looked like Bixby had failed the test on purpose, drowning herself and Wesley.

Just then the Command Center door slid open, and a drenched Bixby Timmons strolled into the room smiling at everyone inside.

"BIXBY TIMMONS!" Pippa shouted at her. "What were you thinking?"

"What do you mean?" Bixby questioned.

"Uhhh, you just drowned yourself and Wesley in a simulation!" she replied angrily.

"I have to agree with Pippa on this one, Bixby. That was a pretty disturbing thing to watch," Marin added, not completely convinced she knew what just happened.

Bixby smirked at their confusion. "I solved the puzzle, didn't I?"

Dumbfounded, the teens in the Command Center looked at each other quizzically and then over to Arthur who was in charge of running the simulations.

Without being able to hold his emotions any longer Mr. Richards piped up.

"Do tell, when was it that you figured it out?" he asked like a schoolboy who had stumped a teacher.

"The first time I climbed..." Bixby paused, searching for her words carefully. "... I got distracted," she continued. "But this time, after racing up the wall, I was able to take a second look around and saw the pressure switch above the exit door. Knowing it was there, it was easy to deduce that the water pressure would be needed to activate it," she said.

"I knew if we didn't add a disturbance in the climb somehow, you would have seen it right away," Mr. Richards gloated. Everyone knew that Wesley wasn't the distraction she was talking about, but nobody else said a word.

"Thank you. He was a very nice floaty," Bixby said sarcastically, knowing it was still an uncomfortable thing she had done.

"So, why did you not climb up to the dead end and wait for the water to rise over the door and swim out?" Tipton inquired to which Bixby chuckled.

"No really, Bixby. That was really hard to watch," Pippa replied to her indifference.

"Come on, you guys. It is a fake Wesley in a fake scenario. I was just trying to have a little fun. I could see the rocks slide away as light started to emit from the adjacent room when the switch activated," she said slyly.

"Then why did you go and raise all of our heart rates?" Tipton shouted still confused.

"It was *sooo* much more fun that way," Bixby proclaimed. She could see that nobody approved of her stunt, so instead of apologizing she chose to turn and walk out of the Command Center.

Marin sat back in her chair and pondered Bixby's cleverness. In a way the two of them had a very similar, twisted sense of humor, but Bixby's climb had triggered red flags even for her.

"I'm not going to be able to focus at school today," Tipton complained.

"Now that you mentioned it, Tipton, you all need to make your way to your Launch Rooms presently," Arthur said, looking at his watch.

"You three created this monster," Tipton said to Harvey, Mr. Richards, and Arthur as he stomped out of the room to get his Ghost-Suit on.

Holo-School Prime and Headmaster Gabhammer awaited them all.

CHAPTER THREE
IN THE HOT SEAT

The only reason Bixby attended school was to keep up the appearance that everything was fine at Pinnacle Manor. Last thing she needed was to have a nosey school social worker come by and find out that she was practically raising herself. Showing up was the only effort she decided to give Gabhammer anymore.

Normally, all students would launch into their seats in homeroom, but today, Bixby, Tipton, Marin, and Pippa found themselves seated directly in front of Headmaster Gabhammer's Holo-Desk. He was standing next to the window in his usual pose: grouchy wrinkled face, hands firmly clasped behind his back, and dressed in one of his finest Pedrodean suits. Normally, Bixby tried to stay as far away from Gabhammer as possible, but when he launched you directly into his office there wasn't even the remote possibility of unlaunching until he had spoken with you.

A hush filled the room for a good minute until Tipton braved the stillness. "Um, sir?"

"Silence, Mr. Ellerby, while I contemplate what to do with the four of you rodents," Gabhammer snarled.

"Hey!" Bixby shouted, standing up for herself and her friends with fresh abandon for rules and authority.

"I SAID SILENCE!" he growled as he darted from the window, slamming his fist into his desk with a gargantuan thud that took even Bixby's confidence down a peg. The sheer force of his voice jolted Bixby back a step. She, however, did not waver in her contempt for his words and stepped back in to meet his gaze.

"Please, have a seat," Headmaster Gabhammer said in a calmer tone as he reached up and started rubbing his head. He properly sat down first in his oversized leather office chair, opened a drawer, pulled out a jar of aspirin, and made two of them disappear down his gullet. Bixby felt invigorated to have just gone toe-to-toe with Gabhammer and not to have been suspended for her outburst.

"The four of you continue to give me a constant migraine. Since I know that you *children*..." He paused to make sure he emphasized the word 'children,' "...have no respect for authority."

Bixby sat forward, ready to argue back against him, but before she could he pushed through his sentence, "...and will ask me, 'What could you possibly mean Headmaster Gabhammer? We are sweet angels sent from above to save the world,' I will tell you why I have a headache... and then I will come up with a way to stop you from continuing to be a thorn in my side."

He reached into another drawer and pulled out two manila folders. Opening them on his desk he faced them towards the foursome who sat in front of him.

"This folder contains a list of the students that have transferred out of my once fine and upstanding Holo-School Prime," he said, pointing to the list of names.

Bixby looked down at the compilation of students. Her eye immediately found the names of the Daggers, and most of the students who were either friends with Wesley and Penny Dagger, or students whose families had important roles with Dragonthorp Inc. Next to each of their names was a listing that ranked each of them in the Business Draft. Wesley was a number one draft pick, and the rest of the students were not too shabby themselves. Most of them were in the top one hundred draftees if not top fifty. She was perplexed as to why he was divulging student information, but before she could say something he began to grumble.

"I have limited staffing and a painfully small budget with all these students going to another school," he said, sitting back in his chair, persistently to rub his forehead before he continued. "Everyone connected to the executive branch of Dragonthorp Inc. has followed the Daggers out the door."

Bixby was intensely trying to scan the sheets while he was distracted by his headache, but her temper got the best of her as she passed several of the names who regularly bullied her.

"Good riddance," Bixby said without looking up at Gabhammer.

Gabhammer refocused his attention and frowned at her as she said, "I'm certain there is a waitlist a mile long to attend the school that Bixby Timmons goes to." Her comment was so arrogant and cocky that even Tipton turned to her in astonishment.

"As much as I hate agreeing with you, Bixby, our waitlist is indeed extremely competitive currently because of the high standards we put on education, but everyone on that list will need assistance, and I can't pay the bills without people paying their full tuition," Gabhammer said, trying to give it a different spin.

"Can you please get to the point?" Bixby demanded. Tipton's eyes were growing larger and larger at every volley of the conversation.

Gabhammer almost smiled at her boldness.

"I was happy to see Marin's name at the top of the transfer list as her scores are most excellent and reflect the standards I expect. I received a second request for a transfer student. '*No problem,*' I think to myself. If they were anything like Miss St. James here..." He gestured towards her. "I would take a hundred new students with her aptitude. So, I look at his scores like any good Headmaster would do, and he is dumber than all three of you put together."

Everyone's mouth in the room nearly hit the floor at his insult of their fellow students.

"Headmast..." Tipton started to protest with the confidence he had building off of Bixby's boldness.

"Silence, Mr. Ellerby!" he shouted.

Tipton shot back in his chair with a whimper. All confidence was gone again as Headmaster Gabhammer composed himself again.

"Bixby Timmons, you are going to bankrupt this school with your arrogance," he said, finally getting his frustrations out on the table.

"I have no idea what you're talking about, and frankly I really don't care what problems you have here at the school. I have a ton of my own to deal with," Bixby said as she grabbed her backpack from her chair.

"Bixby, my problem is that you're letting every student on this list launch into this school using Pinnacle Manor's servers," Gabhammer replied.

Bixby looked at the lists of new students and then back up at him. She was terrified that someone knew about their Ghost program.

"You don't think we had anything to do..." Pippa started as Gabhammer shot her a look that would silence a crying baby.

"My technology staff and Dragonthorp Inc.'s tech team backtracked the signal, and it is most definitely coming from Pinnacle Manor... including you three," he said pointing to everyone in the room. "Did Pinnacle Manor turn into a manor for wayward children, I wonder?"

He was in cahoots with Dragonthorp Inc. Bixby's mind raced; school might have ruined their whole Ghost operation, but then she had an idea.

"So what? Even if we are helping them, there are no rules about how we launch in, only that we are able to launch in. What's to say I don't flood your school with every kid from all over the world?" she asked, setting the verbal trap.

"What's to say I don't expel *you* and your band of misfits for not showing up to school after I send someone to your house to check on the well-being of you and..." He paused intentionally. "...your family?" he said, standing up to meet her gaze. He struck a nerve, but Bixby expected it, because his sentence confirmed Daemon Dragonthorp had been meddling in things. There was no way he knew her family was gone without speaking to Dragonthorp Inc.

"I dare *you* to expel all four of us and try and explain to the world that it was because we were trying to help a bunch of kids get a better education. Do you know what that would do to *you* and your precious school's reputation? And I *double dare* you to send Dragonthorp Inc. over to intimidate us during the interim of the Riddle. How much more bad press would that be for all of you? There is nothing you can take from me that I already haven't had ripped away already."

Bixby could see Gabhammer contemplating her counteroffer. No one else in the room dared move a muscle.

"So, as I said before, send us back to class... we're missing out on *your* high-cost education," she finished with heavy sass.

Gabhammer entered the staring match with Bixby.

"Bixby Timmons," he finally started. "*You* have no idea who you are going up against," he said in a deep tone.

"I've heard that phrase a lot, and yet I'm still here. Tell Daemon I said, 'nice try' for me when you report back to him," she replied, confident that Gabhammer was one of Dragonthorp Inc.'s flunkies.

Gabhammer stared back at her. Bixby wished she could hear his internal dialog, because she knew she was right, even if her attitude was less than appropriate. She was numb. He had no idea what it was like to carry the burdens she had going on in her life on top of all the empty threats he had just given her.

Everything that was once good in her life was all gone. After this morning, she didn't care about her attitude anymore.

"Make sure all four of you report to detention during lunch for launching in late again today," he said as he reached down and pressed a button on the underside of his desk releasing them back to class before any of them could oppose.

"Dude, Tipton. Tell me you didn't ruin Ghost by letting people piggyback onto our launch rooms," Bixby insisted as she plopped down next to Tipton at lunch.

"With how you were talking to Gabhammer I thought maybe you had figured out how to do it just to get under Gabhammer's skin," Tipton replied.

"You're talking to the most tech illiterate person in this school," Bixby said, stuffing her turkey, cheese, and hot sauce sandwich in her face.

Pippa darted down next to her man, Tipton, while glowing.

"I have to say Sugar Bear, that is the nicest thing I have heard anyone do for others. I mean, to create a backdoor into Holo-School Prime. I could kiss you right now!" Pippa exclaimed.

"Well? What's stopping you?" he asked as he slowly put down his hamburger.

She wrapped her arms around Tipton and leaned in for a smooch.

"Perhaps the fact that it wasn't Tipton that did it would stop you from making me yak?" Bixby said with hot sauce dripping down one hand, and a pen to paper in the other.

Pippa pulled away and playfully slapped Tipton on the cheek.

"At least you could have done was let me enjoy a little kiss before you sunk my battleship, Bixby," he said as he returned to his burger.

"And what's to say I didn't do it?" Bixby asked, raising her head from her binder towards Pippa.

"Common Bixby? You think the toaster is too complicated of a gadget," she replied as Tipton nearly spit out his food in laughter.

Knowing that she expressed the same sentiments to Tipton moments earlier, "Touché," was all she could reply.

"What about Marin?" Tipton asked.

"*What about Marin*?" Marin mimicked as she walked up behind him.

Grandpa Richards was able to scare Tipton with his stealth, but Marin still scared Tipton because she was an absolute specimen of intimidation. He didn't know if it was her military stature, brilliant analytical mind, maybe the fact that she knew ten ways to impale him with her pinky, or perhaps all of the above.

As Tipton took a second to cower, Pippa chimed in, "We were just discussing the possibilities of who hacked our Ghost system?"

"It wasn't me," she said gruffly, dropping her tray on the table with a thud. She immediately folded a slice of pizza in half and dipped it in ranch dressing before chomping half of it.

"I'm willing to take her word for it," Tipton said, trying desperately to stay on Marin's good side.

"So, none of us did it, but it came from Pinnacle?" Pippa continued.

"I bet it was Gramps," Marin said, directing her comment at Pippa.

"No way! Grandpa wants nothing to do with the outside world. He was very happy being a hermit at Dragonthorp Inc., and now his only joy is writing riddles for Bixby," Pippa stated with confidence behind her point.

"So, Ghost is compromised?" Marin asked the group.

"I don't think so," Bixby interjected as she continued to pen her letter. "Harvey does an entire system scan, so does Arthur, and so does Mr. Richards. Plus, who wants to get us in trouble so bad that they do something awesome like help kids get into Holo-School Prime? You nerds need to backtrack the signal and find out what is going on once we get home," Bixby said still engaged in her writing. Bixby was still extremely feisty and out of character since she gave up in the simulation.

"*We* can absolutely do that, but the more important question is, what are we so deeply involved with over there, Bixby?" Pippa asked, leaning over the table to catch a glimpse at her pad of paper.

"I'm catching up with a pen pal is all," she said as she slapped her notebook closed.

"You know they have this thing called texting and email for stuff like that, Bixby?" Tipton said as he smashed his fries in mayonnaise and gobbled them down.

"I also live with a super program, three H-bots, two computer hackers, a crazy old man, and a data analyst. Nothing in my digital house is sacred except snail mail," Bixby said as she stuffed the parchment into her book bag, stood up to empty her tray in the garbage, and headed off to her next class.

As she walked away, Pippa slapped Tipton's brownie out of his hand. "How can you eat at a time like this?"

"Wha... Why would you?" he said looking at his crushed brownie.

"Bixby has a pen pal! Who do you think it is? I mean we have been with her for over a year, and I haven't seen anyone besides old friends from Snagleyville or fan mail come through her Holo-Writer. Do you think he goes to this school?" Pippa questioned.

"You go through her emails and online accounts?" Tipton asked.

"You don't? I want to make sure she stays safe is all . . . It's for her protection," Pippa said, sounding like she believed what she was saying.

"Thank God I build my own firewalls," he replied.

Chuckling, Pippa stood up with her tray, leaned over, and kissed Tipton on the cheek. "I broke those down months ago, Bear." She walked away.

Realizing he was left alone with Marin, Tipton slouched a little and whimpered.

Marin stood up, flipped her uneaten brownie on Tipton's tray and proclaimed as she walked away, "Those things will slow my mile time by at least eight-hundredths of a second, and if I catch you in my emails... I know where you sleep . . . *Bear*."

Tipton nodded quickly, and as she walked away, he tore open his new brownie.

CHAPTER FOUR

RIFFRAFF

Bixby was happy to make study hall her final class of the day yet again this year. She could usually get all her work done before enrichment which left her the entire evening to work on her craft. Because Tipton and Pippa were into their tech focused studies, neither of them could join her for study hall. For Bixby, this was a peaceful time. She spent nearly every hour of every day with any combination of her three companions or one of the house computer systems. Finally, she was alone... except when she chose not to be.

Putting the final touches on her envelope, she waved Marshall Grove over to where she sat. He sauntered over to Bixby's table in his usual jeans, sandals, t-shirt with a picture of himself on it, and a blazer.

"You do realize how pompous it looks to wear a shirt with your selfie on it, don't you?" Bixby jabbed.

"Bixby Timmons, if you weren't making me so much money right now, I would consider punching a girl in the arm," he razzed back.

In the past year, Bixby had given Marshall the rights to sell paraphernalia with the Timmons family crest emblazed on it. She figured it was a good way to have a resource for information without having to do any work for the tasks she needed done. Marshall was both loyal to paying customers and very discrete about completing tasks. Since entering Level Two, it was Marshall that caught Bixby up on all her class work. He also was able to procure her several technological updates for her communication systems in the Holo-Simulations that Harvey and Mr. Richards had developed. It was, however, his discretion on delivering the secret letters that Bixby valued the most.

"Ah, another letter to your lover boy," he said as he ran the envelope under his nose and sniffed deeply.

"And now you've crossed the creeper line," she said with a turn of her head.

"I don't get it, Red... I mean, I get why you don't email him; having all those computer hackers in the house and all, but doesn't it suck not being able to see your beau?" he asked as he leaned over the table.

"Let's be clear. First, he is not my *beau*. Second, I will indulge you a little and say that it is very nice to talk to someone who isn't constantly pestering me about improving something about myself or my gadgets in preparation for the next level. Finally, there is something vintage and deeply personal about writing out a letter versus typing it over a computer. It's nice to have some anticipation versus the instant gratification of email."

"Aww, just like you anticipate me coming over to your table and having such heartwarming conversations?" Marshall asked, batting his eyes mockingly.

"You know me so well, Marshall," Bixby said, picking up on his sarcasm and batting her eyes right back at him.

"Now that you continue to take money on behalf of me and my missing family, I believe you may have something for me as well?" she said, holding out her hand with a facetious grin.

"Yikes. You make me sound like such a bad person... But, as a matter of fact, you are unfortunately not wrong on both accounts: I enjoy your money, and I do indeed have something for you," he replied, reaching into his coat pocket.

From inside his lapel, he pulled a single envelope and a small glass data drive. "Because sales have been down these past few months due to the lack of a new level in over a year, I have to say that I will continue to be your little love courier, but I am going to have to put a hold on the data dealing. It is very risky on my end and the rewards are just not there anymore," he said as he gave her the contents of his pocket.

Dragonthorp Inc. undoubtably had him on their radar as well, and she could see why he would be cautious.

"Understood," Bixby said, slipping all but the very top of the newly acquired letter under her book and the chip in her backpack.

"I tell you what though, if you do something scandalous or Level Three starts back up, your wish is my command," he said with a hinting tone.

"Well, I'm not one for scandal, so it looks like we are on hiatus until Level Three," she replied.

"Same time next week, Red?" he asked as he started to slip away.

Bixby nodded as she eyed her new correspondence.

Marshall disappeared back into the crowd, as the letter mocked her for not reading it immediately. Bixby couldn't wait. She pulled it from its brief hiding place and held the letter up to the light to make sure she wasn't ripping the prize inside. With a quick yank, she tore the end of the envelope and pulled out the contents.

Dear Bixby,

I always feel like I write much shorter letters than you do. If you feel as if you're getting cheated, let me know and I can add a few more paragraphs. I don't find my life to be as amazing as yours. I mean you are training every day to do your thing, and last week I went to a comic book convention dressed like Beauregard the Brutal. Which by the way, I looked almost exactly like him, and one of the writers took a picture with me! I promise that one day I will be brave enough to post a photo of myself in my tights to my Holo-Page for you and the world to see. Anyway, my family is doing well. Mom was sick for a few days, but it looks like she will pull through without having to miss any of her shifts. Dad is still working like 70 hours a week at a stupid desk job for Mr. Dragonthorp. It is beyond me how much time he spends shuffling papers and reviewing tech specs on all the little chips that go into the Holo-Systems. Did you know that there are almost a thousand chips that go into every new Holo-TV? I heard that Cody had it down to twelve independent chips per TV, but he vanished before he could publish his specs. I know you hate talking shop, so let's see...

I entered in one of those obstacle races! It looks like the race will be five miles, which includes rock walls, some water obstacles, a ridiculous amount of mud, fire, and some kind of primitive weapons throwing. I'm going to do it with some of my buddies in real life, not in Holo. Oh, I almost forgot that I am trying out for the track team to get in shape for the race. Before you roll on the floor laughing, my dad was a pretty big track star in his high school days, so it's in my blood. Again, I will hold all "me in track shorts" pictures off of my Holo-Page until absolutely necessary, so don't even ask. Maybe one day I will be as fit as the great Bixby Timmons. The bell is going to ring so I will have to wrap this up. I look forward to our next post. It's most definitely the highlight of my week.

Sincerely,
Hemsley

Bixby folded the letter back up and stuffed it in the envelope whence it came. His letters were, in fact, always much too short, but they were sweet, and very boyish. In a way she liked his matter-of-fact simplicity. There was never really a riddle to go along with their talks. It was straight forward and honest. Now if he would just write a two pager like she usually did. She wouldn't care what it said, as long as it was from him. For now though it was time to figure out who was getting her into so much trouble as the room went dark and Bixby found herself in her launch room. After a minute of standing in silence the door hissed open and Arthur entered.

"I hear we have a new riddle to solve."

"The only reason I care is because it means there is some sort of back door into our system. We need to find it and fix it," she insisted in a tone normally reserved for Arthur himself.

"Yes, ma'am," he replied, in shock at her demeaner. "Harvey has already started the scan. The rest of the group is live streaming on your silly game as they wait."

One of their favorite things to do, outside of Holo, was to watch Tipton play old games that used handheld controllers and an actual TV. It helped that Mr. Richards was one of the designers of most of the archaic console games and had access to some of the older systems. Pippa always live streamed the gameplay and the conversation to the Timmons Nation. The nostalgic vibe of the game and inside conversation with Team Timmons made it one of *the* most viewed streams on all of Holo, which kept Pinnacle Manor financially secure for the time being.

Each time they streamed was a well-oiled machine. Pippa guided the online chat, Marin practiced strategy, Harvey seamlessly ran the production to make the sound and video look good, Miss Marmalade provided snacks, Arthur made sure to keep it family friendly, Tipton did the controlling, and Bixby did her puzzle solving while answering some of the questions people lobbed them in the comment feed.

During tonight's episode of Tipton playing *Wamdoodle's Time Warp*, Tipton was the one who asked a most riveting question that had everyone pause a moment to ponder, "Do you guys ever think about what 'normal' is going to look like when the Riddle is over?" Tipton asked as he adjusted his headset which was practically invisible thanks to Marshall Grove and a set of stolen Dragonthorp Inc. blueprints.

"You mean you don't want to get up with me at five o'clock every morning and train when there is nothing left to train for?" Bixby asked, scanning the room in the game he was playing for a sequence key to the cypher written in old tribal symbols on the massive screen over the fireplace's mantle. She was trying really hard not to blurt out the answer to Tipton, because the one thing she learned from the last level was to let everyone play their part on the team, and old gaming was Tipton's thing.

"Yeah. I mean it's going to end eventually, and we can't be roommates forever, right?" he asked.

Bixby didn't fully know how to answer that right off the top of her head, while also deeply enthralled by the video game.

"It has to be hidden somewhere in the wall. Maybe one of those rods over there is a switch that will open a compartment," Marin said, also still focused on the strategy aspect of the game.

Tipton directed the painfully good-looking avatar named Jacque, who somehow just fell out of a plane without a scratch, over to the rods and pushed, pulled, and twisted each one of them.

"Sorry, Marin, nothing here," Tipton replied as he spun the joystick around again.

"I really haven't thought that much about it, Tipton, because every morning I'm up before my alarm ready to repeat what we have been doing forever. It's almost as if my mind and body wake up every day craving these riddles," Bixby explained, trying to answer the best she could in the moment.

"Yeah, well my body craves coffee that early in the morning," he replied as he navigated Jacque.

"Don't forget doughnuts," Marin jabbed, her focus remaining on the Holo-TV.

Bixby chuckled a little bit as Tipton grumbled, "Cute."

"You're quiet tonight, Pippa. What do you think?" Bixby asked as she unslouched from the loveseat.

Pippa was busy clacking away at her Holo-Writer as her ears caught the end of Bixby's question. "Uhm, what did you say, Bixby?" she replied as her mind focused back to reality.

"Just wondering why you are so quiet. There hasn't been a single question about my pen pal, or input on how to get Jacque's Future Orb. Are you feeling, okay?" Bixby asked jokingly while still slightly concerned.

With a long pause and a deep sigh, "We have been at this a long time, Bixby. We are a great team and honestly this has been one of the best years of my life since..." She knew that Dragonthorp Inc. was most certainly watching every one of their live streams, so her words trailed before her thoughts unraveled. "You guys have been the greatest friends I have ever had, but why is Cody taking so long?"

"Pippa..." Bixby started to say before a brief pause. She knew her next words needed to be said for the sake of her friends and the Timmons Nation, but she also desperately prayed that her family could hear them, even if they couldn't respond.

"Right now, every day continues to tick me off even more than the next," Bixby replied.

"Really?" Pippa asked, awestruck that Bixby would share what she was hiding so well behind her new defiant carefree façade to the world.

"Today piled it on with Gabhammer's accusations," Bixby replied frankly.

Pippa's eyes got wide not knowing if Bixby was going to go into why they got a detention and almost expulsion. But she was more concerned that Bixby could slip up and say something about Holo-Ghost.

"The anticipation is absolutely killing me. We are all freaking out in our own way, and for everyone out there who doesn't know, Gabhammer pulled us into his office and threatened to expel us because he thinks we are helping people bring down his precious school. The thought that I would care about stupid stuff like that after even one level of the riddle is ridiculous. Those little things like that annoy me more and more each day," she said, in understandable irritation. Nobody dared interrupt her as she thought out loud what everyone had been thinking about for months.

"The live stream wants to know how we are getting people into Holo-School Prime." Pippa said as the feed started to buzz.

The question gave Bixby an idea on how to really get under Gabhammer's skin. Bixby wanted to create a little chaos of her own.

"According to him, we are helping get people into Holo-School Prime, but there is no way we could possibly help any of you get in if you haven't registered," Bixby said, knowing the school website was about to get blown up with traffic from all over the world trying to put in an application.

Jacques stood at the crux of the rubble pile staring at the sunrise over the desolate landscape. He was looking down over an ancient war zone that nature had reclaimed. Bixby reached over to the live feed and covered the mic.

"I freaked out yesterday, and I'm sorry you all had to see that," Bixby replied in a calm tone directed at only the people in the room. This part wasn't for the world to hear. "And you're right, I'm not sure I am fully in control of myself right now, and I need you all to know that that terrifies me... but Pippa..." Bixby paused to compose herself. She felt the same anxious panicked feeling she had on the side of the simulation cliff that she gave up on. It came in waves, but she was learning to slam the emotion back down as far as she could into her mind so that nobody would ever see *that* Bixby again.

Fight it, was all she could think as she quickly clinched her eyes and shook it off before continuing "...every day I wake up thinking of getting my family back. You guys have been the closest thing to normal that I have, and I don't care who is doing this as long as it helps us make Pinnacle Manor a fortress. Ticking Gabhammer off is a bonus," she said, turning her gaze towards the feed and pulling her hand off the mic and switching back to the webcam.

"There, Tipton, on the ledge below the old bakery," Bixby said, leaving the previous conversation to simmer in everyone's mind.

"I see it, too," Tipton replied, trying to end the awkward moment that he thought was broadcast to the world.

"I don't see it, guys," Marin replied. "Oh wait, duh!" she said, visibly upset she didn't see it first.

After some time to figure out how to get to the ledge that held a shiny metallic orb, Jaques made his way over to a podium that seemed to be the likely place that the sphere was meant to nestle itself into. Once in its old home, the weight of the object pushed the stone pedestal in place within the rock. A burst of light sparked through the baseball sized globe illuminating the wall with the deciphered symbols.

"Okay, Bixby, do your magic and get us out of this room," Tipton said, giving Bixby permission to help him along. She quickly translated the word on the wall into English, and when Tipton painstakingly navigated a qwerty keyboard to type the word, one letter at a time into the game, the mammoth door broke open. As Jaques strolled through the archway, that part of the adventure expired, and the team began packing away their gear before meeting Miss Marmalade for dinner.

"My, that was a quick one this evening," she said, commenting on their ever-growing speed of completing the different levels of *Wamdoodle's Time Warp.*

"Come to think of it, that was a rather easy one compared to the last few weeks," Marin said as she stuffed a pile of diced fruit in her mouth.

"Are you going soft on us, Grandpa?" Pippa shot the question to the back of the evening newspaper that covered Mr. Richards's upper half. It was rare to see him in the evenings, but it was nice to be able to ask him questions about one of the original games that Mr. Richards co-created back when consoles were a popular thing.

Folding the lip of his paper down just enough to expose the top of his head just below his eyes, "Don't ask me," he replied. "When I designed that riddle for Jacques, there were a few large moving distractions that would have made it harder to find the key. It was the game's director that thought it would be 'too hard for teens to solve,'" he said, snarking at the idea he had anything to do with a soft riddle. He flipped the paper back up and continued his reading.

"Anyone seen Harvey today?" Bixby asked, noticing that he had not made an appearance all day, including his usual dinner remarks. She knew he was running the scan and was curious if he had a result.

The room was silent as everyone pondered whether or not they had or had not seen him that day. With no answers returned, Bixby said, "I'll see what's up," as she shoved herself away from the table and headed towards the Great Hall.

"Harvey?" she proclaimed, knowing that he liked to appear in his Holo-Body leaning over the fireplace staring into the dancing flames. Right on cue he assimilated into his usual position.

"I know that look, Harvey. What's troubling you?" she asked.

"I have finished the backtracking that you requested," Harvey replied, sounding glum.

"Let me see the coding," Pippa shouted as she jumped over the back of the chair and logged into her Ghost-Writer and awaited the data.

"I'll save you the trouble, Pippa. The signal is indeed coming from Pinnacle Manor," Harvey replied.

Everyone in the Great Room now looked at each other as if there was a traitor amongst the ranks.

A leader never shows weakness or confusion, Bixby thought as her brain continued to scramble between feeling insecure about who she let into the house and confident there had to be something more to this.

"So, why do you look confused?" Bixby asked.

"Arthur, Miss Marmalade, Hucklebee, and I all have a blind spot to overlook them launching in somehow," Harvey replied.

"You mean all of you are allowing this and didn't know it?" Tipton asked.

Hucklebee gasped that he would have anything to do with getting Bixby in trouble.

"Are you four hacked, Harvey?" Tipton asked.

Before he could answer, Pippa blurted out, "No, they are not, but something else is super fishy about all of this coding," she mumbled, finishing her scrolling of Harvey's work. "All of the tracking information is washed from everything."

"That is not possible," Tipton replied.

"That is also an enigma. They are logging in and somehow are able to delete the trail of how before we can get to it," Harvey added at the same conclusion he had come to as well.

"So is the person who broke into Pinnacle a friend or not?" Marin asked bluntly, standing in the kitchen door.

"I can't compute that answer, Marin. There are too many variables at play here. As I see it right now, the only advice I can give you all is that you must steer clear of Headmaster Gabhammer, be very careful who you talk to outside of Pinnacle, and about what, and always be ready for Level Three. When we know more, we can better analyze our position."

"Ohhhh, shoot!" Tipton blurted out.

Harvey gave him a confused look.

"Bixby may have just done something to make him even more mad at us," he replied.

"Bixby, did you really just crash Holo-School Prime's website?" Harvey asked, replaying the live steam in his head while simultaneously scanning the school's website's traffic.

Everyone turned to Bixby who was lost in another one of her mental puzzle solves.

"Bixby?" Pippa dared to interrupt her thought.

"Are you four hacked?" Bixby repeated softly Tipton's earlier question.

"There is no sign of hacked for any of the four of them," Pippa replied not certain if she had heard her response to Tipton moments ago.

"Who haven't you hacked at school, Pippa?" Bixby asked as she pulled up the list of new students on her Ghost-Writer.

"Honest answer?" Pippa asked a rhetorical question.

"For the sake of time, the answer is 'nobody'. There is nobody she hasn't hacked. She has literally been in every single person's everything," Marin said sarcastically.

Everyone's attention was fixated on Bixby, eagerly awaiting her discovery.

"I know how they did it and why! I'll tell you if I'm right after school tomorrow," Bixby said, as she grabbed her Ghost-Writer and stuffed it in her bag. "Good work, everyone!"

Tipton never really thought before he spoke. Therefore, he never realized how blunt he could actually be.

"Hold up... you're saying that you, Bixby Timmons, the most un-tech savvy person we know, has the answer to the most difficult technological conundrums we have ever faced by a momentary glance at that file?"

As Bixby slung her bag over her shoulder, she reached across the couch and ruffled Tipton's hair, "And I'll have the answer to you in time for dinner tomorrow," she said as she walked away.

CHAPTER FIVE
FIRST CLASS FLIGHT

Bixby completed her afternoon classes and launched into the only course she had with Tipton during the day besides lunch. Math was easy for Bixby, so paying attention was usually not part of her time spent. She pulled out her Holo-Writer and uploaded all of her homework to the proper teachers and sifted through her Holo-Page. She tried not to pay much attention to the hoard of people who daily violated what Bixby called the Holo-Page etiquette. She felt that if someone posted vague things about how bad their day was just to get people to ask you 'What happened?' they had violated Holo-Page etiquette. If they only posted witty self-esteem sayings multiple times each day: violation. People who haven't had a positive thought in the past two weeks irritated her and were in flagrant violation of etiquette. Her biggest pet peeve of all was those whose hashtags were longer than the actual post: deleted from Holo-Page. Daily her list of violations was getting longer and longer, but it was like staring deep into a crackling fire. For some reason, she couldn't help but to break her routine each day and stare aimlessly into the black hole that was her Holo-Page. She rationalized it with the hopes that maybe... just maybe... someone will have done something interesting with their lives. After all that she had been through though, she was disappointed each morning with the same list of violations.

"Did you confirm who it was?" Tipton asked, leaning over to see what she was doing.

"Even if I did, I wouldn't tell you in here," Bixby said, showing her untrusting side of the Holo-Systems. She tilted her Ghost-Writer away from Tipton.

"You do realize that you are the most interesting person in the world, which means that anything anyone else posts will resound as boring," Tipton said, leaning over to give her a nudge. He too found himself mindlessly watching Holo-Pages, but his interests always came back to rewatching Pinnacle Manor's live feeds.

"You really think what we do all day is interesting?" Bixby asked.

"Bixby you have a house that creates detailed holographic puzzle simulations, your family has been kidnapped, you have been on live broadcast for millions of people to see, survived life and death situations half a dozen times, have three of the most watched streams on Holo-Live, and you're best friends with the President and Vice-President of Timmons Nation; your life can't get any more exciting."

Bixby looked down at her Ghost-Writer and switched it off.

"Maybe you are right, Tipton. I've just been thinking about what Pippa said about it being over, and it just scares me that..."

Her pause was long and thought filled. "Honestly, I'm not sure I want all this to end. I mean, I want my family back, and I really do hope that you can stay at Pinnacle Manor with my family, but all this constant changing and not knowing what is going to happen when it's..." She dreaded even saying the word 'over.' "I just want some sense of normal," she finished with a sigh. Trying to make a joke she continued, "Maybe I should start breaking my rules of etiquette just to see what social norm is all about. What do you thi—"

Bixby stopped her rambling mid-sentence as she looked up from her Ghost-Writer. Nobody around her was moving or making a sound. As she looked over at Tipton it seemed as if he had frozen while rubbing his nose.

"Tipton?" she asked while pushing on his shoulder. He was a booger picking statue.

Bixby stood up and started to check the rest of the students around them. Each one held their pose just like the next. It was as if she was at a wax museum of her school.

"Listen, you guys are really creeping me out. Jokes over," she lamented.

Bixby thought maybe the school's program had iced up so she tried to unlaunch but nothing happened.

"Here we go," Bixby said out loud to the room of statues. She was certain that Level Three had just begun. She raced up the walkway and burst through the classroom door. Out in the hallway there were two teachers suspended in mid stride while exchanging stacks of papers. Marshall Grove was elbow deep in his locker as she strolled up behind him. Her first inclination was to search him and his locker to see what treasured secrets for sale were inside. However, if this was really

Level Three, she had no time to dawdle. At the end of the hall Headmaster Gabhammer stood, gaze piercing through the back of Mrs. Gables' head. He was saying something as she was walking away. Bixby could tell that whatever they had previously discussed, Mrs. Gable was not happy about the final resolve. Approaching the Headmaster, she couldn't help but to stop and wave in front of his face. She knew that if this was a prank that Gabhammer could only take so much taunting before he blew a fuse.

"You in there, Quincy?" she asked, standing on her tip toes to look him closer in the eyes. She was certain he was reduced to a state of immobility, so she gently reached up and flicked his nose just to make sure.

"You need to be nice to Mrs. Gable. I like her," she said as she placed her palm on the top of his immaculately groomed head and ruffled his hair.

Certain now that this was in fact Level Three, she raced from classroom to classroom to see if she could see any signs of a first clue or riddle. Gymnasium, cafeteria, auditorium, Spanish room, teacher's lounge, front office... each room she inspected was exactly the same array of people playing a game of freeze tag. Then she saw what it was that she was looking for; a light literally came on.

Bixby was wandering the halls just past the guidance counselor's massive glass windowed office. Any time a student was inside sharing how they felt with Doctor Melissa Schmelney, she would press a button on her desk and the windows would immediately fog up so that nobody could see who was inside. Bixby knew this because after she had finished each one of the levels, she had to do a psychological evaluation with Dr. Schmelney courtesy of Headmaster Gabhammer. If you can think of the most cliché stereotypical shrink it was Dr. Schmelney; thick rimmed glasses with the chain attached to each earpiece, business suit, short strong haircut that shaped her old wrinkly face. Her questions were always something like, 'How did that make you feel?' or 'Would you care to go deeper with that thought?' This time she was in the middle of writing something on a piece of paper, but the massive window behind her was no longer a beautiful view of the school's central garden. A light had turned on in the middle of an empty airport terminal that shouldn't be outside of Dr. Schmelney's office window.

"Airport terminal it is," Bixby said as she slipped through the not-fogged glass door and over to the window. A quick glance down at her desk, Bixby discovered that Dr. Schmelney was signing a letter requesting a transfer to Vex Academy. Bixby knew the name immediately from the transfer papers that Professor Gabhammer had shown her and her teammates a week before. The upstanding doctor was jumping ship to the same academy that the Daggers and their hoity toity friends transferred.

"I never liked you anyway," Bixby said over her shoulder.

She was standing in front of the three picture windows. There was no riddle to be had on how to enter the terminal. Bixby reached up and pulled the latch and pushed the massive glass windows open. She stepped through almost like a doorway, but with a bit of a hurdle. It smelled like stale airport food, and a flight attendant's overuse of perfume. Inside each of the shops the coffee bubbled, and the walking escalators continued to churn out the same message about the walkway ending and how passengers should watch their step.

BIXBY TIMMONS AND THE SNOWENWOOD RENNEN

"A limo, submarine, and now an airport," Bixby declared to herself as she started to pick up the pace looking for a riddle. As far as Bixby could tell, it was an airport terminal in every facet of her expectations except no long security lines, travelers huddled around the single outlet charging their electronics, or standby calls. The human element had completely been taken out of the equation. There had to be something out of place. In the limo it was the dirty glasses, and in the submarine... come to think of it, the submarine took everyone by surprise. Bixby really hadn't traveled enough by airplane to really notice something out of place in a terminal. The next food vendor she hurried by she grabbed a few apples from the basket that was on the counter, and a turkey sandwich from the cooler below. If this was Level Three, food may be at a premium later. She didn't dare risk starvation while she had the chance to stock up now. She crossed over from Terminal B to Terminal C as she continued to scour the airport for any signs of life or oddities.

"Paging passenger Bixby Timmons. Bixby Timmons, please report to your gate: Gate C34 for immediate departure," a typical overhead announcer instructed.

Bixby's eyes darted around the terminal. At the other end of the long runway, she could make out that one of the gate doors was wide open. Spinning around in haste, she squinted to see if any of the doors in either direction was ajar, other than the one under C34: nothing. Bixby was certain that this was the start of Level Three, and she wanted desperately to have the lead. Her legs couldn't take her any faster as she hit the turnstile to run down the ramp to the plane, however she was met with an unpleasant shot to the hip bones. The turnstile didn't budge, stopping her from a dead sprint and nearly somersaulting her to the ground. Clutching her waist in discomfort, a 'BING' rang out from the computerized ticket counter.

"Please, take your ticket," it politely instructed as the clacking of the ticket printer began.

Bixby fumbled over to the desk and in the relay below the machine a paper ticket had been deposited. She snatched it from its home and glanced at it quickly.

BIXBY TIMMONS: ROW 1   SEAT 3

She frantically searched back at the gate for a place to deposit her ticket. A small yellow arrow was blinking on the lower face of the turnstile. Bixby jammed her voucher in, arrow first, and the previous roadblock now clicked. She hesitated slightly as she used both hands to push the metal restraint of the style as it rolled forward allowing her to pass through. The stub popped out of the top of the admittance booth. Knowing she was free to enter, she seized the end, pulled it free, and raced down the gateway. Her heart was racing as her feet pounded down on the metallic floor below her. Making a slight left she slammed on her brakes. They were already here...

"Bixby! Don't be shy! We are securely buckled in our seats!" A shout from Wesley's bitter voice box rang out through the plane and onto the walkway.

Bixby's blood began to boil, and the beast inside that longed for her family started to stir. She had spent months mentally blaming Dragonthorp Inc., and Wesley for their disappearance. The last time Bixby had heard Wesley's voice was in a simulation screaming to let go of him before she pulled him under the icy water and through the exit of a simulation. That same blinding rage had washed over her again.

"C'mon, Bixby! Our tray tables and seatbacks are in their upright and locked positions! Let's see where this trip is going to take us, shall we?" Greg mocked some more as Bixby slowly peaked around the lip of the plane's hatch and into the cabin. She was certain that it was a trap, and that Greg and Wesley would pop out and tie her down just like Maggie did in Level One. Her temper forced her jaw to clench as she readied herself to take action, but just as promised, Greg and Wesley were the only two occupants in the plane. A quick look in the cockpit revealed no pilots or stewardesses.

"Even if he wanted to get out of his seat, as soon as we buckled in, the plane literally locked us into place," Greg said as he yanked on the belt buckle that was wrapped on his hips. "I guess Cody wanted to make sure you two didn't have it out on the trip to wherever we are going," he continued as he rocked back in his chair defeated.

There were only three chairs in the middle of the first-class section of the plane. Each one was just as plush and spacious as those she remembered walking by when she was a child on the family's way to Wallaby World. She never understood why the airlines made the less financially endowed people who had to sit in the cramped accommodations in the last row walk past the rich businesspeople of first class on their way back to their not so comfortable seats. Then flight attendants had the audacity to tell you to have an enjoyable flight moments later. It was a punch in the face from the airlines if you asked her.

Today, Bixby didn't have to walk past first class. However, it was the only option. The seats were far enough apart that even if Greg, who sat in the middle, wanted to reach over and touch Bixby or Wesley, it would physically be impossible. Instinctively Bixby made up an escape plan that involved the fire extinguisher, the complementary blanket, and the floatation device that she saw protruding just below her seat. It was, however, the extended broom, specifically the handle, that transitioned her anger into action. Greg and Wesley gave each other a look as if to shrug off the fact that Bixby didn't believe them. It wasn't that she didn't believe them, it was answers she wanted.

With a flick of her wrist the broom was in her hand, and she spun the new weapon like a helicopter just above their heads, naturally forcing them to duck. As they flinched Bixby slammed one end of the wooden rod against Greg's chest and the brush end against Wesley's. She was pushing against the middle of the broom as hard as she could as it slowly slid up towards their necks. Both were visibly panicked because they couldn't free themselves from the pressure of the broom pinning them against their seats.

"Where are they?" she screamed as she put all of her weight into choking the life out of her competitors.

CHAPTER SIX

THE WINNER'S TROPHY

"My parents are gone because one of you decided to steal Pinnacle's servers!" she shouted, knowing that it was irrational to think that either of them were actually there to take the servers and force her parents to go missing. All three people in that plane cabin had been racing around Shadow Deep to solve the Phantom's riddle when Pinnacle Manor was broken into, but it didn't matter, she needed someone to blame so badly that her ears were now burning with fury.

"We ask that all passengers take their seat before we begin our trip," came a friendly voice over the intercom as the plane hatch hissed closed. Bixby didn't relinquish her pressure.

Maybe one of them would unlaunch and be disqualified, she thought to herself before she crushed her eyes closed and revisited the thought that neither of them could have broken into Pinnacle themselves due to being launched into Shadow Deep. *What am I doing?* She had let her mind wander into uncharted territory and yet again, it made her do something dumb.

She ripped the broom from their airways, snapped it in half over her knee and stuffed it under her seat as the boys gasped for air.

"If either of you come close to me... I may not stop next time," she said over their coughs before settling down into her seat. The seatbelts, like two little snakes, slithered up her waistline and fastened themselves together with a metallic clack. Bixby gave her buckle a tug to confirm the boy's struggles with their own belts.

The tone had been set even if she regretted it a little.

"You're crazy!" Wesley shouted through deep gasps for air.

"You thought we were lying about not being able to get up, didn't you?" Greg asked still rubbing his neckline. Bixby could tell he was trying to avoid the subject of her missing parents, so he resorted to his usual southern charm and banter.

Bixby sat in cold silence.

"Did she not remind you of Maggie just now?" Greg asked Wesley in a boastful manor.

Flashes of Maggie's fierce temper raced through Bixby's mind before she grimaced at the idea that she had indeed let her anger get the best of her.

"Maggie 2.0," Wesley said, joining in on the taunts.

"Do you two ever stop talking?" she asked, knowing that they both could see her stewing. She had already shown her new weakness, and they made sure she knew it wasn't a secret.

The engines of the plane rumbled as the turbines began to whine. From her window she could see that they were pushing back from the gate. The door of the cockpit still remained open as dials, levers, and knobs were adjusting themselves independently.

"I do love Holo, Bixby," Greg started as Bixby shot him a glance, but he blew right though the warning look, and kept talking. He was pointing to the cockpit. "Seriously, people can have an experience like flying in first class, sitting on a warm beach, playing in a silly game of riddles, or whatever your mind can imagine, and it cost those running the program virtually nothing. I mean, if I wanted to sit on a plane like this in the real world, it would cost me thousands of dollars. I don't have that kind of money, Bixby. Well, I will once I win this little game of riddles, but you know what I mean right? The little people won't ever be able to experience stuff like this without Holo. It costs too much for fuel and staff."

Bixby squirmed in her seat because she knew that Greg was right. Her family would never be able to fly on a plane like this to Wallaby World.

"Hey, what makes you so sure you are going to win all of this?" Wesley asked as he laid back in his seat and rested his heating pack gently over his eyes. "Don't get me wrong, you two have made it this far, but I don't plan on leaving these riddles anytime soon."

"What is to say Bixby and I don't just roll over on you and squash you like a bug? She seems to have a bit of fight in her," he replied confidently.

It had taken Bixby a few moments, but there was something odd about Greg's voice as if he were sick. His Southern Cal surfer dude vernacular was still there but was now much more refined. Bixby was certain he was hanging out too long with the uppity people of Dragonthorp Inc.

The plane jumped a little as it started its taxi.

The heating pack slid from Greg's face and down into the awaiting hand as one of his eyes peeked open just long enough to say, "I guess we will find out soon enough."

Finishing his remark, he slapped the pack back over his eyes and the engines dully screamed through the nearly soundproof cabin as everyone was thrust back in their seats. It didn't take long for the plane to reach cruising altitude, and a panel swung open near the cockpit revealing a silver wagon that began to roll from underneath. At first Bixby thought it was a runaway beverage cart and she held out her arm to try and stop it, but it slowed on its own just before it reached her seat and four trays jettisoned out from the sides. In one side was soda, juice, water, and other drinks of choice. Within the other wing were candies, fruits, sandwiches, and nuts. Bixby trolled the cart and selected a bottle of water with a turkey sandwich and a packet of hot sauce. She already had one stowed in her hoodie, but she wasn't going to waste an opportunity to fuel herself.

"Predictable," Wesley interjected about her decisions. "You still eat those stupid sandwiches every day?" he continued. He used to mock her in the cafeteria, "Did your mommy pack you a lunch? Too poor to buy anything more than that little sandwich?" It made him look like a jerk back then and even though it was a different day, he was the same old Wesley.

"You should really mix it up, Bixby. Who knows what delicious things in this world you are missing?" Greg commented as Bixby realized that the two boys were patiently waiting for the cart to make it to their seats.

"I hear that successful people eliminate as many choices as possible from their lives in order to make sure when they actually have to make a choice, their brain isn't cluttered with questions like, 'what should I have for lunch?'" Bixby said, sounding profound.

"Garbage," Wesley said as he started grabbing a handful of everything. As she finished her comment and listened to Wesley's brilliant response, Bixby was presented with her first puzzle.

Greg's face had gone from indifferent to slightly uncomfortable as she spoke. She didn't say anything too deeply philosophical, but Greg was noticeably soured by it. The expression quickly flashed from his face as he took a hearty chomp on his egg salad sandwich.

An hour passed and the trio sat quietly staring out the window or at the limited selection of magazines provided them. There was no turbulence to speak of, and conversations about how each other's holidays went would be kind of pointless seeing as nobody really cared much for one another outside of the Riddles. Just after takeoff, Bixby was slyly working her way around the chair to see if maybe the seat itself could be the riddle and perhaps getting out of it was the first task. She had noticed that Greg was doing the same thing while Wesley sat passed out drooling in the lounge position. Bixby was certain that Greg knew she was also exploring the escape possibilities, but neither of them acknowledged the other. They each used magazines to attempt to cover one of their hands as their fingers walked over every inch of the chair. After lunch Wesley had tried to use the complementary blanket to do the same, but the luxurious reclining chairs, mixed with the heating pack, and the cozy blanket must have overcome him. Bixby hated the anticipation almost as much as she despised heights.

BING

Wesley shot up in his chair launching the heating mask past the galley and to the threshold of the cockpit. He was asleep and prepared at the same time. Greg and Bixby were also on high alert when an announcement over the PA politely publicized, "Your inflight movie will begin momentarily. Enjoy."

A projector screen slowly crept down the wall and gently hovered in place. No video projector could be seen, but the screen flickered on, and the images began to glint like an old black and white movie. Each slide of the film had a brief pause in between the next. It reminded Bixby of a picture book that her grandfather had made her as a child. He would draw hundreds of pages of stick figures going skiing or pole vaulting into a pit of wild animals. Grandpa always had a way of making her laugh when she needed it the most. It was nice to be reminded of him while in the Riddle from time to time. It kept her spirits high.

The film resembled an instructional video she once saw in gym class about how to play basketball. Everyone in the video wore high water pants up around their belly buttons, wave combed over hair, and was generally physically fit. In this rendition they were talking about some kind of Geo Race called Snowenwood Rennen. None of the plane's occupants seemed to really understand what was being said, because it sounded like the narrator was speaking in German. As much as Bixby could ascertain from the video, this was a race that always involved two people. One person seemed to be always the same, but during each event or leg of the race the teammate was someone else. Half of the challenges included a physical element like swimming or mountain biking, but others were more scientific. One team was putting together a model rocket, while yet another team was mixing chemicals in beakers. There were only two banners throughout the video that had any English displayed. Each was a 'Welcome to Snowenwood Rennen '1962' and '1963' respectively. She could see that Wesley was searching for something to write notes with but couldn't find a utensil. Greg simply stared at the screen unflinchingly. Her best guess was that neither of them were prepared for this adventure, therefore not wired to speak with their outside team. Her team was currently frozen in some classroom back at their respective Holo-School Prime.

Bixby quickly recited the spelling of Snowenwood Rennen over and over in her head, and then used it in a sentence multiple times so it would stick. It was a method that her grandfather taught her on how to store pertinent data in her long-term memory. The video concluded with one team standing on a podium holding up a beautiful metal sculpture that displayed 'Champion' on the bottom in bold black letters.

They must have won both years, Bixby thought to herself. She also noticed that the plane was descending rather quickly. There was no doubt that they would be arriving at their destination shortly.

The video screen went dark and, like a spider, crept back up the wall into its hiding place. Before anyone could say a word, the plane rumbled down on the tarmac and yanked itself to a crawl. They were finally back on the ground. Each of the contestant's gears were churning:

Where are we?

Does the race start now?

Get ready to run!

Bixby reached down to unbuckle her seatbelt, but it was still securely fastened.

"My seatbelt is still stuck," Wesley said to Greg as he wrestled with his strap.

A flash of light tore through the middle of the cabin, causing the trio to stop their escape attempts. A small electric blue cylinder of electric sparks hovered three feet above the carpet of the jet. Bixby had seen that light once before, in the secret library deep in the heart of Pinnacle Manor. The light transformed from an orb into its final figure as it did two years before. Cody Dragonthorp now stood pigeon toed before the three competitors. His appearance had not changed in the slightest since the last time she had engaged his hologram.

"Yo, it's Cody," Wesley said in a manner that led Bixby to think he had never actually seen him.

Cody wore neatly pressed slacks and a shirt under the lab coat with the Dragonthorp Inc. logo stitched into one side of it. The other pocket had "Dr. Cody A. Dragonthorp" in bold blue letters darned on it. According to Tipton, when he received his first three doctorates in Applied Physics, Engineering, and Computer Science on the same day, he never took his lab coat off. His hair was peppered just like his brothers, and the only difference between them were the glasses that he wore. Daemon Dragonthorp had Lasik eye surgery to correct his vision, but

Cody denied treatment based on the statistics of failures in the procedure. It was the only way the public could tell them apart.

Bixby scanned over to her flight companions and Wesley watched almost with bated breath for Cody to begin, but Greg's eyes still didn't flinch at the sight of Cody standing before him. He was focused.

Bashfully, Cody began to speak.

"I hope that you enjoyed your flight and entertainment. I want to say congratulations on doing so well in the first two levels. I must conclude that five better contestants could not have been chosen. With that said, I want to inform you that I have made some changes in the rules and layout of my riddles due to the fact that my original rules were being stretched slightly," he said as he rubbed his shoulder to his ear slightly agitated at the thought that each of the contestants were taking some large liberties with how they were interpreting the generic rules. "I am well aware that each of you have been contacting others outside the parameters of the Riddles for help and support. That was not the intentions in these games but seeing as it has brought such great kinship with the supporting cast..." He was now rubbing his head vigorously with the palm of his hand. "I will allow it in accordance with the new rules of Level Three," he said as he slammed his hand back down to his side and with a wide-eyed gaze glared back at the recording device.

"Level Three Rules are as follows: You must follow all the Rennen's original rules. And you must try not to hurt each other like before... I don't like scary movies..." he said, rubbing his eyes harder, if that were even possible.

"That's it," he said as he again slammed his hands back down on the side of his pant legs while his fingers moved as if they were typing on a keyboard.

"Oh, and I have decided on prizes for the winner," he said pointing to the sky as if a lightbulb had just come on in his head.

"Being that there are some people who are allies in this game, I believe that this will help to keep things fair," he said with pursed lips.

"To Wesley Dagger of Black Rock. If per chance you win, I will give you two partner shares in Dragonthorp Inc. As you know I currently hold fifty-one shares, and my brother forty-nine shares. With this trophy you will now have the final say as to what direction any decision Dragonthorp Inc. moves in case of an opposing ballot."

Wesley's eyes immediately lit up and darted towards Gregory and Bixby in sheer joy. This was a huge prize for Wesley and his family who had always been the servant to the Dragonthorp's business need. Now he could potentially be a player. He quickly adjusted the tie of his school uniform and sat happily back in his seat.

"To... Greg Tracy of Dragonthorp Estates. If you happen to finish first," Cody again started to rub the back of his head more forcefully than before. He quickly said his remark, "I award you the same prize—two partner shares in the Dragonthorp Inc.," he said, letting out a deep sigh followed by a strong huff. Greg, too, fell back in his seat as a smile slinked over his face like a Cheshire cat.

Then, with a grin, Cody raised his head with composure and, with a pat of his hips, turned towards Bixby. Even though he was a hologram, he looked richly into her eyes.

"To Bixby Timmons of Pinnacle Manor. Upon completion of these riddles, no matter what place, your family will be safely returned to you, you have my word. However, a victory in my riddles will get you all the pieces to the most fantastic riddle you have ever had to solve. The only way to procure all the necessary pieces is to make it to the end, Spot, where your prize will be revealed," he said with a small grin just big enough on one side to produce a dimple. He jammed his hands down into his lab coat pockets and rocked back and forth while kicking the ground bashfully as he finished proclaiming her peculiar prize.

A raging cold chill electrocuted Bixby's spin. To anyone else on the plane, Cody just said 'to the end spot' meaning a location. However, Bixby heard it the way she was certain Cody meant it as 'to the end, Spot.'

To a pirate an X 'marks the spot' signifying a treasure, and that is why Bixby had to have an X in her name when she was born—she was the newest family treasure in a family of puzzle seekers. There was only one person who called her Spot behind closed doors and she, in return, called him Grandpa.

What did Cody Dragonthorp know about Grandpa that she didn't? was what Bixby began to ponder.

"I hope those prizes will keep you all focused on the task at hand. You have two weeks to build and prepare your team."

With that Cody exploded into a thousand tiny lightning bolts and as they fell to the ground like snowflakes, disappeared.

The cabin lights came up, and each of the contestants again tried their seat belts. Once more nothing budged as they could feel the plane stop.

What if they were released at the same time? Bixby thought with slight panic. For the second time on that plane Bixby rehashed her plan to break the wrist and nose of Greg before knocking Wesley completely unconscious. The plane door handle slapped up and the door shushed open. Everyone could see the electronics in the cockpit turn off, and the cabin start to dim. As soon as the lights went out in the pilot's chair Bixby's buckle let loose. Looking over at the boys who were still struggling with their restraints, Bixby dashed for the door leaving only the cries of her foes behind.

"Bixby, we both agree to give you the hundred million dollars if you drop out right now!" Greg cried out from his seat.

The cabin went silent as Bixby slid to a stop. "Our offer is worth way more than a hundred million dollars, and you could have your family back today. I am sure that if you agree to it, I can have Daemon put it in whatever account you wanted as soon as we get off this plane," he said, trying to convince Bixby.

"And none of us have to compete in Level Three," Wesley said, relieved at the idea that it was once less challenge he needed to do.

Greg was right. A hundred million dollars meant nothing to the two of them with an offer like Cody had given them. The loser wouldn't see a penny either way, and it was a small price to pay to not have to complete a level. Bixby could build her own Pinnacle Manor and have her family back.

"I'll think about it," Bixby said as she turned to exit the plane.

"You know it's a way better offer than what Cody gave you!"

"That's what you think," Bixby whispered inaudibly as she turned to escape.

"Deal's off if we launch in!" was the last she heard as she tore up the ramp and jumped the turnstile. She had no intention of receiving another bruised hip. She looked over her shoulders four or five times as she raced through Terminal C and back into Terminal B. The window back into Dr. Schmelney's was in sight and she glided to a stop on the freshly waxed floor and hopped over the threshold. She left the windows open in hopes that it was a windy day that would blow all Schmelney's paperwork to the floor. From the front of her desk Bixby grabbed a pen and over the shoulder of her shrink, she wrote on the top of the transfer request in bold letters:

GOOD RIDDANCE, YOU OLD WITCH!

Then she drew a mustache on her face in permanent marker and ran out her glass office doors for what she hoped was the last time. Bixby had no clue how long the frozen state of her school would last, but she knew that she had one chore and one last prank to pull before she made her way back to her seat. In a mad dash to the hallway of her classroom she glided around every corner like a racecar driver would drift around a turn. Bixby screeched to a halt right behind Marshall Grooves, yanked the pen out of his hands, and scratched a quick note in the notebook he had flipped open. Now it was on to Gabhammer who was just down the hall from her, still as solid as a statue, while scolding something at Mrs. Gable. Bixby yanked the marker from her pocket and drew two angry eyebrows on Headmaster Gabhammer's face. Next, she added a goatee and sideburns to his normally clean-cut look. Finally, across the billboard of a forehead that he had, she wrote, "TRY NOT TO LAUGH AT ME" in bold black letters. She gave Quincy Gabhammer another, harder, flick on the nose before ditching the marker in the trash bin after wiping her fingerprints off with her sleeve. Bixby rushed back into her math class and nestled down into her seat next to Tipton and stared blankly ahead hoping that things would automatically go back to normal.

"Bixby? Are you even listening to me?" came the comforting voice of Tipton next to her.

"Oh, wait what?" she stumbled. "How long have I been daydreaming?" she asked.

"Only a few seconds, but you were like frozen in place there," he said sounding concerned.

"BOAAA HA HA HA!" came a howling laugh that definitely belonged to Mrs. Gable. It emanated from the hallway just outside the classroom door where she had left them. Bixby chuckled under her breath knowing that she had just made Mrs. Gables' year of teaching well worth it. There was so much that she had to tell her team, but she was going to enjoy the last little bit of school strictly on principle.

"What is going on with you, Bixby? You've been acting really strange," he demanded of his closest friend.

Bixby smiled from ear to ear as Mrs. Gable entered the room and hushed the class with a giggle. "I made things worse and better for us at the same time, but dinner should be really fun tonight," Bixby said with a roguish grin.

Tipton bowed his head into his hand as it shook, "Oh, no."

He knew that grin.

CHAPTER SEVEN
SNOWENWOOD RENNEN

The team had gathered in their customary seats and corners of the Command Center as they waited for Bixby to enter her Launch Room and launch into the latest afternoon mind-bending puzzle. Much to everyone's chagrin Bixby strolled into the sanctuary behind Miss Marmalade and the dinner cart. She had already made a sandwich and was sipping on an iced coffee when she arrived.

"Taking a day off, Bixby?" Tipton asked, eyeing the cart as it went by.

"Nope," she said, cheerfully between chomps and sips.

"Care to tell us why you are not in your Ghost-Suit and launching into the simulation?" Marin asked while gawking at Bixby in sweatpants and her favorite hoodie that had the Space Force logo printed on it.

As Bixby plopped down in a recliner and took another bite, she smiled and reminisced about flicking Headmaster

Gabhammer in the nose. Twice. She wished so badly she could have been there when he or Dr. Schmelney awoke from their state of stillness.

"I met with Greg, Wesley, and Cody today," she said after a brief pause for reflection.

"WAIT, WHAT?" Pippa shouted, nearly shooting coconut water out her nose.

Arthur was doing a digital recollection of her school day from the Launch Room's mainframe, as was Harvey. Marin maintained a cold face as she waited for Bixby to volley back with an answer. Tipton's hands and forehead started to sweat as he thought about being back in Level Two again. One level inside the Riddle was enough for him. Bixby had already confided with Miss Marmalade, so she continued to lay out the food on the buffet. Hucklebee was busy changing batteries in all the electronic devices in the room. He took pride in making sure everything was fully charged for when they puzzle solved.

"Has anyone ever heard of a Rennen?" Bixby questioned as she shined an apple on her sleeve before taking a bite.

"Rennen means 'race' in German," Mr. Richards replied from the corner after a brief silence. Tipton was so focused on his experiences at Shadow Deep, that he wasn't even surprised by Mr. Richard's presence.

"Have you heard of the Snowenwood Rennen?" she questioned Mr. Richards who was on top of his German translation.

Gruffly, he turned to the cookie table and as usual piled it high with only chocolate chip cookies and poured a glass of milk. "Ahhhh, nope, never heard of it," he replied, noticeably trying to hurry along. As he finished making his plate, he gave the group a "Let me know if you need anything," before rushing out of the room.

"Is it only me, or was that odd even for him?" Tipton said with his brows furrowed.

"You two need to knock it off," Pippa replied, before spinning around in her chair, cracking her fingers, and burying her head into her work on her keyboard. The Holo-TV began to do digital reflections of what she was searching. Everyone in the room watched as she hustled through gobs of information for Harvey's system to digest and formulate an answer.

"You get all of that Harvey?" Pippa asked as she slapped her keyboard away from her lap as if she were being timed.

"Just a moment," he replied as he compiled the information into a more manageable bite of intelligence. Upon completion he changed the channel on the Holo-TV and a snapshot presentation of his work began to play.

"The Snowenwood Rennen was a race held in the Swiss Alps in 1962 and 1963," he said as a beautiful view of the mountain range flashed up on the screen, followed by a picture of a man working in a laboratory of sorts.

"Adam Snowenwood had been a scientist all his life. He was highly competitive in multiple fields such as Botany, Chemistry, and Genetics. Due to the immense amount of time he spent doing his research and development, he had absolutely no time to dedicate to physical fitness. He had amassed a large quantity of vacation time with Lausanne University, and when the city of Lausanne had lost its bid for the 1960 Summer Olympics to Rome, he vowed to see what it was that Rome possessed that Lausanne didn't. The city would lose millions of dollars in tourism that came with hosting the Olympics."

"This guy is mad at the Olympics? That is a pretty big organization to be upset with," Tipton interjected as the video rolled on.

"After attending events day and night during the Games of the XVII Olympiad, he reached a conclusion about the structure of how the world viewed competition in general. His observation was that physical challenges were easily solved by tests of strength and endurance over several weeks' time. But every athlete only competed in a very narrow field."

"So, you mean like runners never did swimming, and basketball players never competed in water polo?" Tipton tried to clarify.

"Precisely! The culmination of one's works in physical labors and tasks over a four-year period could be measured logically through a challenge such as the Olympics. Each athlete honed their skills during smaller races throughout the region in the four years between the Olympic games. The world could tangibly see those who were physically the ultimate in the land in very specific areas of physical greatness. But nobody was ever given an award as the single greatest athlete of the Olympics. He could only conclude that the Olympics, though profitable, did not provide a clear picture of the world's finest athlete *overall*."

"Leave it to a scientist to try to figure out a method to calculate the greatest person alive," Marin said, knowing that she had recently relied on mostly physical strategies, but since realized the importance of mental strength as well.

Harvey noticed that the team was getting lost in all the information. Stopping the video reel, he continued in his own words.

"Dr. Snowenwood was upset that we gave awards to people based on how they performed on one particular day in an athlete's career, but scientists were only receiving accolades after a lifetime of work. His first thought was to start a Science Olympics. After thinking about the concept deeper, he wondered who the strongest person would be both mentally and physically in the world simultaneously."

"He wanted to see who the best all-around human was?" Pippa asked, making sure she understood.

"Indeed," Harvey affirmed and then continued.

"He first looked at how smart the strongest athletes were and found out that most of them only possessed average intelligence. Upon looking at the scientists, most could only perform basic physical endeavors. In a compromise he developed a team system of physical and mental strength. Snowenwood Rennen was born."

"How did Snowenwood get the athletes to compete with the nerds?" Tipton asked bluntly.

"The good doctor was a master of marketing," Harvey started as he pulled up a few pictures of Snowenwood's plan to meld the two worlds together.

"In 1961 a convention was held in Germany that attracted brilliant minds from all over the world. During the same week, a European International Track and Field meet was held in the very same city. Most of the athletes who attended were those who had competed in the Olympics a year earlier. Snowenwood posted hundreds of fliers inviting scientists and athletes to attend his first ever Snowenwood Rennen to be held in Lausanne, Switzerland. Every bulletin board and hotel throughout the city had a flier posted for all to see. He had printed one hundred additional fliers detailing the race and its rules. At a table set up near the convention center entrance his fliers were all but gone within the first hour of arrival. Snowenwood promised to publish the same information in the next day's morning paper. The German equivalency of the Tribune had to do a midday reprint due to shortages of the script based on the concept's popularity. A New York City paper received a copy of the rules by Snowenwood with a note saying, "A race for only the smartest and fastest." Because of its international buzz, they printed the rules on the front page the next day. It was an overnight smash."

"So, what were his rules that made it so attractive?" Bixby asked, wondering what would make anyone want to do a silly race.

"Here is a copy of the original advertisement place in the paper if you want to read it," Harvey said as he formulated a yellowed newspaper excerpt.

SNOWENWOOD RENNEN

"A race for only the smartest and the fastest."

Entry Fee: *$5 (all proceeds will go to trophy, prize money, and beatification of Lausanne for future Rennen's)*
Cutoff Date: *May 15th, 1962.*
Lodging for the contestants will be in the dormitories of the University of Lausanne.

Race will begin at the gymnasium of the University of Lausanne at 5 pm. on July 18th, 1962.

THE SNOWENWOOD RENNEN

Rules:

- All teams will consist of six human team members of any age, gender, and nationality.

- One of the team members, who will be designated as team captain, has to complete all tasks.

- He or she must compete with one team member during each leg of the race.

- A team member can only complete one leg of the race with the team captain.

- Each leg of the Rennen will consist of one scientific trial which the team captain will then choose from his team members a partner. Then a physical event will be made known to the team captain and team member after the team captain has chosen his/her partner for the scientific part of the leg. Together they will compete in both the physical and scientific aspects of the race together. No substitutions can be made after the science portion has begun.

- No outside help is allowed for the pair once the challenge has commenced. Violators will be immediately disqualified. Conversations within the team can only be done between challenges.

Bixby Timmons and The Snowenwood Rennen

- If a team captain or competing team member is unable to finish a task or challenge during any part of the race, the team is disqualified.

- Challenges for the Rennen will be developed under lock and key by the University of Lausanne in cooperation with its science and athletic departments.

"I still don't get how it became so popular in only a week's time? You mean that add got so much buzz that papers started writing articles and the whole thing blew up?" Tipton asked as he was now at the buffet making a plate.

"It's like the first viral Holo-Social post," Marin said. Everyone looked at her because it almost sounded like she was trying to make a joke. Even though that wasn't her intention, it was kind of funny.

"I'm sure back then they printed what they had based on how popular the buzz was around it?" Bixby asked.

"That is the brilliance of Dr. Snowenwood," Harvey said. "He created the buzz by word-of-mouth by going around to all the scientists and athletes while they were out and about and saying that other countries were already entered in the race. Then he would say that those countries were proclaiming that they would beat any of their competitors into the ground. He used the passion for competition that was already brewing in the city to recruit participants."

"I would assume that it worked if we are talking about it," Pippa said as she continued to file her nails.

"Not only did it work, but by the time Professor Snowenwood had returned home from Germany, his office had nearly four hundred team entries delivered by mail. By the day of the race not only were the University of Lausanne's dorms completely filled, so were several of the universities in the local area."

"Okay, so they had a bunch of people sign up for the race. That happens all the time these days. What makes this race so special to Cody that he would make this scavenger hunt an entire level in his Riddle?"

"Part of it had to do with the caliber of people the race attracted. For example, a Russian shot-put hurler who competed in the previous Olympics had four teammates from Lomonosov Moscow State University. They were the best of the best that Russia could send. The United States had chosen several teams to attend, but most notable was the 400-meter gold medalist paired with the bright minds of Oregon State University, and a basketball player who teamed up with some of his college roommates at The Ohio State University. The buzz around the unknown parameters of the Rennen mystified everyone and stirred the excitement all the way up until the starting gun."

"Ok, so what happened? I have never heard of this Rennen before today, and I don't think it's going on still, right?" Marin questioned as the concept intrigued her.

Harvey almost seemed excited as he explained this part. "Excellent question. The Rennen only occurred twice. The first-year captains had chosen what they believed to be the smartest in the scientific worlds they knew. Each country was selecting only athletes that were from *their* country, as well as scientists who were brilliant in one specific field. Many teams fell out of competition within the first round, because the physical aspect proved to be too much for the scientist, or the scientist didn't have the background in the field in which the scientific question was composed. By the final leg, there were only six teams remaining. Much to everyone's surprise, a team from Australia led by a boxing medalist had made their way into the lead and ultimately claimed the trophy. When the other teams dissected the unlikely victor's methods, coaches quickly could see the pattern for success. The boxer strategized that instead of guessing at which scientific field would present itself during the race, he instead chose five teammates that were leaders in several fields, but not necessarily the best in one or the other. This logic was quickly adopted by all other teams moving forward into the next Rennen. The brilliant field specific scientists were now replaced with men who were smart in a vast blanket of topics."

"It makes sense," Bixby started. "I mean, Dr. Snowenwood *was* trying to see who could do a wide range of physical activities, why not also do the same to the scientific world?" she concluded.

"You are absolutely right, Bixby, but although athletes ate the competition aspect of the race up, the science world was split on the Rennen. Half of them believed a race with such parameters would water down the desire of men and women to become scientific field specialists taking away the chance of lifelong devotion and discovery in a field of study. Others in the science ecosystem deemed it cutting edge thinking that would lead to an excess of wide thinkers to tinker with many fields and concepts that otherwise would never overlap. Either way Lausanne, Switzerland was now the home of the annual Olympic sized cash cow that was the Snowenwood Rennen."

"It must not have been that cool if it only lasted two years," Tipton interjected between bites of his corndog and the dipping of it in mustard.

Harvey corrected, "Oh, it was cool alright for those two years. The city of Lausanne raked in enough tourist money from the athletes, their families, and the potential investors that it secretly became the meeting spot for the Olympic Committee who wanted to adopt it into their overall Olympic cycle. In fact, the committee fell in love with Lausanne so much so that once the dust settled after the last Rennen, they opened the official Olympic Museum there in 1993."

"That still doesn't explain why it stopped," Marin interjected as she tried to get back on topic.

"Yes, about that," Harvey continued. "It was thought that athletes of both the winter and summer games should have a chance to compete in their respective climates, so each year it was held in opposite seasons. That would be the downfall of the gem that could have been. The first leg of the Rennen only eliminated three teams in 1963. The second leg was a climb up one of the Swiss Alps' peaks to recover a beaker containing a chemical needed to complete the next scientific task. On the summit of the mount while teams were securing their prize, a rare and unexpected storm of tremendous size and strength bashed the side of the mountain. Five days later rescuers were able to scale the mountain that was lambasted with snow. Twelve pairs of competitors and four individual scientists were found frozen to the side of the Alps."

"Wait! You're saying twenty-eight people died during this race?" Marin asked.

"That is correct, Marin, but there were six people who had found a way to survive the ordeal with some hypothermia and a few missing appendages, but their teammates succumbed to the harsh elements. The two unaccounted scientists have yet to be found to this day. The race had lost some of the most talented minds and bodies in the world because of Professor Snowenwood's ideas. He was immediately deemed a madman. Quickly and quietly, he was tried and held liable for all twenty-eight people's deaths and those two that had gone missing."

"Great. We are going to participate in a death race," Marin lamented.

"This *was* a very dangerous race created for the fastest and smartest, but they didn't call it a death race," Harvey continued. "But the race was dubbed 'Rennen Übersetzung' which roughly translates to 'Madman's Race.'"

"That name is really not much better," Tipton said, adding his two cents.

"The memory and all its potential have been swept under the rug and forgotten by everyone because of its disgrace. The trophy awarded to the Australians hasn't been seen since it was removed by the Prime Minister of Australia from the capital building shortly after the news of the deaths was made public to only the leaders of the countries that lost men," Harvey said, completing his explanation of the Rennen.

"So, each of us has to go in with Bixby to compete in this 'Snowenwood Rennen?'" Pippa asked, knowing that she most likely knew the answer to her own question.

"You mean Rennen Übersetzung?" Marin chimed in.

The occupants in the room spun around and looked at Bixby who was now holding the rest of the information that they needed.

"Nobody says you have to go in. Cody did say that each level would get much harder and more dangerous," she said before briefly recapping the events of earlier that morning: how the school had completely frozen, how she found her way to the plane where her archenemies were already waiting. Then she explained the video but skipped the part where she told them what the prizes were for each contestant. She was not certain that if she won everything, another riddle about her grandfather would sit well with her friends. She wanted to know more before sharing it with the group.

"Cody also sent me this list of fifty potential challenges he will choose from for the five legs of the race. It should help us at least focus our training," Bixby concluded.

"Fifty is an awful lot of challenges to train for in a week," Harvey said from the corner.

"I agree, Harvey. That is why I need you, Arthur, and Mr. Richards to combine as many as you can into each training session," Bixby replied, hoping he could create a good plan.

Harvey scanned the list as he spoke his thoughts out loud, "I could do a parachuting excursion that lands you on top of a mountain, and you could ski down. I'm going to have to teach you how to drive for this one to work..." he said as his voice faded off down the hallway towards the launch room.

"For those who are coming into Level Three with me, tonight you should eat and catch up with as much homework as you possibly can. Holo-School Prime may not see you for a few days or weeks. We will all need to train these simulations because the Snowenwood Rennen rules state that I need to go in with a partner," Bixby said.

"Hate to put a damper on all of your battle plan there, but you are a little short on manpower," Arthur said, from his corner, making an obvious observation of his own. Being the H-bot programmed for rules, he never missed an opportunity to let Bixby know she was outside of the boundaries.

"He's right, the rules say you need a total of six people to make a team. Other than Bixby as the team captain, we only have three humans as team members," Tipton said, concerned by the math.

"What about Pops?" Marin asked.

"You all know as well as I do that my grandpa is not physically able to go into the level," Pippa said almost immediately.

"Couldn't we ghost Hucklebee, Miss Marmalade, Harvey, or Arthur in?" Tipton asked as he reviewed the rules.

"Cody specifically said that they have to be human," Bixby said, recalling his three rules: follow the original Rennen rules, human teammates, and having to complete all tasks to finish the race.

The reality of the situation sank in with the remaining three.

"Where are we going to find teammates that we can trust that will go into Cody's riddle in less than two weeks?" Tipton moaned.

"What about one of your ROTC buddies, Marin?" Pippa asked, hoping she had other friends outside of the three of them.

"Do I look like someone who goes out of my way to make friends?" Marin asked rhetorically. "You all are hard enough to keep up with."

"You seem to not be rattled by any of this, Bixby. What's the plan?" Pippa asked, concerned.

"They will be here for dinner tonight," Bixby interjected at the highpoint of the group's anxieties.

"How'd you find them?" Tipton asked, baffled at her speed in assembling a full team.

"Bixby, you're keeping way too many secrets," Pippa said sarcastically with a pouty tone. "Who are they?"

"A lady never reveals her secrets, am I right, Miss Marmalade?" she asked.

Already knowing who the guests were, Miss Marmalade walked by Bixby's chair and gave her a fist bump.

"You bet, Sugar," she said and then let out a beautiful southern chortle.

"You all have three hours before dinner. Everyone needs to prep for a lot of training before Level Three," Bixby concluded before she made her way to her room. Knowing when the riddle would start gave her peace enough to feel free to take a much needed nap.

She propped up her pillows, turned off the lights, pulled Cody's clock from under her bed to illuminate the void, and from underneath her pillow she pulled out Grandpa Timmons' riddle book. It was the last relic she had left of his after the ransacking of Pinnacle Manor. It was the only thing she had belonging to any of her family members that she could hold close to feel as if they were there with her. A hundred million dollars and her family back would be very nice to have right now, but the idea that this entire riddle involved a secret from her grandfather helped her stave off the temptation of quitting, for now.

CHAPTER EIGHT
THE NO-SURPRISE SURPRISE

Pinnacle Manor smelled of every possible dinner food. Bixby could tell that Miss Marmalade had been cooking since the moment she said guests were coming.

"Coffee is on, Sugar," she announced. Bixby loved Miss Marmalade's voice when she called her 'Sugar', and she liked her even more when coffee was ready. Bixby had begun to drink way too much coffee since sleep wasn't an option for her.

She was not surprised to see everyone at the dinner table anxiously awaiting the arrival of their new teammates.

"Any idea when they will get here?" Tipton asked through a face full of hamburger.

"No," was all the answer he got in return as she poured herself a cup of coffee.

"Oh c'mon, Bixby. What's with all the secrets lately?" Pippa asked.

"To keep everyone safe," Bixby replied after the first sip of her black coffee hit her soul.

"You don't really think we believe that, right?" Marin asked.

"Nope," she said before taking another sip.

"Based on how you're dressed, I'd say it's your boyfriend," Pippa said, realizing Bixby had freshened up a lot since leaving them last in her grunge look.

"Nope," she again said with a straight face. Their banter wasn't going to phase her. The two new colleagues were there to take care of business, and she couldn't let anyone in the group think that there was time in the next two weeks to do anything more than focus on training. Finishing Level Three was one step closer to getting her family back, and figuring out what Cody knew about Grandpa.

"Arthur just got back from the front gate with our guests," Hucklebee announced as he rolled through the kitchen. "Dibbs on helping with the luggage!" he shouted. It reminded Bixby of the first time she met him—he had been rummaging through the family van trying to help bring in her luggage.

"All yours, Big Guy," Marin replied as she pushed up from the table.

Bixby reached the door first and pulled it open while the remaining three took their place in the Great Hall, kneeling over the back of the couch.

"Thanks for coming on such short notice," Bixby said to the guest that was hidden by the massive door.

"You really didn't give me much of a choice now did you, Red?" Marshall Groves' voice could be heard as he reached the threshold of Pinnacle Manor. He was in his everyday outfit of sandals, jeans, blazer, and this time a green T-shirt with "Eat, Sleep, Hustle" in multicolored letters across it.

"Raise your hand if you saw that one coming?" Tipton asked, astounded.

"How much did you pay him, Bixby?" Marin followed with a logical question through a concerned voice.

"That's your boyfriend!" Pippa exclaimed, appalled at the thought of Bixby hugging him let alone a kiss on the cheek even. "Eww!"

"Definitely the hacker," Marin said, proposing the idea that Bixby did indeed solve the conundrum as to who was Ghosting students in.

"You are the hacker!" Pippa exclaimed as Marshall smiled from ear to ear. Her outburst and his cheesy grin confirmed that he had outsmarted the best tech minds in the school.

"Again, didn't see that one coming either," Tipton said in shock.

"And he will tell you all about it before we start training," Bixby said, making sure he knew there was going to be no new secrets at Pinnacle Manor.

"Pinky promise," he said holding out his hand, to which nobody put their hand out in return.

"I will show you to your room, Mr. Groves," Miss Marmalade said, motioning him to follow her.

"Give me just a sec, I don't want to miss this next part. Your other..." he paused to make sure he didn't spoil the surprise, "...friend is a real sweetheart and was trying to help Hucklebee with the luggage," Marshall replied as he took a seat on the arm of the couch next to Marin.

"Does Marshall realize that he will actually have to go into the Riddle this time, which is dangerous and potentially deadly?" Tipton asked his housemates as if Marshall was invisible.

"You guys do realize I'm standing right here? I'm literally right here," Marshall grumbled cynically.

"Marshall has every reason to cooperate with us," Bixby said as she turned to see what was taking Hucklebee so long.

"She's right, and to answer your question, Tipton, I know that there is a possibility of going into the Riddle, and being seen by millions of online viewers, and potential customers," Marshall finished.

"That's the Marshall we have come to know and love," Marin said, connecting why he would even consider entering the Riddle which will be teeming with peril.

"And Bixby may have threatened to make my client list public, which would destroy me!" he said with a raised voice of disapproval.

"Blackmail. Now that is the new Bixby Timmons we are continuing to figure out how to love," Marin replied.

Bixby looked over her shoulder with her eyebrows furrowed. It was what needed to be done to get Marshall to comply with Bixby's needs. "He will be fine with our arrangement."

"No complaints from me," he said as a thud could be heard outside the door.

"Please, let Hucklebee take those the rest of the way in," she implored.

"Marshall packed his entire house," huffed Hemsley as he propped himself up against the door exhausted. He was smiling a big gushing smile at Bixby.

"I'm glad you could make it," she said in a tone that nobody had ever heard her speak in before.

"I wouldn't miss this for the world. I mean the last Riddle was awesome, but this one is going to put that mud race to shame," Hemsley said, stepping through the threshold and giving her a little hug.

"Definitely saw that one coming," Tipton said of the most recent guest.

"Hey, I didn't get a hug," Marshall said softly as he now stood next to the couch that had the onlooking team.

"You're not her boyfriend," Pippa said to Marshall. "I knew it was Hemsley," she also whispered to Tipton giving him a warm nudge.

"Just friends," Bixby insisted.

"Good to see you too, Pippa. Is Grandpa around?" Hemsley asked his cousin.

"Good luck finding him. He only shows up every now and again," Pippa replied as she got up and went over to hug him. Tipton followed with a hearty handshake.

"If there is partner dancing like in the last level, does that mean Marin is my date?" Marshall jested now sitting alone next to her.

"Ohhh, the pins and screws the doctor put in my leg are killing me," Marin winced. "Not on your life, Marshall," she followed in her normal crassness before putting some distance between the two of them.

"Y'all need to finish eating before you start practicing. Harvey just told me to tell you that he will have your first challenges ready to go in a half an hour," Miss Marmalade shouted from the kitchen.

Everyone did as they were told. The guests set up their new rooms and everyone met up outside the Ghost-Rooms to start their training.

Harvey stood arms crossed like a coach ready to put in a hard practice with his team as all six made their way to meet him.

"There are three separate simulations. You will each take a turn in the mockup while your teammate is in the Command Center helping you. Then you will switch with your partner and redo the whole level. Based on the fifty different potential challenges, I tried to help you learn several skills during each Launch. Bixby can't learn it all, which means that everyone will need to become an expert at different things," he instructed.

"Who's my partner?" Marshall asked.

"I have Bixby with Hemsley..."

"Oooooh," Pippa said, taunting them, to which Bixby elbowed her in the arm.

"As I was saying, Bixby is with Hemsley. Pippa you are with Marshall, and Marin is with Tipton," Harvey listed.

"Aw! I wanted to be with Bear," Pippa whined at the idea that she couldn't be with Tipton.

"I need you and Bear to focus on the riddle, not each other," Harvey said.

"So, you put Bixby and Hemsley together?" Tipton asked, stating the obvious.

"If you don't get in your Ghost room right now, Tipton, I am going to add a lot of running into your simulations," Harvey said with a growl in his voice.

It didn't take much convincing as he raised his hand and volunteered to Marin, "I'll go first."

"Good choice, Lover Boy," Marin replied as she turned towards the Command Center.

"I'll go first as well so that I can at least spend time with Bear in the Command Center afterwards," Pippa replied as she ducked into the room in front of Marshall. He turned to go to his post, but before she went in, she spun around. "And you and I need to have a conversation on how you Ghosted everyone into Holo-School Prime without *me* knowing about it," she said, miffed at both situations.

Marshall smiled. "Can't wait to tell you *all* about it."

"See you in there," Bixby said to Hemsley, sounding all business to everyone in the hallway.

As Bixby shut the Ghost Room door Hemsley followed Harvey into the Control Room, which had now been sectioned off into booths so that each team could navigate their own challenges without being distracted by other teams. He closed the door behind him and settled into his chair.

"Alright, I'm in," Bixby said over her com as the world around her was made visible to him through a computer monitor.

"Do they always harass you like that?" Hemsley asked about her housemates.

"You have no idea how bad it has been with your cousin, Pippa," she said as she started her search of the mechanisms around her.

"I haven't really seen or spent any time with her or Grandpa Max since we were really little kids," he said, recalling times when he would play in Max Richard's backyard on a rusted, old swing set with his younger cousin.

"Honestly, when she called and said she needed my help in Level Two, I thought she was joking. In fact, I was in disbelief that it was even her. I had no idea how deep she was in with the Cody Club or Timmons Nation or whatever you call it now."

Bixby was scaling the side of a wall and looking down at all the gears. She found that discovering a highpoint in Harvey's riddles was the best way to see all the different objectives and to reach a solution. On the platform next to her was a harness and a clip in point. Bixby was certain that this level was going to help teach her more about using the harness to scale up and down the clock.

Using her best Dr. Schmelney impression, Bixby asked, "How does that make you feel?" as she finished clipping on her safety gear.

"Well, if she hadn't, I would have never met you, and definitely wouldn't be here helping you with Level Three," he observed.

"Are you up to the task?" she asked as she grabbed ahold of the massive second hand as it moved its way up to twelve.

"Well, yeah, but there has been one question I have been afraid to ask in our letters..." he said, hoping that she would allow him to speak freely.

"Now is better than when everyone is around us," she replied, almost certain she knew what he was going to ask.

"Why are you doing all of this? Why don't you quit and get your family back? It's not for the money, is it?" he asked, needing to know.

Bixby was standing on the base of the two in the number twelve while holding onto the one for support.

She was at the very top of the clock looking down. Her mind stopped focusing on the riddle and thought back to Greg's offer to give her the prize money. What he didn't know was that the money had always been secondary. The thought of getting her family back with a hundred million dollars made it sweet, but she was very successful with the streaming they were doing, and money never seemed to influence her.

"A hundred million dollars is a good motivator," she said, surveying her next move.

"So, it *is* for the money?" he asked cautiously.

"At first. But when I stood in the library debating on whether or not to sign the paper and take Cody's challenge, it was as if Cody was talking directly to me. Not like a recording, but a real conversation. It's hard to explain, but it seemed like he was asking me to help him. The money doesn't mean anything to me anymore."

"Why would a tech billionaire genius need help from you?" he asked, but immediately clarified. "It just seems odd to put you through all of this."

"For the longest time I thought about the same question, and I almost quit the whole thing multiple times," Bixby said as she looked out over the peaceful city below her.

"So, why didn't you?" Hemsley asked.

"There are three things that keep me moving forward," Bixby replied.

"You're really going to have me ask?" Hemsley asked, knowing Bixby was dragging the conversation out for some reason.

"I guess someone should know besides me," Bixby began. "When my family was taken, my dad left a message that said that no matter what, I *had* to keep going. Before all of this I didn't really like my dad a whole lot because he wasn't around. But after Level One, I realized that I love my family even though we weren't perfect. I had to keep going. And the second..." Bixby paused. She had not told anyone her prize offer yet. "The second one is that my grandfather keeps showing up as part of the riddles, or part of things that have been promised to me through these levels." Bixby started to scan her surroundings for the first clue to solving their conundrum.

"You're not going to tell me the last one?" Hemsley asked as he also engaged the riddle. He was acclimating himself to the controls as he did a three-hundred-and-sixty-degree spin of the surroundings.

"You ever done something just because you know that it will tick someone off?" Bixby asked as she swung herself down to the loop of the nine. Harvey had built in the tutorial like an old school video game so that she could learn as she went.

"You're kidding, right?" Hemsley asked, sounding like he didn't believe Bixby was capable of intentionally making someone irate.

"The school shrink says it's my coping mechanism with all the trauma the Riddle has brought me," Bixby replied as she continued her way down the clock. Hemsley was silent at her confession that she was using her emotions to elicite reactions from other people as a way to deal with everything going on inside of her.

She swiftly moved towards the clock tower's only window near the large number six. It was now shattered into a few shards hanging on by the wooden frame. The drop was steep and most likely deadly if she fell. She made her way around the corner to see if there was another way she could climb in. There were absolutely no footholds to latch out on. It also seemed to be a dead end.

"There," Hemsley said as he sat forward in his chair.

"Where?" Bixby questioned not knowing what it was that Hemsley had discovered.

"When the second hand hits the thirty second mark it skips a tick," he said directing her back to the clock. "I thought it was just me the first time around, but after the next few times I could see that time literally stopped for one second at the thirty second mark.

"So, the second hand pauses on the thirty second mark for one second?" Bixby asked for clarification.

"Yes, I swear. Just watch," he replied.

Bixby made her way back over to the clock and waited for the second hand to make its way back down over the number six in the clock. Just as Hemsley had observed, the clock briefly paused every minute as it reached the halfway point on the clock.

"It's almost as if it becomes a handle that you have to either push or a pull," Hemsley said with options of what to do next.

The first guess to push, which was met with no result. After the pause, it kept making its way back up the left side of the clock.

The second time around Bixby reached out and grabbed the hand. As it made its customary pause, she gave it a great heave. The six on the clock opened like a door. The hand of the clock was briefly unlocking the door's mechanisms. This allowed Bixby to duck through the passageway and then the simulation unlaunched her.

Hemsley crashed back into the leather chair and said to himself out loud, "This is all madness. What have I gotten myself into?" He lamented.

Hemsley rubbed his head in nervous anticipation of what was said and now what he had to do in the simulation to complete his turn. Silence was at a premium because the quiet observer in the back of the cubical made his presence known.

"That is a great question, Hemsley. A question I need you to answer before you go any further," Harvey said somberly.

Hemsley spun around, again astonished that he wasn't alone. There stood the little Scotsman in his flat cap and tweed vest. This time, Harvey was in his holographic body.

"Careful what you say, young man, I am everywhere," Harvey said, leaning against the wall.

"I didn't mean anything by it. I'm sorry, okay... you're not going to tell her I said that, are you?" he asked nervously.

"Hemsley, Bixby has asked you to join this team because she is willing to put her life and her family's lives in your hands. Everyone here has something at stake in these games except for you," Harvey stated.

Hemsley looked at the old man quizzically.

"Aye... you don't know," Harvey began, sitting on the edge of the end table next to him. "You're in a house filled with orphans and pirates, Hemsley. Everyone here either wins their lives back, money, fame, and prestige, or they lose everything, depending on how Bixby performs in the next two levels."

Hemsley's head cocked sideways like a confused puppy dog.

"When this is all over, Hemsley, you get to go back to your, home, family, and friends. Maybe you are even looked at as a hero for competing in Level Three alongside the great Bixby Timmons. Your parents have no ties to Dragonthorp Inc. because you all run your family grocery store that is in the real world. You don't have to worry about the Business Draft because you will most likely take over the family store someday if you so choose. You have nothing to lose and everything to gain by being here. However, for the rest of the students here at Pinnacle, there is little to go back to if Bixby doesn't succeed."

"What do you mean?" he asked.

Hemsley's eyes darted to the ground as Harvey explained, "Bixby will no longer live in Pinnacle Manor and most likely will never be the same if she loses without getting the answer to the question, 'Why the riddles?' Tipton lost his parents a long time ago and will be on his own like he has been for many years prior to Cody's Riddle, and Marin's family is already scraping bottom to get by after being kicked out of Plumberry Island."

"Marshall seems like he will do fine," Hemsley interjected trying to make it sound like not everyone had it so bad.

"Once Dragonthorp Inc. finds out Marshall has been creatively using their technology to help Bixby, if they don't already know, he will most likely be kicked out of Holo permanently. They don't take too kindly to people who data breach them. And don't forget that your grandpa no longer works for Dragonthorp so your cousin and he could be out on the streets."

"They can come work at the store and live with us," he interjected, trying to make things sound hopeful.

"This isn't a game, Hemsley," Harvey replied, hoping the words were sitting heavy with him. "Do not go into Level Three unless you are absolutely sure you are willing to lay it all on the line for Bixby and the others in this home. No more puppy love, Hemsley. You're in or you're out."

As best as Harvey could compute, he loved Bixby like a father would love his daughter, something that his system was unable to do for the longest time. For fear that this boy would cloud her judgment in the games, Harvey had said what he needed to say to make sure Hemsley's intentions were pure.

The Command Center doors shushed open, and Harvey's tone change as Bixby strolled in and the cubical door pushed open.

"I have a few early insights on what is happening at Dragonthorp Inc. currently. I'd like to bring you up to speed on that info, when you get a chance, of course," Harvey said, changing the subject.

"As soon as Hemsley completes his harness course," Bixby said.

"Very well," Harvey replied, flashing Hemsley one last stern glance before vanishing, leaving the two of them alone.

Chapter Nine

The Ghost of Snowenwood

"He hacked me!" Pippa shouted as she blew into the Command Center like a tornado touching down.

"What happened?" Tipton shouted, standing up to defend her honor, even if he had no idea what was going on.

"Give it a second, Lover Boy," Marshall said as he strolled out of his booth.

Pippa grabbed her Ghost-Writer and started furiously typing. Marshall sat with his fist under his chin, began batting his eye lashes, and grinning a snarky grin.

"There's nothing here," she said, confused.

"Because you deleted it," he replied quickly.

"I deleted..." she said as she began to stare off into space. It didn't take her long to realize what she had done. "He knew that I hack everyone I come in contact with except..." She paused.

"Except yourself." He finished her sentence.

Tipton was the second to understand what was happening. "You ghosted them into her Ghost Room knowing she wouldn't precheck it, and she would delete all traceable files afterwards?"

"My Ghost-Room had like twenty people in it every time I launched in?" Pippa asked.

"You're holograms, so it's not like you could actually bump into each other. All they needed was to get their hands on a Launch-Suit and a backdoor program I wrote that allowed them to use the original Buckberry system to project themselves in."

"That is a lot of profit you could be making on a rig like that. So, what's in it for you?" Marin asked. Marshall never did anything for free.

"I hand selected them because of what they could do to help Bixby, but also because of the access they would get me," he replied.

"Access?" Marin asked. She knew that he was playing chess while everyone was playing checkers when it came to strategy.

"I may have left myself a backdoor so that once they were logged in, I had access to their whole house's Holo and could replay all of what their parents were working on at Dragonthorp Inc. I now have unlimited access to Dragonthorp Inc., and no chance of being caught," he said with a smile.

"There *was* no chance of being caught," Bixby interrupted. They both knew that if Bixby revealed his client list and all that he had done to exploit Dragonthorp Inc., he would be a dead man.

"And that is why I am very happy with our current agreement," Marshall replied.

"Okay, so how did Bixby bust you?" Tipton asked more curious than ever.

"Somehow she broke into my locker and left me a very well worded note, that I cannot repeat, that convinced me to join the team."

"I may have been a little upset when I made the connection that you were the one making life difficult with Gabhammer," Bixby replied.

"That doesn't explain how you knew it was him," Marin said, refocusing the conversation.

"The first kid on Gabhammer's list was Devereaux. His dad worked with my dad on the gloves that allowed my dad to pet holographic polar bears. It was the first project that I asked Marshall to lift when we rebuilt Harvey so that we could create a whole suit out of it," Bixby replied.

"The second thing we worked on was the command center logistics, and does anyone remember the second name on the list?

"Brix," Tipton said with a bit of a gush.

"She has one of the most insane gaming rigs on the planet," Pippa added, slightly gushing herself.

"Her mom helped create multi-player gaming centers that worked together as if they were all playing on the same controller. The blueprints Marshall gave us was for a basic controller, we simply made it into an entire ecosystem," Bixby said, boasting that all she had to do was follow the list down. "There was only one person outside of Pinnacle Manor who knew our builds."

"Marshall," Marin said in surrender that she too had been duped.

"Correct," Marshall replied, bowing his head slightly with a sense of pride. "I do what I can to please my customers."

The word 'customers' stirred the leviathan inside.

"You need to get past everyone in this room being customers and start looking at us like the ones who could save your life," Bixby said, leveling with everyone in the room. "And if I find out that you left even a single backdoor into any of our work, let's be clear, I will burn your business to the ground... with you in it," Bixby said, stonefaced.

The room fell silent, and the mood shifted. Everyone knew she had an obligation to check his loyalty, but nobody had ever heard this side of Bixby before. Not one person dared challenge her, because they could all tell she meant every word of it. The leash that kept her internal beast in check was starting to fray.

Marshall, for the first time in the few years Bixby had known him, had nothing to say. She didn't know if it was shock, or if he was weighing his options, but he knew she meant business.

"We don't have any backup on this level, so everyone needs to be ready to go into Snowenwood's Rennen," Bixby said, passionate about why they were training.

"Wait, Level Three is a Snowenwood Rennen?" Marshall said in shock. Up until this point, nobody had told him the details of the level.

Bixby nodded in return.

"Whoa! You know the ghost stories about that race, right?" Marshall asked.

"Just because contestants died, doesn't mean there are ghosts," Tipton replied.

"Dude, I'm not talking about the dying part," Marshall responded.

"There is something more concerning than everyone dying?" Tipton asked under his breath.

Marshall slowly inhaled. "Way worse. Snowenwood was secretly tried for the deaths of all the people who died up in the Alps and was found guilty. He was quietly sentenced to life in prison with no chance of parole. After that there is no record of what happened to him—no jail record, no nothing. I searched death records, inmate records, and even all the insane asylums in the area; this guy is a complete ghost. Most people now talk of him as a myth rather than a real person. Some say he haunts the Alps looking for the remaining dead bodies that were not recovered. Others believe he is still haunting the Chateau St-Maire where his hearing was held because a courthouse would have been overrun by angry mobs," Marshall said in an almost scary-story like voice.

"No wonder why everyone doesn't think he exists," Tipton said, commenting on how hush-hush everyone had kept the trial and sentencing.

"I'm not sure that he deserved to go to jail for their deaths. I mean didn't everyone sign some kind of waiver in a race like that?" Pippa inquired.

"I don't think those existed back then," Marin said, looking over his data.

"Probably not, but at each leg of the race the team had to check in with Snowenwood and tell him who was going to enter with each team captain. Snowenwood recorded it all in a journal that has never been found. I figured that if I could locate the journal..."

"We would know who survived and could ask them about the parameters of the Rennen," Bixby concluded for him.

"There is no way that journal is floating around out there somewhere," Tipton said in disbelief.

"I'll get The Timmons Nation on it right away," Pippa said pulling up her Ghost-Writer.

"No need, dear Pippa," Marshall said, halting her clacking with a hoity voice. The table gazed at him in wonderment.

"Whoever made the Snowenwood Rennen disappear from history did a really good job. Even though I don't have the actual journal, one of the moms of a kid I helped ghost into Holo School-Prime is in charge of a massive mining expedition into some sort of hard drive vault. They started right around the time Bixby learned about the third level. They believe that Cody already knows the answers to the questions we are asking, so they are drilling away day and night."

"How much do they know?" Bixby asked.

"Don't know. Her feed went dark two days ago, and her son hasn't been back to school since. All I know is that they are spending a lot of time trying to open a file that seems to be a list of something.

A massive crash interrupted it all.

Everyone at one end of the table jumped up from their seats as iced tea splashed all over the table. Mr. Richards was wiping an excessive amount of the liquid from the front of his pants. Embarrassed, he dashed from the dining hall to go change.

"Grandpa?" Pippa cried after him.

"I'm fine," he shouted back. He was already down the hall heading for his room to change.

Miss Marmalade made quick work of the mess and dinner was back to normal in no time.

"Ok, where were we?" Marshall asked.

"You think they opened it?" Tipton asked.

"If Dragonthorp Inc. has gone dark, maybe," Marshall replied.

"Can you give the Timmons Nation access to those other parent accounts?" Bixby asked, formulating a plan.

"Can we not burn my entire empire to the ground by giving everyone access to it? At least give me some time to work it myself?" Marshall asked, knowing that one wrong move and his gift of stealth was a strongpoint of his.

"You have until we launch in to figure out what it is, and if you don't have anything, I need to turn the Timmons Nation loose on whatever it is Dragonthorp Inc. is mining," Bixby insisted.

Marshall huffed and nodded in approval.

"The hackers will help you to make sure you are no longer hiding anything," Bixby added, to which Marshall rolled his eyes.

"Don't worry, you will get paid if we mess up your illegal operation," Bixby said, batting her eyes at him. She knew that he understood that he had no choice but to have a little bit of help in his search.

"Looks like Pippa and I will be working closely together," Marshall said with a devious tone.

"Over my dead body," Tipton said, asserting his disapproval of them working together alone. He quickly added, "She said the *hackers*. Plural. Which includes me."

"Anyone with a computer chip in their head needs to work with Marin to make sense of all the data they pull," Bixby instructed.

"Even me, Sugar?" Miss Marmalade inquired.

"You do what you do best and help them when you can," Bixby replied.

Miss Marmalade smiled and winked back at Bixby.

"We don't have any more time to dwell on ghost stories. We have less than a week to learn a lot of new skills and keep an eye on whatever Dragonthorp is up to." Bixby urged the group back to focus.

"I'm not so sure we aren't going into Snowenwood's ghost story, Bixby," Marshall replied.

"It's only a ghost story when you're not the scariest thing in the story," Bixby said, as the leviathan was stirring on the inside of her.

CHAPTER TEN

LAUNCH DAY

Bixby's Ghost-Writer went off next to her bed, even though she had it on Ignore Mode. For the first time in a long time, she had slept long and deep. Rolling over with only one eye open, she clicked on the Ghost-Mail titled, "Updated Rules and Regulations" and glanced over it quickly.

"Forward to Pinnacle Manor inhabitants," she commanded her Ghost-Writer as she dropped it back down on her nightstand. Bixby was familiar with the jitters that came with launch day and hoped to be able to grab a few extra hours of sleep. Once in any of Cody's levels, sleep became an afterthought. Her mind and body were always on either the offensive or defensive. She was never really able to take a moment to calm herself, because if she wasn't thinking about the next move in the puzzle, she was running full speed into the next bone-jarring activity. This may be her last few moments of peace before her world began to spiral out of control. Again.

"Knock-Knock?" Hucklebee jovially asked outside her bedroom door.

"TEN MORE MINUTES!" Bixby shouted back, pleading for just a few more moments of silence.

Without a reply Hucklebee was gone as requested. Bixby's mind wandered to her family and moments they shared as she looked out from her pillow over Worthy Lake.

"Bixby, please, it's time to go. We are all prepared and waiting for you," Max Richard's voice said from a cracked door. She figured he was the only one brave enough to knock on her door this time. She didn't care who it was though.

"Didn't I say I would be there in ten minutes?" Bixby grumbled as she covered her face with her pillow.

"Yes, Bixby, you did. That was nearly an hour ago," Mr. Richards lobbed back.

Pulling her pillow back and looking up at the picture windows that overlook Worthy Lake, she could tell that the sun had gone up over the horizon a great deal more than the last time she looked at it.

She pulled the Cody Clock from under her bed, plopped it on her nightstand, and confirmed the time.

"Uggghh," she grumbled as she scratched both sides of her head while sitting up.

"Where did you get that... magnificent clock?" he asked gob smacked at the sight of it.

"It was Cody's and the final key that led me to the library and the start of this whole thing," she said with a big stretch before putting her feet on the floor.

"Didn't the story say that he made that clock and sold it?" Mr. Richards asked again, sounding confused.

"Listen, I have no idea how it got here, or even how it works. All I know is that this clock was the key that started it all."

"Right... yes, you're right. Well then, we will see you in the Great Hall in fifteen minutes. Everyone is ready and waiting," he concluded as he walked out her bedroom door.

Bixby pushed up out of bed and did her normal morning routine with the exception that instead of her everyday Holo-Suit, she reached to the back of her closet and pulled out the Holo-Riddle Suit held together by strong, thick, silver threaded seams. She had not touched it since Level One because Cody tricked her into putting on a Holo-Dress in Level Two.

"Good to see you again, ol' friend," she said as she slipped it from the hanger. As she pulled it up over her shoulders, she noticed that it didn't fit her like it did in Level One. She had changed. As she pulled up the last zipper, she realized she looked slightly ridiculous in her high water, tight fitting Holo-Riddle Suit. She had grown both in height, but also strength. The instant the final zipper went up, the suit self-adjusted to her body as it did the last time she put it on.

"That's better," she said, giving herself one last look while pulling her hair back. "Keep me safe, Grandpa," she prayed before pulling open a back zipper and tucking his leather notebook inside for safe keeping. Bixby took one last look around her room before she made her way to the Great Hall.

Hucklebee was the first to greet her sheepishly. "I am sorry that I woke..."

"Who's there?" Bixby said, cutting him off with a smile.

"Cows go," he said, perking up knowing Bixby wasn't mad at him.

"Cows go who?" she said, thinking she may already know the end as she rolled her eyes with a sneer on her face.

"No, silly. Owls go hoo. Cows go moo!" He laughed at his brilliance.

Bixby gave him a big hug and thanked him for all that he had done for her over the last year. "You have been the closest thing to a brother to me since mine have gone missing."

He savored the thought of being as close as a brother to Bixby.

"You all read the updated rules and regulation email that I received this morning?" she asked, talking directly to the team that was sitting around the coffee table enjoying a big breakfast and lattes. Harvey brought it up on the big screen as she took her seat next to Hemsley on the couch.

"I'd like to review it really quick so that we are all clear," she said grabbing her plate.

UPDATED RULES AND REGULATIONS:

- *All of the original rules from Snowenwood's Rennen still apply.*

- *No contact outside of Level Three once you and your chosen teammate have begun the challenge.*

- *Failure to comply will trigger an electromagnetic pulse or EMP in the game rendering your communication devices useless for the remainder of the level. This is not negotiable in any way.*

- *You will have exactly one hour of transportation time in between exiting one challenge and arriving at the next challenge.*

- *I will publish the videos of each competitors on-demand once all three teams have completed the challenge so that nobody can steal answers from anyone else.*

- *Please enter your launch rooms at 0900.*

The clock was ticking down as they finished reviewing the rules.

"Does anyone have any questions?" Harvey asked.

"What happens if someone accidently leaves their microphone on?" Pippa asked, fearful that someone would make a mistake and cut off communications.

Arthur stepped up to squash any anxiety. "With the help of Tipton, I have put a breaker in the system of the second person to launch that will allow us to automatically cut off all communication devices to and from the launch rooms. I have thoroughly tested the hardware and it is fool proof," he comforted.

"What order do we go in?" Marin asked, knowing that everyone else in the room other than Bixby was thinking the same question but afraid to ask.

"It will depend on the challenge. We will discuss it as a team and decide who is best for each riddle. If we need to, we could also lean on some of the Timmons Nation if we are stuck on a riddle and possible solutions before we select a teammate," Bixby said.

"I trust each one of you to be there for me just like I will be there for you," Bixby continued. Unknown to the rest of the group, Harvey's eyes made contact with Hemsley as he stared intensely at the wooden table. Harvey wanted to make sure that he heard every last syllable that Bixby was saying, and that he was taking it to heart. He didn't yet know if Hemsley had really digested the sacrifice that he may have to make standing next to Bixby.

"From the looks of it, we will be hitting the ground running right away, so I need everyone ready not only in the Command Center, but also stretched out and ready to enter the Riddle right away. Two of us are going to get an early start in this thing," Bixby reminded everyone.

"Miss Marmalade, I am going to need you to whip up something with a lot of protein, sugar, and/or caffeine in it to keep me going. Every time someone new launches in, I will need you to send them in with more of your concoction. There will be no rest for me until this is over, so I need as much help as I can get."

"I'll start on it right away," she said, bounding towards the kitchen.

"Are we all ready?" Bixby asked with a smile, trying to build the team's confidence. She could see that everyone except Marshall was a bit rattled. He had just checked his websites stock of Timmons paraphernalia to make sure that everything was ready to ship when Level Three launched. Seeing what he was doing while looking over his shoulder, Tipton tapped him on the shoulder and whispered, "You realize you have to survive the level in order to cash in on all of that right?"

Suddenly, Marshall was just as on edge as the rest of the group.

"Alright, let's go," Bixby said as she stood up from the couch and led the group down to the Command Center. She gave everyone the traditional launch hug, but this time instead of saying "See you afterwards" she said, "See you inside."

Shutting the door behind her, she met Arthur outside of her customary Launch Room.

"Any words of advice?" she asked him nervously.

"Bixby, I think they fear you more than you fear them," he said as he pushed open the latch of the Launch Room with a swoosh.

"You think so?" she asked as she began to step inside.

"Heck, I'm even scared of you when you get inside of this thing," he said with a smirk. "Keep them all safe, Miss Timmons," Arthur finished.

Bixby affirmed him with a bob of her head as the Launch Room door swung closed. She knew deep down inside she couldn't promise she could keep herself safe let alone other people, but nobody needed to know that.

She centered herself in the room as a time clock appeared on the wall across from her: forty seconds remained. She closed her eyes as she began to slowly recite her family creed that her grandfather etched into all of his journals:

"I am a Timmons: Rich in history, faith, and love. You were born a fighter. Nobody messes with a Timmons' faith, family, or friends without arousing the bull inside. Those loved by a

Timmons will never feel a greater kindness from anyone else in the world. That is our name and how we live our lives..."

As she finished, she could hear the humming of the Launch Room as it warmed up. Her heart was now in overdrive as she breathed in and out slowly trying to control her vitals. She could see the first flash of light through her eyelids. Four of her five senses did their regular launch checks.

Smell. Nothing particular. Maybe a hint of plastic, or ink from a printer, and stale carpet.

Taste. This sense was never really needed when she launched in, but she licked her lips anyway. This time there was a hint of salt.

Feel. It was cool on her face and hot on her back, as if she was standing in the doorway of an air-conditioned room on a hot day. A gentle breeze could be felt across her cheeks.

Sound. Mechanical clicking and scratching as if a child was coloring with pencils on a paper.

She gathered all of her information in a matter of a split second. It was time for her to open her eyes and begin.

Sight. On the door of the tent, that did indeed have a small breeze pulsing through the crack, she saw the scribbling up close. She quickly stepped back to see the whole riddle.

I look flat, but I am deep, hidden realms I shelter. Lives I take, but food I offer. At times I am beautiful. I can be calm, angry, and turbulent. I have no heart but offer pleasure as well as death. No man can own me, yet I encompass what all men must have. What am I?

Bixby only paused a moment because the answer was still fairly easy, and she knew Cody said that each level would get harder. She knew she couldn't fall behind and needed to trust her puzzle solving skills that had not failed her yet.

"You are an ocean," she replied under her breath, hoping that her competitors, if they were near, wouldn't hear her. She winced slightly in anticipation of a burn to appear on her arm, but instead Bixby heard the clanking of metal chains falling off the tent doors, inviting her to go inside. She obliged immediately.

"Ok, team, it looks like I am in some kind of business office that was moved into a large tent. There is an A/C unit cranking in here but outside you need to know that in the brief few seconds I was there solving the riddle, my back started to sweat. So, we are someplace really hot. I tasted salt in the air, and the answer to the riddle was ocean," she rattled off as she turned on her communication device.

Moments after Bixby launched, the team could see what she saw up on their Holo-TV just like in their simulations from Harvey. According to the rules, cameras broadcasting to the world were not allowed to be inside of the Riddle tent, only outside to watch the physical challenge. The rules did say that the teams could communicate from inside the tent all the way up until a teammate launched in. Thanks to a stolen blueprint, courtesy of Dragonthorp Inc. via Marshall Grove, the collaborative efforts of Harvey, Pippa, Arthur, and Tipton were able to recreate a device that went into Bixby's eye like a contact. Advanced far beyond anything they had ever worked with, the ocular piece was able to filter out her excessive eye movement and blinking giving the team an exact view of what Bixby was looking at in real time. It must have been what Greg and Wesley had been using the previous two levels.

"We see you now," Marin said, taking charge of the team as usual. She was a natural born leader, and the rest of the team had no problem letting her do what she was good at doing. "Please turn and give us a 360-degree view of the room so we can log it."

Bixby complied with Marin's request and turned completely around, giving the team a snapshot of her surroundings.

"It looks like a computer lab, but I don't know what those big machines are that are doing all the scribbling," Tipton said, analyzing the room first. "It looks like a gigantic lie detector test."

"What is in those lockers in the corner?" Mr. Richards asked from the buffet.

Bixby raced over to the lockers and pulled on the handle. It creaked open with an ear-piercing squeal. Most everyone squirmed at the sound.

"Scuba gear?" Bixby said, unsure of how they fit with the rest of the room. As she shuffled through the items hanging neatly in the metal cubbyhole Pippa finished banging away on her keyboard.

"You're in a Seismic station, Bixby," Pippa shouted, making the connection.

"A what?" she asked back as she kept searching the lockers.

"It is a station that measures the seismic activities of the earth. It's used by earthquake scientists and volcano scientists..."

"Seismologist," Marshall interjected the accurate term. Pippa side eyed him at the correction before continuing.

"Those machines measure how much seismic activity is happening around them at any given time," Pippa replied.

As Pippa spoke, the earth under Bixby's feet began to shake violently knocking her to the sand below. It only lasted a few seconds, but it was enough to convince Bixby that what Pippa was saying was most likely what was in the room with her.

When the ground ceased to vibrate the machines that were bolted to the counters began to gyrate almost out of control. The needles on the paper leapt into action making page wide scratch marks on the parchment that kept feeding into it.

"I don't know how to read this," Bixby said as she made her way over to the machine. "The number on the top of the machine reads 7.2." She continued feeding data to her team.

"That is the number that it registered on the Richter scale," Tipton chimed in as he too was surfing the web on seismic activities. "The Richter scale measures the magnitude of an earthquake on a scale of 1-10: 10 being the largest. 7.2 is a pretty big earthquake, Bixby."

"I am well aware that it was big; I was here for it," she replied acutely.

"I don't think you are going to like what you have to do, Bixby." Marin spoke up nearly cutting Bixby off.

"What did you find?" Bixby asked, looking around the room.

"You're going to want to look at the map on the wall," she urged.

Bixby raced to the other side of the tent and hanging above a metal desk was what looked to be a topographical map of a mountain. Its circles noted how high each landing was as she climbed up.

"Great, we get to climb the mountain first," Bixby huffed, thinking about the stories she learned about mountains and the original Rennen.

"Not exactly," Marin replied.

"Then what am I looking at here?" Bixby asked.

"You're not climbing *up* a mountain, you're gonna need to dive *down,* below the ocean and reach the base of the underwater mountain," Marin corrected her.

"Huh?" Bixby asked.

"It's a map of the ocean's depth. Each one of the rings on the map has a number written along it. That means how far below the ground is opposed to the water surface. You can see that one of the rings overlaps with the other set of rings?" Marin started to point out.

"Yeah, I see it," she answered as she reached up with her finger and traced over where they were overlapping.

"That is a cliff that hangs over a huge void or what looks to be a fault line. Underwater, there are fault lines that slide against each other. As they slip, they cause earthquakes. Now see the two red flags on the map on either point that bisects the fault line?" Marin asked.

"Yeah, I see them," Bixby replied hurriedly, knowing the clock was ticking.

"That is where you will have to place the explosives," Marin finished.

"Explosives!" Bixby shouted.

"Ahhh, yep," Marin said with a huff, knowing that it was bad news. "Those blocks on the table right below you with the wires coming out of them. You're not playing bingo, Bixby. C-4 is an explosive," said the military expert.

"I am seventeen years old! I am not messing with explosives. I haven't even had a chance to learn how to drive a car!" Bixby shouted.

"Bixby, I realize these riddles are a little bit different than the ones we practiced on, but I'm sure it is going to be alright," Harvey said, trying to calm her down.

"Says the people sitting in leather chairs eating cookies!" Bixby shouted as Mr. Richards looked down in his hand and realized he had a cookie in it. Slowly, his hand disappeared behind his back.

"Who's going in there with her first?" Harvey asked the group as Bixby paced the floor collecting her thoughts.

"Marin? You seem to be the weapons expert," he said, offering first dibs to the one with some experience.

"Claustrophobic. If I get in that wetsuit and go underwater, I will freak out like you have never seen before," Marin replied, certain she was not the one for this job.

Harvey quickly moved on. "Tipton?"

"No can do. I can't swim," he replied.

Reaching out to the last member of the original training team, "Pippa?"

"I can't either; I have tubes in my ears. I even have to wear earplugs when I shower for fear of getting water in them."

"Looks like it has to be one of you two," Harvey said, turning to the reinforcements.

"Rock, Paper, Scissor you for it?" Marshall challenged Hemsley.

"Best two out of three?" Hemsley asked, confirming the parameters of the challenge.

"Rock, Paper, Scissors, Shoot," they said in unison as Hemsley won the first round.

Marshall came back to win the second round with paper, but in the end, he ultimately lost with rock to Hemsley's paper.

Marshall quickly dialed a number on his cell phone as Arthur directed him towards the Launch Rooms.

"Yeah, Marty! Those shirts we have in the stock room with my face on them... Yes, those ones... Put the caption 'I'm the Bomb' on it anywhere and get it online now... No, no, I trust your creative genius... It needs to be on the site in less than five minutes in every color and size and call in some of your guys. We are going to get extremely busy," he shouted into the phone as he strolled out of the Command Center while Miss Marmalade followed him with a big armful of protein bars to stuff into his Holo-Suit.

Arthur snagged his phone out of his hand and hung it up. "I need you to focus!" he scolded.

"Hey, that's my phone," Marshall cried out.

"And that is my Launch Room which will blow up if you bring it inside. So, if you are quite ready, Bixby is on a time schedule here."

Understanding Arthur's urgency, he slipped quickly into the Holo-Suit, grabbed the snacks that Miss Marmalade had finished packing, and made his way to the center of a Launch Room. He crossed his heart and kissed a saint that was dangling on his neck under his suit.

"Does this thing..."

Before he could finish his question, the bright light shot into the Launch Room, and Marshall was now part of the Riddle.

CHAPTER ELEVEN

LURKING IN THE DARK

"Are you ready?" Bixby cried out from the opposite side of the tent.

After a moment of getting his bearings, Marshall could see Bixby already putting on her wetsuit and pulling diving gear out of her locker.

"You did the scuba diving simulations?" he asked.

"Tell me you did the scuba diving simulations as well?" she demanded.

"I went swimming with dolphins once at Wallaby World," he said as he hurried over to his locker so that he could copy everything Bixby was doing.

Bixby also had only been scuba diving once at Wallaby World on the one vacation her family ever took. She saw picture instructions on how to put together the dive equipment, but one glance brought her brief two-hour training course back in a flash. But Bixby had also taken at least ten of Harvey's diving instruction courses before the race.

"Okay, here is the crash course because we don't have time to mess around. The deeper we go underwater the more pressure our bodies will feel. Your ears will start to pop, and you may even feel a little foggy in the head. It is totally normal, just gulp every few feet as we go down to clear your ears. It is not a race to the bottom or the top. Each way we swim has to be slow and steady or we will get what is called the Bends, or decompression sickness—"

"Like Mercedes Benz?" he interrupted.

"More like your bubbles of gas start to form in your body and if you don't equalize your bodies inner pressure slowly and regularly you will bleed from your nose, ears, and eyeballs."

"Not really something I want to hear right now, Bixby," he said as she helped him put on his buoyancy compensator and tank.

"Then it might be a bad time to tell you that we are both going to be carrying a cube of explosives?" she tried to say in a joking way, but the thought freaked her out as well. Marshall just looked at her with discord in his eyes.

"I think after this we need to renegotiate our contract," he said nervously.

Finally, the two divers were suited up and made their way over to the plastic explosives. Each one had a Velcro arm band so that they could carry the cargo attached to their arms leaving their hands free to swim.

"The instructions next to the C-4 says that this green button here under this safety flap is what will spark the magnesium timer which is waterproof. As soon as the magnesium gets to the C-4… kaboom," Bixby said, pointing to the laminated paper.

"How much time do we have to get away?" Marshall asked.

"Not enough for you two to mess around. Get to the surface and get home," Marin said as she researched magnesium burn times while estimating the length of the wire.

"I'm sure it will be enough to safely return to shore. Remember that if you surface too fast, you will get sick and end up either dead or in a compression chamber for at least a few days," Bixby said as she pulled her last zipper tight.

Marshall nodded, but not very convincingly.

With flippers in one hand and a mini bomb in the other, the duo made their way to the tent's exit.

"See y'all on the other side," Bixby said to the crew a few feet away from her in the command center. But to Bixby and Marshall, everyone was a million miles away.

"Be safe," was all that Tipton was able to muster as he reached down and cut the communications early for fear of getting it taken away from them. The team watched as Bixby pulled back the tent cover and dashed out onto the beach.

For the first time in Level Three the world could see Bixby Timmons and her dive partner. "Wave to your audience," Bixby whispered to Marshall.

"Where?" he said, nervously looking around.

"I don't know where the cameras are, but they are here somewhere," Bixby replied.

With his flipper filled hand he started flapping his arms like he was trying to excite a crowd at a rock concert and started screaming at the top of his lungs, "C'mon y'all, make some noise! Bixby Timmons and your boy Marshall Grove are about to drop a bomb on this Riddle, y'all!"

Bixby couldn't help but smile knowing that she couldn't see or hear anyone cheering, but she was sure that in cyberspace the crowds were going nuts. Looking down at the sand she could see four other footprints shuffling their way out to the ocean.

"Hey, hot shot! Let's pick up the pace; the other teams are in the ocean already," she urged, knowing they were already in last place. Coming to the realization that if Bixby finished in last place his business would go belly up, he scrambled to the edge of the water, secured his explosive to his left arm, put on his flippers just like Bixby, and shuffled backwards into the sea.

Bixby had taken a mental picture of the topographical map and knew once they entered the water, they had to veer just slightly to the right to find their ledge. Several times she could tell that Marshall was swimming on pure adrenaline because she had to grab his ankle and pull him back so that he wouldn't dive too fast. Eventually, she grabbed his wrists to help him pace as they made their way into the belly of the ocean.

At the halfway point Bixby pulled Marshall to an abrupt stop. They were not alone...

Unable to communicate with their rebreathers in their mouths, she started to use hand signals as she reached down to her ankle and pulled out her knife. Marshall freaked out a little bit knowing that he didn't have a knife on his ankle. He tried to pull away from Bixby's grip and as he did, something large and firm rammed him in the back knocking the rebreather, his only oxygen source, from his mouth. Desperate to recover his lifeline, he thrashed his arms over his shoulder as it floated behind him. Knowing he was panicking, Bixby took a deep breath in and then pulled her mouthpiece out of her mouth shoving it into his. He breathed as deeply as he could and then several short fast breaths followed. She reached around behind him and caught his rebreather and held it in front of him after he had regained control. With a deep breath he made a quick switch replacing each of their lifelines back into their correct place. The calmness didn't last very long as Bixby clicked on her underwater flashlight connected to her life vest. It was only on for a brief second, but they both realized what was currently swimming near them. They were roughly the size of a cow with hundreds of razor-sharp teeth.

Marshall's eyes started to water as his hand raised between them and he started reluctantly making a chomping motion.

Bixby flattened her palm all the way out and starting at her forehead made a motion slowly down, signaling him to stay calm.

Sharks are attracted to shiny objects, so they circled the pair hoping that it would again make an appearance. As Bixby and her companion huddled close to each other in the murky water, Bixby grabbed hold of Marshall's jaw and had him focus on her. She knew that his inclination would be to surface, but there were three problems with that plan: One, sharks surface much faster than humans can so they couldn't outswim them. Two, they had not completed their mission. And lastly, surfacing too quickly would certainly give them the bends, and an untimely end to Level Three. Bixby had to think of something quickly, or they would be ragdolls in the teeth of monsters.

Then it hit her. Very slowly Bixby unbuckled her buoyancy compensator which was also her life vest with her air tank attached. In the dimly lit water, and with detailed hand motions, she laid out her plan to Marshall.

Bixby deflated her vest, and on the count of three she turned on the light connected to her shoulder strap. The shark's full attention was now on the bright LED bulbs as they moved in to attack. With the blade of the knife, she sliced through her airline which sent most of her scuba gear tumbling out of control towards the bottom of the ocean. Every cold-blooded beast surged down below to take a stab at the gyrating oxygen tank. As it came close to the bottom, Bixby and Marshall could see their flags thanks to the flashlight that was also dancing along with her tank on the ocean floor.

Letting all the air out of his vest, the pair slowly sank to the murky depths, unnoticed by the ferocious man eaters. As they descended, they shared breaths from the single working rebreather. Bixby gasped one last deep breath of air before pointing Marshall to his flag, while she stayed and attended to hers. She slowly crept towards her marker and fixed her C-4 to the base of the metal pole with the Velcro that held it to her arm. Bixby let out a few bubbles as she watched Marshal complete his work at the second pole, repeating the same steps with his package. He held up his fingers and counted back from five as they both opened up their security flaps and pressed the green buttons simultaneously when he had no more fingers up. The faint audible *'clicking'* noise like her dad's electric grill could be heard. The magnesium burst into flames. The spark lit up the sea floor like a floodlight. Bixby only caught a small glimpse of the flame, but it was like looking at the sun: burning her eyes and spinning her around enough to discombobulate her directionally.

Bixby was certain that the clicking noise and mini floodlights would immediately draw the shark's attention. She could hear Marshall's squealing through his rebreather. She was certain he had also looked at the light and was panicking. She was too a little bit because she didn't have any air, and if he decided to surface, she was done for. Bixby whipped around and swam towards his shadow that was aimlessly flapping in the ocean. He must have looked at it longer than her because he was noticeably trying to find a way to rub his eyes even though he had his mask on. Once she reunited with Marshall he flailed and screamed through his mouthpiece. She was certain he thought she was a shark. She pulled him in with a bearhug and rubbed his arm. It was all she could think to do to show she wasn't a shark while he was blinded. She then tapped his mouthpiece begging for air. Upon realizing it was her, he relaxed a bit, took a deep breath and she was able to pull the rebreather to her face and suck out the sweet oxygen she had gone almost a minute without. It was the best breath of air she had ever taken.

The sharks had taken notice of the new light sources as Bixby slowly added air into Marshall's vest. They were now a black blob slowly rising to the surface, while the magnesium held the shark's attention. Switching the breathing apparatus back and forth was taxing on both of them. Each ten feet or so Bixby would put her hand in his palm and give him the 'Okay' signal just to see how he was fairing. Each time he would return the signal. She could tell his large blind spot in his vision was fading because he started to look sideways at her as they swam, giving her the 'okay' signal before she could reach his hand, but Bixby could see he was looking a little green from all the action. With about twenty feet to go Marshall's eyes went wild, and as predicted, he panicked darting to the surface. Bixby had taken a large breath each time in anticipation of this reaction.

As she was instructed by her diving instructor at Wallaby World as they prepared to dive with the sea turtles, in case of a situation like this, she started to hum a tune as she let her body slowly float to the surface. Somehow humming allows a diver to not only conserve air as they surfaced, it seems as if the oxygen lasted longer as well. It was pure speculation, but Bixby stayed true to her training. Again, as predicted, when Bixby poked through the water Marshalls mask and face was covered in blood.

"It is not as bad as it looks!" she shouted to him as she grabbed his vest.

"I'm gonna bleed out!" he cried back.

"Knock it off!" she shouted back, pulling him in close. "Anytime a little blood mixes with sea water it seems worse than it really is," she said comfortingly. "It is called a sinus squeeze," she continued, trying to keep his focus.

Because he seemed a little disoriented, along with the blood dripping from his nose, she knew he had a mild case of the bends.

"Tell that to the sharks," he cried back with tears in his eyes.

Bixby's eyes flashed wide open as she realized that they were a good distance away from the shore and Marshall was now bleeding in open water that contained a whole lot of hungry sharks, and two bombs that were about to go off. A plan began to form in her mind, but even she didn't like it.

Bixby was a huge fan of shark series on the Wild Channel and knew some sharks could smell blood from a quarter mile away. They were well within that distance.

"Get your weight belt off," Bixby said as she took off her belt, grabbed a handful of blood from his face and smeared it all over the belt before dropping it into the pitch-black abyss.

"Let's hope they think that is the only thing bleeding," she said as he caught on to her plan and as fast as he could repeated the process with his belt.

"I don't feel that great, Bixby," he said after completing the task.

"Let's get you out of this level," she said. "I'll need your vest!" she shouted, unclasping the buckles. Bixby worked quickly to flip the tank on his vest upside-down before she fitted the vest to herself and leaned back into the water.

"You're going to want to hold on to me like a boogie board," she cried through the choppy sea. He reached up and grabbed the collar of the vest, still woozy from the decompression sickness. She wrapped her legs around him tightly in case he passed out, reached down to the valve on the side of the tank, and slowly opened it. Much to her surprise they gently crept towards the beach. It was working, but Marshall through his haze started stammering, "Bixby, please hurry up, they are getting closer." Looking over his shoulder she could see their dorsal fins raised out of the water. In her brief glance she counted at least eight sharks beginning their stalk. Without hesitation she opened the valve as far as it would go. They were now skimming the water as Bixby was using her arms to steer them the best she could. However, they were not going fast enough to outrun the predators that were gaining on them. Bixby retrieved her knife from its sheath.

"I need you to wipe some of that blood on this knife and then throw it as far as you can." Without arguing, Marshall reached up and obliged her request. It worked... slightly. Two of the sharks darted after the blood covered knife leaving a handful more who were nearing Marshall's flippers. The tank was running out of air as they began to slow. There was only a hundred yards between the shore and Bixby, but she doubted that they would be able to make it.

The explosion was terrifying.

The water mushroomed out of the depths of the ocean like a scene from a war movie. The kings of the deep scattered at the sheer vibrations that it caused. It punched Bixby in the back lifting her and Marshall out of the water. The tank had let out its last gasp of air as the mist from the blast blew inland. Bixby and Marshall could feel the soft rain as it showered down. They were left floating within earshot of the beach as Bixby leaned back to check on Marshall.

Bixby could see that he was getting more discombobulated as he turned his head and looked as if he were going to fall asleep.

"Marshall! Marshall, I need you to stay with me! Hey, look at me!" she shouted as she had to turn his face for him. "We are going to make it, but I need you to stay with me."

She knew she didn't have long until he passed completely out, and it wouldn't take the flesh eaters long before they would be back on the hunt. Bixby turned him over and wrapped her arm under his shoulder region and started to back paddle towards shore. It was her only option left. She settled into a rhythm of pulling at the water and occasionally glancing over to see if he was still with her—it was exhausting. But in the cadence of swimming, Bixby felt an overwhelming sense of uneasiness. Something didn't seem right. Unless the sharks were preparing to swim up from underneath them and breach the surface with them in their jaws, the ocean was very almost calm... for a moment.

The rocks under the ocean's surface must have fallen into the crevasse below the tectonic plates. That was the cause; its effect was the summoning of a massive wave to displace the water that it had removed.

Bixby saw her ride home, and it wasn't going to be a pretty one.

"Tsunami," she whispered.

"Marshall! Marshall!" she said, slapping him. "There will be several smaller waves coming towards us, and most likely one very large one after that. The first ones we need to catch and ride into shore," she started.

"I do love a day at the beach, Bixby," he said, sounding a bit spacy.

"Keep up with me, Marshall," she urged, giving him a flick on the forehead. "Once we get to shore, we have to hurry to the tent, because if that very large wave gets to the tent before we do; we don't get out of this level!"

He began to nod as if he understood. She knew she would have to help him, but she figured a threat on his life would be enough to propel him to the finish line and his big payday.

The first waves were exactly as she had predicted, large enough to give them a ride.

They were able to body surf close enough to the shore that she could put her feet down in the sand. Though it was encouraging to be back near land, they had to hold her ground as the undertow wanted desperately to pull her and Marshall back out to sea. They could both tell that the next wave was going to be bigger than they could have imagined, because they were now standing in knee deep water nearly fifty yards from what used to be the shoreline. All that water was now gathering a few hundred feet below the ocean's surface, and in a few moments, it would come crashing back to the sandy beach they were trying so desperately to get to.

"We need to run!" she said terrified.

"Yes, yes, we need to run," he said through the muddy feeling that was in his head pointing up to the wave that had started to build in the distance. It grew so fast that the sun sank below its horizon in an instant.

With one arm over Bixby's shoulder, they wobbled to the beach. They didn't need to look back as they reached the dry part of the sand, because the power of the wave made the ground below them shake almost as bad as the original earthquake. Part running, part stumbling, but mostly pulling, Bixby lugged Marshall with all of her might.

They could see the shadow of the wave in the sand as it rose above them as they punched through the tent's flaps and braced for the end.

Nothing...

Knowing that they had most likely completed the challenge, Bixby let out a cry of joy as Marshall rolled over, took his last big breath before he hurled and then unlaunched.

Chapter Twelve

Job Interview

"Bixby!" The shout came over her intercom.

Catching her breath and doing a full body review to make sure all her appendages were still working properly, Bixby sat up. "Yeah, guys, I'm here."

"That was insane!" Tipton shouted.

"How do you feel, Bixby?" Harvey chimed in, hushing the room.

"I'm good. I honestly wasn't sure if we were going to make it out of that one," she replied as she rolled up to her knees and stretched her back out. "Where do we stand?"

Pippa took the lead on this question. "Everyone has completed that challenge. Greg had some super fit oceanographer diver guy go out with him. Not really a challenge at all for the two of them. They were out of the water before the first wave rolled up on shore. Wesley was pretty quick, too, but

140

his partner was the cousin Barnaby; the guy who tried to tie you to a chair," Pippa said as Bixby rolled her eyes at the thought of him. "Anyway, he has a really gnarly bite on his leg from one of the sharks. The explosion was what saved them too."

"How's Marshall?" Bixby asked as she reached her feet and started making her way to the tent's exit. Her knees were still a little shaken, but she knew she had to press on.

"Arthur already has him in a decompression chamber helping to stabilize him," Pippa replied.

"He should be okay, but Arthur wasn't too happy about having to clean up a large pile of vomit on the Launch Room floor," Tipton interjected.

Bixby smiled, knowing that the sounds of someone getting sick immediately led to her wanting to get sick. She was glad he waited until just before he unlaunched to do it.

"Bixby, I know that you have already been through a lot, but Greg is already on his plane, and Wesley got into his car a few minutes ago. You have to get going," Tipton urged while looking at the live feed of the race.

Knowing that Tipton was right, she didn't take off her wetsuit, but decided that it could wait until she got to one of her transports. Darting out of the tent she spotted the black luxury car with the back door open. She ran a similar pace to the one she maintained only moments before a massive wave was ready to crash down on her. She dove into the back seat of the car and the door glided closed behind her. The vehicle lurched forward, and she was on to her next challenge. The cool leather seats felt great on the back of her neck as the team hustled into gear.

"Bixby, the news feed is on a timed delay so that we cannot see what is happening to all three teams until everyone has started the challenge. This way we can't see what the person is doing in the first place and copy their method of solving the riddle. Right now, the feed is dark and won't start up until the last team has started the challenge. While you are spending the next hour getting to your next destination, they are broadcasting and reporting on all three teams' time under water. Brilliant if you ask me," Tipton said, glued to the feed. Tipton was wise enough to keep the fact that the world had practically stopped, and *everyone* was currently watching the feeds of Level Three.

"Bad news for last place, and good news for first," she said as she rested her eyes with her head tilted back on the headrest. "Cody seems to be keeping things relatively fair this round."

"Bixby, we don't really know what to do here," Marin said point blank. "We practiced getting you through riddles just like the last two levels. We helped you *as* you went through the riddle, not sitting and watching. Now we have to stay here and wait to see if it is our turn to go in or not. I feel like a reserve basketball player waiting to go into the big game."

"Take me out to the baseball field and eat a bunch of snacks..." Hucklebee started to sing, trying to remember the correct words to an all too familiar song while he was tidying up, but he quickly realized he wasn't making Marin smile and abruptly stopped. Bixby, however, found his on key, wrong word, singing rather entertaining.

"Marin, I get what you are saying. We trained hard, but we trained wrong," Bixby shot back just as candidly. "It's nobody's fault, but now we must deal with it. If we don't push forward, we don't finish this level, and we lose. I hope everyone knows that

Marshall could have unlaunched at any point during that challenge and sank our entire team?"

"That's right," Tipton said, appreciating that even though Marshall struggled to make it to the end, he didn't give up.

Bixby was feeling the surge of confidence flowing through her veins that was mostly missing from Level Two. Her job was no longer to carry the team, but to lead alongside. She was motivating a team to press on towards the goal, and it felt good.

"We are a team, and to be honest, this is a pretty crazy Riddle. So far, the danger factor has been taken to a whole new level. You all know the risk now. Take the next hour and make sure you're ready to compete or not. If you don't want to launch in, I understand. We all have something to fight for in this, so when you have been pushed to your limits in here, think of those things that you are fighting for and use them to drive you forward. That's how we make it to the final level together." Bixby's sentence slowly faded off as she drifted off to sleep.

Harvey muted the mic in the Command Center as she rested. Knowing the motivations of most of the team members, Harvey's quick glance to the corner revealed a boy rubbing his sweaty palms together as he stared at her on the Holo-TV.

"Is she alright?" Pippa asked.

"Her vitals are steady, Pippa," Harvey said as his gaze was now on the Holo-TV with the rest of the room. "Let's let her rest for the few moments she has before the next challenge. And if I were all of you, I would make sure you're ready to go in when called upon."

The car and plane rides were nearly equal in length of time. Regardless, the hour was much too short of a period to catch a breather for Bixby, but she pushed up out of her seat ready to face the next challenge.

"Y'all excited about the berserk danger behind door number two?" Bixby asked as she stood at the airplane hatch and waited for it to swing open. The whole of the Command Center was either pacing or quietly in prayer as the hiss of the door could be heard when the locks released. At the foot of the jet's stairs was another tent.

As soon as Bixby entered it would be "go time" again.

"Let's see what fun is hiding behind door number two," she said right before turning off her com device. She didn't want to risk anyone blurting out a wrong answer, giving her a burn. She skipped down every other stair and bounded towards the entrance to the next riddle and challenge that ensued. Slowly she read aloud every word to herself quietly.

A Japanese ship was en route in the open sea. The Japanese captain went for a shower removing his diamond ring and Rolex watch, putting them on his side table. When he returned, his valuables were missing. The captain immediately called the five suspected crew members and asked each one where and what he was doing for the last 15 minutes.

The cook, in a heavy overcoat, said, "I was in fridge room getting meat for cooking."

The engineer, with a flashlight in hand, said, "I was working on generator engine."

The seaman said, "I was on the mast correcting the flag which was upside down by mistake."

The radio officer said, "I was messaging to company that we are reaching the next port in 72 hours. From now that is Wednesday morning at 10 AM."

The navigation officer said, "I am on night watch, so sleeping in my cabin."

The captain caught the liar. So, who is the thief?

She read it again, even more slowly this time. She didn't want to miss a detail, give a wrong answer, and put herself further in last place.

"Think, Bixby," she said to herself, closing her eyes and envisioning herself on the bridge of a ship listening to each of the alibies of the ship's crew.

The cook makes sense. The engineer, I think, makes sense. She thought through each scenario before her eyes flashed open, and she read the first line of the riddle again.

"It was the seaman, because the Japanese flag is the same no matter which way you hold it," she shouted, envisioning the bright red circle in the middle of the white backdrop.

The chains began to unshackle themselves from the tent door. Bixby turned back on her com and was pulling on the handle before the last link hit the ground.

Inside the tent the layout was very basic. On the side wall was a wardrobe rack that stretched the entire length of the tent. In the center of the room was a separate tech table from the map table; to which Pippa didn't hesitate to dive right in as the coms came back up.

"Whoa! Give me a look at that tech table, Bixby!" she hollered into her mic as she gawked at it from a distance. Bixby hurried to oblige.

"Do you know what any of that is?" Bixby questioned the room.

"I'm sure Pippa is about to enlighten us," Marin countered.

"Okay, I will dumb it down for you all," she snarked back excited to see gear that wasn't even on the market yet. "The thing that looks like a digital watch is a mini Holo-Writer for your wrist. It can create a holographic image if you need it to. The things that look like glasses are actually body heat detectors for looking through walls to see who is on the other side. Police use it on hunts for bad guys. The gloves are a digital lock reader. Simply put your hand over a digital coded device and it will do a scan to see if it can come up with the combination based on skin cells on certain buttons, frequencies, hacked stored databases. After it cracks the code, it will show it on the digital read out on the back of the hand. Then there are two cell phones, but the rest of it I have no clue as to what it is," she finished.

"I do," Marin said, taking over the conversation. "The small black cylinder that looks like pepper spray is called 'NitNit'. It is an aromatic spray that puts someone to sleep for roughly fifteen minutes. Cover your mouth and nose when you spray it. Even a small whiff of it will put you out for a few minutes. The clear plastic sheets are actually fingerprint paper. First, you have to use the dust in the container next to the plastic strips to cover an area where there may be fingerprints. Next you will need to put the clear plastic strip over anything that looks like a fingerprint. Finally, you remove it from the surface, and stick it to the white cards which will allow you to successfully remove a fingerprint and use it elsewhere. The last thing on the desk."

Bixby didn't wait for an explanation as she picked the object up and pressed the button. A large arch of electricity made a half circle over the rods that protruded from the top. "Taser... Nice," she quietly said aloud.

From the back of the room, Hemsley imputed, "Can I see those maps?"

He didn't yet have a chair in the Command Center so as Bixby made her way to the map table he reached over Tipton's shoulder.

"Care to sit down?" Tipton asked, startled by the arms that were now reaching over him and typing on his keyboard. Harvey did one better and created a fourth chair in the room that replicated Tipton's. As she thumbed through the maps, Hemsley was loading them into a program he had on a glass chip that he brought with him.

"What is he doing?" Marin leaned over and asked Pippa. Harvey stood in the back of the room with Arthur amazed at the kid's skills as his fingers danced on the keys. With a final stroke he pulled out the glass chip. "Whoever goes in there can launch with this chip and put it into that mini Holo-Writer. It has 4-D images of the building structure, security features, and what I believe to be the target."

"Target?" Bixby asked over her headset.

"On the top floor of that building there is a vault in the penthouse office. It is the only digital safe in these schematics. The problem is to get to it you will have to get past two guarded checkpoints, a biometric scanner to enter an elevator, and all of the workers in the building. That would include the CEO who is sitting at a desk in front of the painting that has the vault, with a digital lock, hidden behind it."

"Oh, is that all?" Bixby snarked before she had an epiphany. "Thief," she said aloud so the room could hear her.

"Say what?" Tipton asked.

"The first tent riddle's answer was ocean, and the second riddle was about a thief," Bixby said, explaining her data.

"The tent riddle is giving you an idea about what the challenge is. Clever," Marin said to the rest of the group.

"Let's get inside and get whatever is in that safe," Bixby said, bringing the group back into focus.

"Getting you in the building will be the easy part. The paper on the table says there is a presentation on the third floor about being a possible candidate for an internship. After that I can't help you much," Marin replied while continuing to analyze the data.

"Marin? You up for this one?" Bixby asked, immediately going to her strategist for help.

"I can create the plan for you, but to have the two least tech savvy people doing a raid on a high-tech building is mathematically guaranteed to fail. You're going to need someone who is better with technology and way more into dramatics than me to pull this one off," Marin said as she started crafting the tactical steps to get them higher into the building.

In an instant the entire room's focus was now on Pippa.

"Ready to get your nerd on?" Bixby asked, knowing she was her best shot at pulling off the heist.

Confident that she was the right person for the job also, Pippa retrieved Marshall's phone from Arthur's jacket pocket. Hitting redial button, the room could hear it click as a man picked up and shout, "Marshall! You're alive!"

"Yes, he is alive, but he is in a decompression chamber right now, Marty," she started as she reached out snapping a photo of herself on the camera portion of the phone. "I'm calling the shots on this one. I just texted you a selfie of me and I need you to put that face along with the words 'Get Your Nerd On' on shirts of all colors and sizes..."

"I only take orders from Marsha..."

"Listen, I just hacked your inventory and see that you're already twenty thousand units backordered with Marshall's 'bomb' shirts. This one will get you at least that many as well, and I get cut in on a third of the profit."

After a moment of pause as the guy made some sort of comment she finished with, "Good man, Marty! I trust your creative genius." and hung up the phone.

Looking around the room at all the eyes gawking at her, she said, "What? If I'm going to put my life on the line, I might as well get paid too."

Nobody could really argue with that as she gave her grandpa a big hug and promised him she would be back soon. Marin finalized a strategy with Harvey and uploaded it to the chip that contained the schematics of the building from Hemsley. Pippa stuffed the chip in her pocket as she left the room with Max Richards following Arthur into the Launch Room area.

"Remember that I am proud of you and what you are doing," Mr. Richards said to Pippa as he gave her one last big hug.

"I will, Gramps. You and Tipton are the reason I am doing this," she said as she made her way to the center of the Launch Room.

As the door hissed closed, Mr. Richards shouted, "Never give up, Pippa! There is always a way to make it out!"

With that the team was again cut off from the real Bixby and now Pippa.

"Pippa!" Bixby said as she populated next to her. With a quick hug of encouragement Pippa went right to work suiting up. They each clipped on a mini Holo-Writer to their wrists. Under any sleeve it would be an everyday digital watch. Pippa slipped the chip into hers first as the program uploaded. She quickly repeated the same step with Bixby's, and they both brought up the plan that Marin and Harvey compiled.

"Ready to get all dolled up?" Pippa said as she went over to the wardrobe to play a game of dress up.

As the two girls put on an all-black base layer that would be part of the latter half of the plan, they each found distinguished business suits that fit like a glove. Finishing first, Pippa rushed back over to the gear table and grabbed the 'NitNit' from the table and brought it back to the cosmetics table.

"No... No... No... Perfect!" she proclaimed as she was sifting through cosmetics.

"What?" Bixby asked as she pulled her coat closed with a button. Bixby could see that she was pulling out the red lipstick from a vial. "What are you doing?"

"When we get to the security checkpoint, I think they will be a little suspicious of 'NitNit' in our purses but hidden inside a lipstick tube... nobody will know the difference," she said as she had finalized her plan to conceal the sleeping agent. She had spun the red lipstick all the way out of the container and removed the actual lipstick. Next, she dropped the tube of 'NitNit' in the empty space, and then cutting off the top of the lipstick she fixed the tip of the deep red gloss to the top of the 'NitNit' canister and spun the tube back down to normal.

Without missing a beat, she put the stick up to her lips and applied a coat to her pucker.

"Ingenious," Bixby said, impressed as Pippa was already repeating the steps to hide Bixby's 'NitNit'.

Once complete Pippa grabbed the two girl's heat detectors and instructed Bixby on how they worked.

"But I don't wear glasses," Bixby started.

"Put them on and I'll explain," she said as she slipped hers on. "To the naked eye, when we go through security, they look exactly like reading glasses, but they are connected to an app in your watch. The outside of the glasses takes in the inferred signal, sends it to the watch for a readout, and then transmits it back to the inside of the lens as a projection you can see."

"So, basically we can see warm things through walls," Bixby summarized.

"Yeah. Pretty much that." Pippa nodded. "The taser though... I have no idea how to get that past the guards," she finished, rolling it around in her hand.

It was quite a riddle for the two of them, but in the end, it was Bixby who solved the puzzle. Opening the taser, she pulled out the battery and attached it to the back of her cell phone. It now looked like she had an extra charging pack for her phone. She then removed the top of the Taser that held the metal brackets where the shock would come from, and she hid it inside the base of the Taser. It was now a makeup case that held her cosmetic needs like eye liner, nail file, bobby pins, and the tube of lipstick and a barb that would stun anyone into submission: all the stuff she never wore.

Pippa followed her lead but instead of makeup she turned hers into a hard-shelled wallet complete with a few dollars and her driving permit.

"You ready?" Bixby said as she did one final check in the mirror and reviewed the next few steps in the sequence of events that were to happen.

"Bixby, you look smashing," Pippa said over her shoulder as they looked in the mirror at each other.

"Okay, let's go," Bixby said, making her way to the tent opening. She reached up and cut the communication feed.

Out on the street they were no longer on a tarmac at an airport, but on a busy downtown street. Buildings had risen up all around them, each with banners talking about the latest art exhibit that was going to happen that night. Passersby sipped coffee, talking on cell phones, and hurrying to their next appointment with briefcases in hand. It smelled of pollution piping up from the subway tunnels below. It didn't faze Bixby much because all she could hear was the sweet music that was the rhythm to the dance of the city. Horns blared, people chattered, planes flew overhead, plates clattered at the sidewalk cafés, and Bixby loved it. She had gone into the city once to see a play with her drama group at school. The bustle of life in the city brought her creative spirit alive. She had always dreamed of making it back, and here she was about to rob a company of something inside a secure building.

"We go in separately and ask for the Snowenwood Intern presentation. According to the maps it will get us through the first security checkpoint, and up to the third floor. I will meet you in the bathroom on the far end of the hallway," Pippa said, going over the map on her wrist one last time.

"See you in there." Bixby nodded in return. It was weird having to trust Pippa. Bixby hated the idea of even letting her take part of Level Two.

Pippa pushed out into traffic first leaving Bixby to take in the sights of the city a little while longer. The plan was to get to the third floor and break off from the intern group to the service elevators at the very end of the tour.

It would let them off close to their target.

As Pippa climbed the stairs of the towering high-rise building, Bixby spotted Wesley at the information desk, and he had a date: his sister Penelope Dagger. Bixby darted out into traffic, nearly getting hit by a cabbie who thought yellow traffic lights meant to speed up. The screech of his braking tires across the pavement brought attention to everyone standing nearby but was out of range to grab Pippa's attention.

"Watch where you're going, lady!" the cabbie shouted from his window. "I almost squashed ya!"

"Sorry, sorry," was all Bixby could reply before she skipped every other step up to the landing in front of Snowenwood Industries. *Ironic,* she thought as she hurried through the revolving door to catch up with Pippa. As Wesley and Penny were about to turn to head towards the security checkpoint, Bixby brushed past Pippa and knocked her purse from her hand.

"Oh, ma'am, I am sorry," she said in a southern drawl to hide her real voice as the two of them crouched down to pick up the contents and hiding their faces from Wesley's view.

"What was that all about?" Pippa whispered as they scrambled to collect the contents of the purse.

After pausing to let Wesley and Penny stroll by, "You almost ran into our competitors, and it wouldn't have taken them very long to raise a red flag about us to the guards."

Pippa slowly looked over her shoulder and saw the Daggers smiling at an officer as they collected their belongings on the other side of the security checkpoint.

"C'mon, really? I could have buried them if it was something to do with coding," Pippa grumbled.

"New plan, we go up to the desk together but act like we are not together, then through security a few people apart," Bixby instructed. "We need to stay out of their sight."

They rose and headed to the information table next to each other, and Pippa took the lead.

"I am here for the Intern presentation; can you direct me on the right path?" she asked sweetly.

"Wow, this is the biggest turnout for the Intern presentation I have ever seen," the guard said aloud.

"Is that good or bad?" she asked, sounding worried.

"Listen, lady, I wish you luck, but we have only had two interns selected to start a job here in ten years, and one of them quit the second day," he informed.

"Oh my, is that right?" Pippa continued with a polite tone.

"Anyway, you are going to have to go through security right over there, and then take an elevator up to the third floor. Once you get there, take a right and the receptionist will get you settled in," he said as he finished giving air directions with his hands.

Pippa thanked him and shuffled on her way.

"How can I help you, Miss?" he said to Bixby who was standing behind Pippa the whole time acting as if she were patiently waiting.

"I am also trying to be lucky number three... intern that is," Bixby replied.

"Follow that young lady. She is going where you are," the officer finished with a smile.

The two trundled through the process of taking off their shoes and placing metallic objects in a bin. Pippa made it through easily collecting her belongings as she headed for the elevators. Three people later the red alarm sounded, and the officer held Bixby at the gate. As the man behind the X-ray machine moved her bag back and forth, he squinted and waved one of his co-workers over to take a look in her bag. Bixby's heart raced but she maintained a confused look on her face as the man searched her bag with a wooden stick. Reaching in he pulled out the shell of the Taser and peaked in.

"I'm sorry ma'am, but we are not going to be able to let you keep this metal nail file," he announced as he pulled it from its hiding spot among other beauty products.

"My nail file?" Bixby asked, befuddled.

"It's new policy with all the crazy things going on in this world. If you stop back in on your way down, I will return it to you, but don't bring things like this in again," he sternly instructed.

"Understood. Thank you for your diligence," Bixby replied as politely as she could.

From a distance Pippa could see that Bixby had made it through the checkpoint and took the next 'UP' elevator. Bixby collected her things and let out a huge sigh of relief as she made her way into the next crowd of passengers.

"I was pretty sure they had you there, Bixby," Pippa said as the two of them stood at the mirror in the third-floor women's bathroom.

"Me too," she confirmed as she double checked the stalls for eavesdroppers. "I also took a peek into the Intern presentation and Wesley and Penny most likely have the exact same plan as we do," she said as she pushed the door open on the last stall.

"There goes the easy route," Pippa said, frustrated that things were not going their way. "How about we alert security to *their* presence?" she proposed.

"I thought about that, but they wouldn't just let us go after we made a report about them. I think we steer clear of those two, and take a different route," she said as she brought up the 4-D image on her wrist band and started to spin the diagram around.

"How about we wait until the group leaves the room to go on the tour and we tail them at a distance?" Pippa suggested.

"Too risky; if they stop to semi-circle the group to talk in any room, Wesley may spot us," Bixby said as the image continued to baffle her.

"And where is Greg?" Pippa asked the question Bixby had yet to think about.

"Focus, Pippa," Bixby replied not wanting any more anxiety at the moment.

"There!" Pippa said, looking at the building as she spun it around.

"I'm not sure what I'm supposed to be looking for," Bixby said, confused at what it was that Pippa had spotted.

Reaching over to Bixby's Holo-Writer, Pippa spun the building around so that they could see the side of the building opposite of the entrance.

"There is a kitchen on this level that has access to a service elevator. We could sneak into the kitchen and up to the penthouse now that we are through the security checkpoint." Pippa pointed at two hollow shafts in the image.

Bixby's mind weighed the possibility, and it was a decent option. "Let's give it a try. We can say we are with the health inspector if anyone asks."

"We could snag a few of the clipboards from the intern desk and make ourselves look a little more official," Pippa said, liking the new plan. "And leave the sassy mouth to me," she continued as she slapped on a fresh coat of lipstick and dropped it in her blazer pocket.

OOF!

Bixby had raced out of the bathroom door and directly into a heap of man in a black suit and wearing an earpiece. Pippa had sandwiched Bixby between her and him.

"Terribly sorry! Excuse me," she said as she tried to skirt around the guard with a shiny badge that read 'Chief of Security.' He immediately stepped into Bixby's path and as she tried to go the other way his gargantuan hand reached out and obstructed her movement.

"I'm sorry, ladies, you will actually need to come with us," he said as Bixby had to lean to either side of the Chief to see that there was indeed two slightly smaller men standing behind him.

"Wesley!" Bixby exclaimed under her breath, knowing who was behind this conundrum.

Chapter Thirteen
Breaking the Rules

"Ladies, I must again insist you come with me," the chief of security repeated.

"I don't think so. We have an internship meeting to attend," Pippa said aggressively.

"I would be happy to let you attend the meeting as soon as you open your purses and show me you don't have tasers inside," he replied.

Bixby and Pippa's eyes flashed to each other as their lips pursed in frustration. They didn't have to say it out loud, but it was obvious that Greg or Wesley knew they were in the level all together and snitched on them.

"How did they know that..." Pippa's words trailed off in befuddlement.

"If you *do* have a taser in your possession, I'm not exactly sure how you got them through security, but we will need to detain you until we can make sure that this is licensed properly before we escort you out," he said as he pointed to their purses in a calm, deep, and oddly assuring voice.

"I have never been so offended in my life! You have no warrant to search our purses like this!" Pippa chimed in.

"For the safety of my staff and all who work here at Snowenwood Industries I must make sure everyone is compliant with the rules. And if you resist, we would be happy to have the authorities resolve this issue."

Bixby was stalling for time as she clutched her purse. Her mind raced at all the options, and then she had one of her most amazing ideas ever.

"You're gonna need to put us in the slammers before I will comply," Bixby said confidently.

"Yeah... Wait, what?" Pippa replied in disbelief.

"As you wish," the man said politely to Bixby. The shiny name badges of the other two security guards were hard to miss. Officer Lucky and Myers fell in behind Bixby and Pippa as they moved towards the service elevator. The large man reached down and placed his thumb on the biometric pad where normally an 'up' or 'down' arrow would be. The doors parted and the five of them entered the elevator. He pressed 'B' for what they were sure was basement and headed downward.

Once in the security center their purses were placed on a table ten feet from the door.

"Wait here a moment," the Chief said, directing them to two hard plastic chairs as he joined the Lucky and Myers who were already rummaging through their bags.

"Do you trust me?" Bixby whispered out of the corner of her mouth.

It was the question none of Bixby's friends wanted to hear back in morning simulations because it meant they had lots of work to do to keep Bixby from killing herself, but it was a whole other level of stress to hear it *while* in the level *with* her.

"We are going to do something dumb aren't we?" Pippa asked, reluctant to hear the answer.

"I like to think of it more as aggressively disregarding instructions," she said confidently as she began to whistle.

"I guess it can't be as bad as swimming away from sharks," Pippa huffed as she slunk down next to Bixby.

"Sir, it looks like the taser has been taken apart and ready for reassembly," one of the guards said as she sprawled the pieces on the table in order of assembly. They fidgeted with it for a few moments and then with a final snap it was back together.

"And what should we make of..." was all the Chef got out before Officer Lucky passed out with a thud against the table.

Bixby had popped up from her seat and lunged at the guards with her hand held out and her finger pressing hard against the lid of her Nit-Nit spray. She had stolen it from inside of Pippa's pocket shortly after getting caught. Pippa closed her eyes and had immediately began holding her breath. Bixby hit Officer Myers in the face with it to complete her first wave. The Chief stumbled back at the small amount of spray he was hit with, but he had dodged the majority of the mist. Realizing her Nit-Nit was now out of juice, Bixby lowered her shoulder into the Chief and drove him back into the table where the girl's purses had rested. It shattered at the weight and the both of them toppled to the ground with a thud. He immediately secured the hand with the spray in it but neglected her other hand.

"I'm really sorry about this," Bixby said as she squeezed the Taser's trigger that she had taken from the table before it shattered. The pulse immobilized the Chef so that Bixby could grab her own Nit-Nit.

With a few squirts everyone was out.

"That was your plan!" Pippa shouted in total shock of Bixby's boldness. She was still sitting on the bench inside the cell. The shock of what she did had her pinned to the chair.

"I couldn't do it in the elevator because we would all be asleep, so this was my next best option," Bixby said as she ripped open her purse and grabbed the finger printing kit.

"Get the chief's thumbprints; we will need it to get upstairs," Bixby instructed as she flipped open her Holo-Writer and started spinning the blueprints of the building.

Pippa worked as fast as she could before asking, "What's next?"

Bixby grabbed the chief's keys, and I.D. card before instructing Pippa, "Follow me."

"If we get caught, will this level keep us in jail for our full sentence before we are allowed to unlaunch?" Pippa asked.

"It's a simulation, Pippa. I'd never do that in real life," Bixby said as they approached the same service elevators they came down on.

"You had me fooled," Pippa snarked back.

"Put the fingerprint here," Bixby pointed to the glass pad ignoring her observation.

Pippa pulled the chief's thumb prints from their sleeves and held it to the glass. The square around it lit green and the doors glided open.

"Top floor," Bixby said as she entered the elevator and slapped the stolen credentials against the security plate before putting the thumb print on the glass pad below it.

What seemed like hours passed as they made it to the tower's penthouse. The doors opened up to a kitchen area where several chefs were bustling to prepare what looked to be a rather large meal. Knives were chopping, meat was sizzling on the grills, and they were yelling at each other to hurry up with one dish or another.

"It must be pretty common to have people show up through the service doors," Bixby whispered to Pippa because not a single one of them looked up from their work. Trying to look as official as possible, Bixby took the lead and headed out towards a set of double doors towards the dining area.

"Follow me," she instructed as they began to move. Bixby reached up and turned on her glasses. She could see that the house was filled with people. In the distance she could see the heated silhouette of a familiar gate and stature.

"Wesley," she hissed again.

"He's here?" Pippa asked.

"Yep. And we are going to arrest him as a thief," Bixby said, flashing the badge she stole from the officer.

Bixby raced inside the dining hall but stopped abruptly enough that Pippa again bumped into the back of her.

"What gives?" Pippa said, rubbing her nose. As she looked around Bixby's shoulder, she could now see that they were standing at the edge of a luncheon with about thirty people sitting in the space enjoying the food as a man stood at a microphone giving some type of speech. From the head table a man in tuxedo rushed over to greet them.

"How may I help you two... ladies?" he questioned.

"Ah, well we are sorry to bother your meal," Bixby stammered as she thought of her next lie.

"Why are you here?" he insisted quietly as he leaned in between the two real thieves.

"Sir, we got a call to be an extra security detail for the Art Show fundraiser event tonight," Pippa said through the slight pause as she remembered the banners outside the building talking about an exhibit taking place later on that evening. The Chief of Security let us up."

"This is hardly official attire," the man in the tuxedo insisted.

"We will be better dressed this evening to blend in, but we have a tip that someone may be trying to lift something from here presently," Bixby added. Looking through her glasses she could see Wesley heading away from them.

"We were told to not wear our uniforms in order to blend in," Pippa interjected.

"You may want to try a little harder next time, though I appreciate your attempt to pay attention to detail, but everyone here is on the list," the snooty man replied.

Bixby hated the smugness of rich people more than anyone could ever imagine.

"Oh, we are terribly sorry... and we trust you on that, but besides the dining room, can we take a quick look around at the layout before we leave? We promise to stay out of sight from your guests," Pippa requested.

"Normally, I would have Brian our Chief of Security, do something like that, but seeing as he let you up here and neglected his duty to keep everyone off of this floor," he started as Bixby's heart raced. "But I would hate to draw more attention towards this party, and it would be a disaster if something was actually stolen between now and tonight's gala..." Bixby could see him weighing his options. "...Please follow my personal assistant to the other wing of the house, see what you need to see, and disappear through the front door? You have two minutes," he begged.

"Absolutely," Bixby agreed as the butler ushered the two girls out of the dining room.

"Two of our fine security details I guess didn't get the memo about not interrupting our lunch," the man announced to his group of guests as the crowd burst into a bit of laughter.

As Bixby was ushered into the living room, two familiar faces were backing into an elevator across the room. Wesley's eyes were surprised to see her, but one hand hit an elevator button as the second one taunted her with a wave of the golden flag he must have recently obtained. He was dressed in a janitor's jumper. Bixby took a rushed step forward, but her mind pulled her back with a flurry of questions. *Who would we call? We are security. If I call them out, who would call the rest of security to their aide without giving up that they were fakes?*

Before Bixby could spurt out a syllable the assistant proclaimed, "That was fast." as he wiped his finger across the glass table. "And not very good."

"You should call their boss," Bixby said, trying her hardest to get Wesley caught without giving up her own disguise.

"I most certainly will, after you two hurry along," he said sourly.

His answer made Bixby's teeth clench because she had not only been outsmarted and put in jail by Wesley, now he is ahead of her, and will stroll to his tent untouched.

"Tell me, sir, what will this space be used for?" Bixby asked trying to buy time while scanning the room.

"It's Mr. Veen, and this is the living area where we will be serving Champagne and escargot on an aged butter cracker for those who have donated anywhere over a million dollars to the event. It will be a much smaller crowd," the stiff old butler proclaimed in a snobbish voice.

"Right, Mr. Veen. Will anyone be allowed to go anywhere else in the penthouse besides the dining room or living area?" Bixby asked to keep the conversation sounding like they actually cared.

"Besides the loo, nobody is to wander to any of the other rooms," the old man explained.

"Speaking of the bathroom, may I use it?" Pippa asked, recognizing her chance to make her way down the hallway towards the study that contained the safe. She was tapping her chin with a glove on that Bixby recognized as the lock cracking device.

"You may. However, I will ask you to hurry as the Master of the House has given you only two minutes, of which you have already used one," he replied in a pompous voice.

"I understand. Which door?" she asked, looking down the long hall.

"First one on your right," he replied.

"Oh my, is your boss big into airplanes?" Bixby asked, looking around at the décor that was dominated by aeronautical artifacts. She was stalling for Pippa the best she could.

The topic piqued the Veen's attention. "Yes, he is, as is all of his staff here. I was hired originally after being the Master of the House's flight instructor. We hit it off so well that he offered me this job which allows me to fly any of his planes at a moment's notice. I see to this penthouse when we are not traveling."

"Really? I have only been on a plane twice: once for vacation, and once for... business," she said, thinking about her family vacation to Wallaby World, and the most recent flight with Cody. "With work and all, I can't seem to find time to travel. Have you ever had to jump out of a plane?" she asked.

"Oh my, heavens no. Knock on wood," he said as he began to admire the work around the room himself proudly. "We do have a couple of parachutes in the owner's office from World War II, but they are antiques to look at now, I guess."

"Parachutes always fascinated me. I mean you only have to put them on and pull a cord. Sounds pretty simple," she said, trying to keep the façade of interest up. In reality, Bixby skipped the second course that Harvey had created for her because it involved parachuting from high in the air which was still the biggest fear she had in the world.

"The technology has been roughly the same except the material has become stronger, and the toggles used to control the chute are much more maneuverable. Other than that, I would say it isn't much different," the butler educated.

"Do you still fly now that you have moved up to the..."

"Calling all units, we have a breech in the building. Two officers down, and the Chief of Security…"

Bixby reached down to her waist band and clicked off the radio she stole to monitor when the security detail awoke. She didn't expect it to go off this fast, but the damage had already been done. With terror in his eyes Mr. Veen dashed for a panic button below the light switch by the door. The sirens began to wail, and Bixby raced for the back office. Bursting through the door she locked it behind her.

"Did you get it?" she shouted.

"I almost lost my hand!" Pippa shouted back as the door to the safe had smashed closed when the alarm sounded. "But I got this…" she said with a smile as she pulled a small golden flag with Bixby's name embroidered on it. Bixby was happy on the inside, but now they were trapped in the office sixty stories up, and an entire security detail and police were about to break down the door.

"That wasn't part of your plan, was it?" Pippa inquired, realizing that Bixby had not set off the alarm intentionally.

Bixby's eyes darted around the room.

"No, but we now need to make a new plan," she said jumping into action, searching the room.

Bixby screeched to a halt mid search of the desk as she looked for a latch for a secret passage or an escape hatch. Her eyes settle on a picture frame on the corner of the desk.

"If this is Snowenwood Industries and we are in the CEO's private office…" she started as her eyes settled on a picture of three men standing in ski gear on a mountain. To the best of her knowledge, they were young and happy. Each of them had goggles on their heads and wind masks across their noses, but

Bixby thought for sure she knew one of the pairs of eyes. "I know you," she said as she took the picture, held it up, and spun three-hundred-and-sixty degrees so that at least one of the cameras would capture it for the On-Demand. She then tucked it in her waistband before continuing her search.

"Wait. What about that window washing rig we talked about earlier? We can pull it up and go down the side of the building," Bixby said trying to avoid looking over the ledge of the building.

"You got to pick the last strategy and it almost got us locked up for several years in this level," Pippa replied.

"I'm all ears if you have a better idea," Bixby replied as she nervously walked over to the patio's edge sixty stories up.

"Great!" Pippa said, noticing Bixby beginning to panic a little.

Bixby looked over the edge of the building and there was a controller that she seized. Pushing the up button, the platform from the bottom floor began to slowly crawl up the floor.

"Put this harness on and we will be fine," Pippa said as she helped Bixby who was focused on keeping her eyes closed as the platform drew closer. Bixby was not looking forward to the ride down.

BAM!

"Again! Break that door down!" Bixby could hear the security guard that had originally captured them cry out.

"Hurry," Bixby urged the wooden planks below. She peeked over the edge, and they were nowhere near close enough to jump down to.

"Get on the edge. We may have to jump down to the platforms if Brian gets in here!" Pippa shouted, standing behind Bixby and helping her to her feet.

"I can do this!" Bixby shouted to herself as they climbed to the edge. She hated the idea of having to jump ten feet down to the window washing scaffolding, but they were now out of options.

BAM!

This time the door burst open with shards of wood splintering everywhere. Bixby and Pippa looked back and made eye contact with Chief of Security Brian before he began running full sprint after them.

Bixby could hear a double click sound on her harness, and looked down at what Pippa had helped her put on when she had her eyes closed.

"Pippa!" Bixby shouted as her eyes widened to dinner plate size.

"You may not like this next part," Pippa replied as she pushed her full weight into Bixby and the tandem began their free fall.

Chief of Security Brian almost grabbed ahold of Pippa's ankle as she went over. If it wasn't for the guard who had come into the room after the chief, Brian may have also fallen over the edge with his momentum.

"They got away and are heading towards the ground floor in... a parachute! Catch them when they land!" the chief yelled into his radio.

Tumbling down, Bixby could feel her whole body yank up as she looked up and saw as spectacular canopy above her. Pippa was franticly pulling on cords to keep them from crashing into buildings as Bixby naturally squirmed at the forty stories below them.

"I'm going to kill you!" Bixby shouted as the wind of the city and the horns blared below them.

"Your way would have been too slow and got us caught again!" Pippa insisted. Bixby knew she was right but didn't want to admit it currently because Pippa had indeed busted them out of a tough jam.

"As soon as the chute opens, it's kind of like turning a horse," Pippa proclaimed as she handled the guidance toggles well.

"How many times did you do this simulation?" Bixby asked.

"As many times as I could! This is fun!" she shouted back as a huge gust of wind slammed into their canopy from in between the buildings they had passed.

"Oh no!" Pippa shouted as one of the stabilizing cords snapped. They were now in a steady tailspin. "I can't control it!"

Bixby had been praying that they could hurry to the ground in part because she hated being up so high, and secondly because she wanted this leg of the race to be over. She never thought it meant tumbling to her death. But in zeroing in on the things below her, she saw their painful, yet best chance to survive during their third three-sixty twist.

"You're going to want to hold on to me!" Bixby shouted to Pippa on her back.

"Don't do something crazy!" Pippa pleaded, knowing Bixby had just taken over their escape plan again.

Bixby reached behind her and grabbed the one toggle that Pippa had in her hand. Focusing all her strength on just the one guide that was still giving them some direction, Bixby pulled as hard as she could. She was certain that the only way to survive was to direct the canopy on a collision course with the side of a building that had one of the Art Show banners draped twenty feet from the ground. Bixby braced for the impact against the strong glass window that would sandwich her between Pippa and an abrupt stop that caused the window to spider with cracks. The impact naturally caused Bixby to cry out in pain as she grabbed ahold of the banner with every ounce of strength she could muster. The weight of her and Pippa pulled the banner loose as they began to fall to the ground. As they streaked down the side of the building, only one cord that was connected to the banner kept anchored to the metal upright that held it in place. It was all that kept the two girls from falling the last twenty feet. Bixby's arm screamed with pain as she dangled above the concrete below. With her good arm she slid down the banner like the rope in gym class and toppled to the ground.

Guards began pouring out of the building yelling for Bixby and Pippa to 'Stop right there!'

As soon as Pippa's feet hit the ground, she disconnected herself from Bixby and scooped her up under her arm. The duo headed towards the coffee shop doors that would lead to their escape from this leg of the race.

Wincing, Bixby's arm dangled at her side.

"Listen to me, Bixby. It looks like you dislocated your shoulder. It used to happen to my dad all the time. You can either try to put it back in place yourself when we go through those doors, or you can let me help you now before I unlaunch!"

Nearly crying now, Bixby agreed to Pippa's help as the officers were closing in with taser guns drawn, ready to fire.

"Quick, lie down on the café table," Pippa shouted as Bixby obliged.

"This isn't going to hurt a bit," she said, grabbing Bixby's arm, placing her foot in her armpit, and yanking.

Pippa had lied: it hurt a lot.

"AHHHH!" Bixby screamed, but then the pain was gone. Another cabbie skidded to a halt as an officer was now halfway across the street, "Freeze!" he screamed, aiming his Taser and firing as the two girls burst through the doors of the coffee shop that was a façade to their tent. Twelve-hundred volts of pain hit Pippa in the back and crumbled her to the ground of the tent.

Bixby, still painfully uncomfortable, was looking into Pippa's eyes as the voltage pulsed through her body before she unlaunched. The golden flag lay in the spot Pippa once occupied. Slowly it too burst into tiny balls of light and disappeared.

CHAPTER FOURTEEN
TROPICAL HEAT

"Pippa!" Bixby screamed into her com as she turned it back on.

Nobody responded.

Bixby pushed herself up with one hand and with the other she kept it tucked tight to her body.

"Essshh," she gasped at the throbbing pain that came with sitting up.

Not wanting the pain of her shoulder to grow before she made her way to her transport, she grabbed some ice from the small fridge in the tent, wrapped it in a towel, and tied it to her shoulder. As she pulled the sling around behind her, the concealed picture frame that she had stolen from the office that she had just robbed fell to the ground at her feet. Bixby knew that it would disappear along with the rest of the challenge as soon as she left the tent, so she picked it up and was immediately drawn to the eyes that called to her to steal the picture in the first place. She assumed that the CEO of Snowenwood Industries had to be Lewis Snowenwood, but she had no idea which of the two other men he was in the picture. However, she was now certain of the man on the left.

Even with his face partially blocked by ski equipment. "Grandpa?" Bixby said aloud.

Bixby was no longer convinced that it was hacking or coincidence that her grandpa had been interjected into the riddle on every level. "What about my grandpa do you want me to know?" Bixby said into the empty void of the tent in hopes Cody would appear to reveal an answer. Her mind wandered back to Cody's alleged prize that he offered Bixby on the plane a few days earlier: *'However, a victory in my riddles will get you all the pieces to the most fantastic riddle you have ever had to solve. The only way to procure all the necessary pieces is to make it to the end, Spot, where your prize will be revealed.'*

"I'm coming, Grandpa," she said, wincing again as she rose to her feet.

Outside the tent was the same tarmac that she flew in on. She didn't know where she stood in the race after this leg, and she didn't want to fall further behind or let a lead slip. Bixby dashed up the stairs into the jet.

"Somebody, talk to me!" she shouted into the emptiness of the cabin.

"Bixby! How bad does it hurt, Sugar?" Miss Marmalade shouted back.

"Miss Marmalade, it is so good to hear your voice. How's Pippa? I think they caught her with a taser," Bixby said as the last moments played over and over in her head. Bixby couldn't tell what happened as it transpired so fast.

"They got her alright… with every last volt of electricity from their stun guns," she pouted.

"Is she in pain?" Bixby asked, burdened by Miss Marmalade's answer.

"No, ma'am. It only caught her for a second or two. Those tasers are made to stop people, not kill them. She practically danced out of her Launch Room, but all the boys are all down there trying to carry her to her room. You should have seen Tipton and Mr. Richards fighting over who gets to take care of her."

"I do actually wish I was there to see that," Bixby said as she cracked a smile thinking about what that argument would sound like.

"How did we do?" Bixby inquired next.

"You managed to move into second," Arthur informed.

"I forgot to mention the walking rule book is here as well," Miss Marmalade jeered.

"Hey, Arthur. Give me the rundown as I am sure you have already reviewed all the footage."

"We know for sure that Greg didn't do any training for this level. Dragonthorp Inc. simply hired fifty professionals to go in with him and skip him through. The professional thief did what you should have done and taken the lift up and back down without even being noticed by anyone."

"Figures," she replied, wishing her trip was as uneventful.

"Wesley and Penny completed the scenario that you had originally planned. While you were in the security cell, they broke from the tour and using the taser to fry the security panel in the elevator, they stole some cleaning outfits and badges and rode up to the penthouse arriving only moments before you. Using the distraction of two officers in the dining room..."

Bixby shook her head, now knowing she was the distraction Wesley used to escape.

"...they slipped in and out unnoticed. Your jump from the balcony was what helped move you ahead of Wesley who was slowed down by the security breach. They locked down the lobby while security ran after two girls in a parachute," Arthur finished.

"Sometimes you're good, and this time, maybe even a little lucky," Bixby joked, realizing the lockdown actually helped her move up in the competition.

"Keep that ice on your arm and the next person that comes in is going to have a little something for the pain," Miss Marmalade said as she digitally searched the house for the best prescription for her ailment.

"BIXBY!" Hemsley shouted as he burst through the doors. "Did they get her too?" he questioned after her response wasn't immediate.

"I'm here, Hemsley, and I am okay," she comforted.

"I thought they got you too," he started. "Pippa was hit in the arm with one of the barbs and the shoulder with the second. She said that she could feel that she was being shocked, but her muscles all stopped working."

As he finished speaking, the Command Center doors again burst open, and it was Pippa this time.

"Bixby, I'm fine!" she shouted as Max Richards and Tipton were right behind her trying to convince Pippa to rest.

"Listen you, two, Bixby separated her shoulder and was almost eaten by sharks. If you expect me to lie in bed while being pampered because of a little electric jolt, you have another thing coming."

Pippa no longer sounded like her delightful self. She had a seasoned tone in her voice now that she had suffered a little at the hands of the Riddle.

"I'm glad you're okay, Pippa," Bixby said, removing the wet towel from her shoulder.

"Are you kidding me? I've had hangnails worse than that," she gloated.

"Bixby, I recommend some rest before the next level," Harvey spoke up. "You have only had a little under an hour of rest in the past eighteen hours. If that is any indication of how long these games will last, you have well over a day to keep going."

"I agree. I'm going to try and close my eyes for a bit," Bixby said as she tucked a pillow under her neck and reclined her seat.

The bounce of the jet's wheels on the tarmac is what jostled Bixby awake. She sat up and let out a big stretch favoring one side over the other. Her shoulder was still sore, but nothing compared to the anguish from when it was dislocated.

"How long have I been asleep?" Bixby inquired of her team.

The team gathered from couches, the buffet, and bathroom to their usual posts in front of the Holo-TV.

"Pretty much the whole hour," Hemsley said. He hadn't left her virtual side since she dozed off.

"Then are we ready to start?" Bixby asked confused about the travel being only in an airplane during this level.

"Most likely," he said as he watched her rotate her arm a few times to try and loosen her shoulder up. Bixby pulled her shirt aside to reveal the bruise that had formed. It was a lovely shade of purple from where she made full contact with the office building.

"You guys ready? Almost to the halfway point," Bixby said, sounding positive and trying not to alert anyone of her injury.

"We are if you are," Harvey said, looking at the three who had not yet been in the Riddle. Each one was dealing with their nerves differently. Tipton ate, Marin was cracking her knuckles, and much to Harvey's surprise, Hemsley seemed only focused on Bixby and her wellbeing.

The plane slowed to a stop and Bixby made her way to the hatch. Bixby gazed outside the jet's window and her jaw nearly hit the carpet.

"You guys are seeing this right?" Bixby asked, hoping that she wasn't alone in her shock. She grabbed the latch of the plane, but it did not open.

"I'm sure the churning volcano with red hot magma bubbling slowly from the top of it has nothing to do with this riddle, right?" Tipton asked.

"I don't see a tent," Marin said, scouring the landscape.

"I don't either, and the door to the plane is still locked," Bixby said. "Hemsley, you are sure it has been an hour?" Bixby asked as he looked at his logs.

"You have one minute, and it will be exactly an hour," he replied.

Bixby darted from the door back to her seat and began scouring the plane.

"What are you doing?" Tipton asked, confused at her sudden spurt of energy.

"I think the plane itself is the tent," she concluded.

"You mean like the limo in Level One?" Marin asked.

"What is the riddle then?" Hemsley asked.

"Nothing has changed since getting on the plane," Bixby said, confused at what she was supposed to do next. She sat in her chair and slowly gazed around the cabin, and even the landscape outside.

"That volcano outside doesn't look very happy," Marin said taking a screen shot of Bixby's view outside the window.

Turning from the buffet table with a bowl full of ice cream, Tipton nonchalantly interjected, "Actually, I think you are going to have to repair the Rube Goldberg on the side of the temples. That was one of my favorite simulations during Harvey's training."

Everyone looked at Marin's screenshot as Bixby still searched the cabin. On the side of the volcano was a temple. It had multiple towers that made a zigzag pattern up the mountain to the lip of the volcano. Several of the paths were quite obviously obstructed by fallen buildings or shifted in out of order sequences. It was obvious that it was a broken Rube Goldberg puzzle.

"What exactly is a Rube Goldberg?" Marin asked, obviously admitting she did not take that part of Harvey's training course.

The occupants of the Command Center all turned to face Tipton as he stuffed his face.

"What? I eat when I get nervous," he said, pausing to finish chewing.

"He was a brilliant cartoonist and engineer among other things. He would make complicated machines to complete basic tasks like getting a marble across a table or turning on an old TV. He won a Pulitzer Prize for his cartoons depicting his machines. People started making these machines and calling them Rube Goldberg's after the concept's inventor. Wicked fun to make if you ask me," Tipton said, shoveling another bite of Rocky Road in his mouth.

"He is right. I took the Rube Goldberg training too," Bixby said, mentally going over the possible solutions.

As the words 'Rube Goldberg' left her mouth the door on the plane unlatched. The riddle was simple, "What is your next challenge?"

Arthur grabbed Tipton's arm and pulled the bowl out of his hand. "Looks like you have work to do, Tipton," he said as he placed his bowl down on the countertop.

"Wait... you don't mean it's my turn to go in there?" he asked as Arthur was already nodding his head 'yes.'

"Hey, I was in *allll* of Level Two... I don't think it is fair to hog the spotlight..."

Arthur was already dragging him to his Launch Room.

As the doors closed behind him, he shouted, "I want a T-shirt about me too!"

Within moments Tipton was reunited with Bixby inside another level. As soon as he appeared, the stairs to the jet flung down from below the open hatch unfolding themselves.

"You ready?" Bixby asked, getting right to business.

"These are for you," he said, buying himself a few more seconds inside the plane. "Miss Marmalade said you need to take them right away." He finished handing her the pain pills for her shoulder.

Bixby took them and gulped them down without water. "Let's go!"

Begrudgingly, Tipton hurried after her.

The two had worked their way down into the dense jungles on the way to the carved rock temples. Swiping vines and debris from their paths, Tipton questioned, "Are you at least a little scared to find out what is trying to kill us in this leg of the race?"

"I am trying not to think about it, Tipton," Bixby said as she yanked down another vine in her way.

"I'm guessing it is the lava that is going to try and kill us," he continued.

"If you keep it up, the lava isn't going to get a chance to murder you, Tipton," Bixby said as she was still trying to avoid talking about dying.

"I'm picking up what you're putting down, Bixby. You don't want to talk about impending doom. So, let's talk about relationships... how is yours and Hemsley's going?" he said through the sweat that was now rolling off of his face.

Swiftly Bixby spun around, slapped her hand over Tipton's mouth tightly, and pinned him against a tree. Slowly, she raised a finger up to her lips to signal silence. Bixby was looking around, trying to see if she could hear what she thought she heard only a moment ago. He nodded vigorously in agreement. Bixby crouched down and picked up a baseball sized rock. Turning to the path they had created through the brush; she threw the rock as hard as she could off to the side of the trail. Cringing in pain a little from her sore arm, she carefully watched as it crashed through the dense jungle thirty or so feet deep into the brush.

Something roared.

"We are being hunted!" Bixby blurted as she started to climb the tree. "Come on, Tipton!"

Following her up the tree he could see the brush start to rattle. Three 'somethings' were barreling at them through the jungle. Whatever they were, they were fast, and seemed angry. Ten feet up the first predator crashed into the clearing.

"Tiger!" Tipton shouted, spotting the large cats emerging from the brush as he fumbled for the next branch.

"I'm seriously considering punching Cody in the face when I meet him," Bixby said as she started to assess the situation. The cats were clumsy as they each started their way up the tree. The problem wasn't their ability to climb; it was their inability to be patient enough to let one feline get out of their way before trying to advance up the tree.

One nearly had Tipton's leg, but a second cat had pounced at the same time knocking the other all the way to the ground. Injured from the fall, it hobbled back into the brush.

"We can't go much higher, Bixby," Tipton shouted, realizing there wasn't any more room, and the branches were starting to get smaller and weaker.

"Neither can they, Tipton. They each weigh hundreds of pounds. These branches won't be able to support them," she encouraged, hoping she was right.

"Fun fact, tigers don't usually hunt in packs," Tipton nervously spewed information.

"That's a mother and her cubs. Luckily they are not great at climbing yet," she said as she looked around.

"Any ideas?" Tipton asked seeing that the remaining two tigers had a better grasp on the teamwork aspect of hunting.

Her eyes were darting side to side as they had reached the canopy of the trees and could see out for some distance.

Spotting their escape route, Bixby looked down at Tipton. "Do you like bananas, Tipton?"

"Umm, I guess so," he said as he shimmied up a few more inches away from the cats that were closing in on them.

In front of his face came a hand that was full of vines. "Time to do your best monkey impression. Next stop is that tree over there."

Tipton didn't hesitate, trusting Bixby implicitly, but it would have done him good to see where he was going as he snatched the vine and jumped from the tree without abandon.

"AHHHAAHAHH!" was all she could hear as the first part of the swing went rather smoothly, but it was the two trees he bounced off on the way over to the pine that did most of the damage. Luckily for him, he crashed into a soft foliage of the tree where he was able to grab ahold of a branch, stopping his pinball act. Bixby also made her way over to the tree, but her trip was much more calculated to avoid the other trees between point A and point B.

"You okay?" she asked as they both were safely in the cover of the branches.

"I think I landed in a puddle of sap," he said as his pants were nearly glued to the tree. "The tigers are going down their tree, I'm positive they are going to come climb this one!" he freaked.

"We have one more swing and they won't bother us anymore," she said confidently.

"How do you know that?" Tipton questioned as his fingers were sticking together.

"I'm not sure if tigers are able to jump over lava moats," Bixby said pointing down at the river of hot magma that was flowing around the two temples that they were trying to reach.

Bixby reached up and pulled a few more vines loose from the sappy tree's branches. They were attached to another tree inside the ring of fire, so this was their chance.

"Wait until they climb the tree a little way so that they don't snag you out of midair. We are going to come close to hitting the ground and the lava so only let go after you have cleared it," Bixby said watching the two beasts begin their climb up the fir.

"See you on the other side!" she shouted as she pushed off. Bixby was correct in gaging the trajectory of the vine. Nearing the ground, the vine and the branch it was holding on to, bent slightly, but held her weight. Bixby could feel the tremendous amount of heat pulsing from the red river that was flowing ten feet below. On the upswing she let go of her grip and skidded to a stop on the other side.

"Tipton, jump now!" she shouted, seeing that the tigers had caught on to their escape plan.

Terrified at what he was being asked to do, he hesitated as the large cats were cascading down to the bottom of the tree and began to make their way over to the river's edge.

"You have to jump, Tipton!" Bixby was now screaming.

Knowing she was right, he didn't necessarily jump, he more so fell forward out of the tree gripping the vine with all his might. He picked up momentum fast as his eyes crushed closed with the fear of smashing into the ground. What he didn't expect on his fall was the third cat, which was injured earlier, had also rejoined the hunt and was sure that he was in line to knock Tipton from his swing. As the cat rose up to make the tackle, so did the two other cats that were coming from the opposite directions. Tipton's vine went right between their outstretched claws as they smashed into each other. His weight had pulled the branch that he was swinging on down a few more feet than Bixby's, and the intense heat was now less than five feet below him. He could feel it searing his skin as he zipped over top of it.

"Let go, now!" Bixby shouted as he cleared the molten rock. The tigers had no way of reaching them while on the inner banks for the Rube Goldberg.

Tipton also realized he was now out of danger and tried to put his feet down and stop his momentum but quickly realized a problem.

"BIXBY! I'm stuck to the vine!" he screamed in terror. Bixby could see that the sap from their previous tree was now on his hands, pants, and caking the vine as well. If he didn't unstick himself and went back over the lava, the cats were not likely to miss a second time.

"I got you, Tipton!" she hollered back as she raced to grab the end of his rope in hopes of stopping his momentum from swinging back over the moat.

With all her might, Bixby buried her feet in the dirt, and, like a game of tug-o-war, she pulled against his weight. Her feet glided along the dirt as she struggled to keep him on this side of the lava. Her shoulder was again screaming in pain. It felt like it was about to pop back out of place, but Bixby held on. It didn't help that Tipton was viciously trying to wiggle free from the vine. Bixby's feet caught a rock jerking her shoulder and Tipton hard enough that she heard a loud ripping noise before she blacked out in pain.

CHAPTER FIFTEEN

Too Hot

"Bixby! Bixby!" Tipton was shouting as he tapped her on the cheek. "Oh god, I don't know CPR. Here goes," he said as he bent down to blow air into Bixby's lungs.

Terrified at the approaching face of Tipton, Bixby screamed, "AHH!"

Tipton, startled himself, also screamed, "AHH!"

"Holy cow, you're not dead," Tipton said as he bear-hugged her.

Realizing that he was not trying to kiss her, but instead give mouth to mouth she gasped in pain when he squeezed her around the shoulder area.

"Oh! Sorry, sorry! How bad does it hurt?" he asked, seeing the bruise had worked its way from the shoulder to the collar bone region. "That looks pretty bad," he said as he went to take a look.

"Thank you, Tipton," Bixby said, pulling her shirt near to her neck to cover the bruise. "I will be fine," she added as she got to her feet.

"Awesome then," Tipton replied oddly.

"Tipton... where are your pants?" Bixby asked, looking at Tipton who was now standing in front of her in his T-shirt and a pair of boxers with the 'Tickle Tart' logo all over them.

"It is too hot for pants. I figured shorts would be more appropriate for this weather," he said, trying to play off the fact that he was now in front of millions of viewers pantless.

Bixby looked across the mote and could see three tigers viciously tearing at the trousers that once adorned Tipton's lower half. The sap he sat in must have glued his jeans to the rope. Her final tug on the vine must have dislodged him from his denims.

The awkwardness of the moment all but shadowed the pain in Bixby's arm.

"Okay, let's get going," she said, pointing to herself in the direction of the temples. "And no more trying to kiss me," she jested as she took lead.

"I was trying to save your life!" he said, looking at her and then to the sky hoping that the cameras would pick up his comment. "Honestly, Pippa, I thought she was dying!"

"Let's go, lover boy!" she shouted as he raced to catch up.

At the foot of the temple Bixby found several banners attached to rotten wood poles. Reaching up she tore one off and handed it to Tipton. "Wrap this around you so the world doesn't have to look at your love for 'Tickle Tarts'," she said, gazing up at the two temples.

Tipton didn't pause at the gesture to hide his pasty white legs. He now looked like he had just spent a long day at the beach and was walking home with a towel wrapped around his wet swim trunks. Feeling a little more comfortable about his wardrobe, he focused his attention on the Rube Goldberg.

"Okay, Bixby, I am pretty sure I see how it works, but it is missing a few of the gears that would help us move the misplaced pieces back in place," he said, holding his hand over his eyes to keep out the sunlight.

"Talk to me like I have never seen or worked with a Rube Goldberg, because I really haven't except for the one on my grandpa's office wall and twice during Harvey's simulations."

"Well, in this Rube it looks like that giant boulder that is sitting at the top of the mountain with lava slowly spewing out the cracks around it, that's the marble."

Bixby gazed up and found the lava ball that was sitting in the very top of the volcano like a large marble wedged into the top of a soda bottle.

"That is one huge marble," she replied.

"Well, it looks like we have one chance to get this thing right, or the lava on top of the mountain is going to run into the river we just swung over and burn us alive in the process.

"And if all goes to plan?" Bixby asked as she was mentally starting to repair the volcano.

"The lava ball falls in that pit, and after that, I have no idea!" he said confidently about the thought. His knees were still shaking from the whole experience.

Tipton continued to walk Bixby through the process of how the lava was going to affect the entire puzzle. Bixby could see exactly what he was saying, and he was right. There were two separate gears missing from each of the temples. If the gears were replaced, it looked like they could adjust all the misplaced pieces by turning a giant wheel at the top of the second landing near where the lava was churning. She could also see that there were a few missing pieces in certain areas of the lava flow that would redirect it to where it needed to go next. Bixby saw a pile of trash tucked behind a pile of overgrown weeds.

"Here is how this is going to work. I am going to go get those gears and bring them back here. I am then going to give them to you, and you are going to put them in their correct place in the puzzle. Got it?"

"That is a lot of stairs, Bixby," Tipton said, dreading working out any more than he had already today.

"Stairs or lava bath?" Bixby countered.

"You have a wonderful way of convincing me to do things," Tipton concluded. "Where is the first gear?"

"On the top of that peg wall," Bixby said looking up at a forty-foot totem pole. The very top face was hiding the first gear in the design of its face paint.

The peg wall was going to be difficult for Bixby with her shoulder's condition, so she quickly devised a plan.

"Tipton, I need you to start breaking these old branches in half," Bixby instructed.

"Bixby, these sticks are not going to hold anyone's weight. They have been drying in the sun forever," Tipton said, observing their brittleness.

"I don't need them all to hold my weight. When I jam them in the holes, even if most of the stick breaks, as long as a little nub is still sticking out, I can take some of the pressure off of my shoulder," she finished as she ran over and tore off another flag making it into a sling for the nubs they were making.

"Put the first two sticks into the holes and then climb up on my shoulders so that you don't have to pull yourself up the first few feet," Tipton offered as the mini climbing sticks were secure in her pouch.

Bixby didn't hesitate at his offer as she jammed the first two pieces of kindling into the bottom holes. Tipton leaned up against the rock's face, and Bixby put one foot on his thigh as he helped hoist her up to the point that she could get the first rock pegs into the holes.

"I've got it," Bixby said as she had the dowels in place and her feet were resting gently on the first set of sticks. It didn't take Bixby long once she had the right rhythm going. "Peg up, stick in, pull up, repeat," she said to herself making sure not to forget any steps along the way. Only several sticks cracked or let loose as Bixby was climbing, which strained her shoulder each time, but it was manageable as she reached the top. With a stone peg in each of the eye holes of the totem's face at the top, she grabbed ahold of the golden sprocket that was doubling as the man's cheek. To Bixby it was obvious that she had to turn it counterclockwise to remove it from its home. It was a challenge at first, but once the dust shook loose a bit it slid right out.

The ground below Bixby and Tipton shook. Bixby was falling straight down with the totem. It wasn't gravity that had ahold of her this time... The totem was retracting into the earth.

"Uhhh, jump! I'll catch you!" was the only thing Tipton could think to say.

Realizing she would probably break a leg if she let the totem take her all the way to the ground quickly, she tossed the gear aside and before the rock completely disappeared into the ground, Bixby pushed off the idol in Tipton's direction.

"OOHHFF!" Tipton cried as he caught Bixby more like a wrestler would catch his opponent while jumping off the top rope.

"You alright, Tipton?" she cried as she coughed from the blow to the gut that she received as she hit and rolled over him.

"I'm not dead yet," he said checking to make sure all of his body parts functioned.

"Good. I'll find the next gear while you get that one up to its rightful place," she said without skipping a beat.

"Yep," he said, with a belly groan of pain as he sat up.

Bixby quickly located the next two gears and made the handoff to Tipton without much hindrance or injury to either of them.

"Last one, Bixby," Tipton said as he gathered gear number three.

"Do you see it?" she asked, stumped.

"I honestly haven't been looking for them," he said as he turned the golden circle in his hand.

"I have been all over the grounds here, and I don't see it anywhere," she said, confused.

"Have you thought about climbing up the tower to see what's up on top?" he said, wiping the sweat from his brow.

"I did break rule number one from the Command Center, didn't I?" she said disappointed in herself.

"You mean 'go to the highest spot and survey your surroundings' rule that Marin made up?" he asked.

"Yep, that one," she concurred.

"I'll climb the stairs with you to the landing where we put the gears while you visit that creepy multi-armed statue at the top," he said, pointing to the highest spot on the temple.

Bixby realized he was trying to catch a breather and sympathized with him. "See you at the gearbox, Tipton."

Skipping every other step, Bixby paced herself up to the top of the temple. Reaching the pinnacle, she was standing at the foot of the figures that Tipton was describing. He was not creepy at all. Bixby saw him for what he was: a statue of masked warrior. Looking over to the other temple she could see the same figure. The only difference she saw was that each of them was holding a sword in one of their six hands, but each arm was in a different pose.

"A mirroring puzzle. Excellent," she said to herself as she pulled down on one of the arms. When she did, one of the arms on the other statue also shifted. The goal of this puzzle was to get each of the arms in the exact same position as the other so that the statues would look like they were mirroring each other. This puzzle was a little more difficult than the other puzzles in this level, but Bixby kept at it for about ten minutes. As she worked, she realized that this was really the first puzzle that was traditional like the one her grandfather taught her how to solve. The strategy puzzles during the first two legs of the Rennen were new and fun for her, but it was puzzles like these that made her feel more in her element.

CLACK. CLACK. CLACK.

The warriors were now exactly the same in posture. Rising out of their pedestals, they moved as if they were marching towards each other. Stopping at the edge of the mountain, they raised all their spears into the air and paused. She could see the last gear under the statue's previous spot. Reaching down she picked it up and the stone fighters' hands dropped down to their sides simultaneously.

Then, boom.

The top of the volcano broke open like a shaken soda pop and the lava ball creaked over the edge, following down the carved path.

"Bixby! The gears are moving!" he shouted from halfway down the mountain.

The three gears that were in place began to spin and the different obstacles formed from stone columns rumbled into place. The Rube Golberg was fixing itself except for the bottom section. Bixby's eyes flashed down at the gear in her hand and back at the boulder. It had made contact with the first section that the gears had repaired.

"Oh, fiddlesticks!" she moaned. "Tipton! RUN!" she screamed, dashing down the stairs and across the face of the temple in the direction of the last gear's home.

Not questioning Bixby's order, Tipton started to run down the stairs as fast as he could. Nearing the bottom, he realized that the banner that he was wearing as a kilt was now a hindrance to his strides. He decided it was better to run in boxers for the entire world to see, than to die a horrible death because the lava caught him. Tipton had always had an issue with the last step on most things. The temple was no exception, as he stumbled as he stepped off the last stair. It was his patented tuck and rolling move that brought him back to his feet, continuing his mad dash.

Bixby put her foot under her rear and glided down the side of the pyramid. Raising her hand before reaching the gear's destination, she slapped it into place seamlessly as she continued her fast decent down the side.

With the final gear in place the four freshly found sprockets began to spin rapidly causing the ground again to rumble. Up ahead Tipton was approaching the lava river, slowing, not knowing where to go.

They could feel the tremendous heat all around them.

The final section of Rube locked into place as the boulder was now going at a breakneck pace down towards the finish.

"I'd like to spend time admiring our work, but what happens next?" he inquired as they were still trapped on the wrong side of the river, and a massive amount of lava had started to churn its way down the mountain.

"I'm hoping that giant marble will give us that answer," Bixby said as it rolled down into the funnel like hole and disappeared without a sound.

"Bixby?" Tipton was nervously asking for an escape plan.

"Bridge!" Bixby shouted, pointing at the stone bridge that started to push out from the lava river. The rock lave ball must have triggered some sort of mechanism to begin raising the bridge.

Tipton saw where she was pointing and made a beeline for it, running as fast as his legs could move.

The volcano let out another burst of power, shaking the duo to the ground again. Bixby looked back over her shoulder and lava had begun streaking down the side of the mountain. It was about to engulf the warrior statues as she got back to her feet and pushed forward.

Tipton had made it to the bridge and as he crossed, he could feel the surging heat on his bare legs and smell the rubber on the bottom of his shoes start to melt from the heated stones that were now the bridge. He feared the lava much more than he feared the tigers at this point, barreling into the forest in the direction of the plane.

As Bixby ran something caught her eye that caused her to slow down. Inside one of the temples the lava had poured down into the ceiling of the temple that was carved into the mountain. Three statues of men stood shoulder to shoulder. Bixby never noticed them because it was fairly dark inside and her only focus was to find gears. Now the three statues were illuminated red from the sweltering heat. They must have been made from rock because they buckled under the lava's flow.

What is going on? was all she could think before the lava became too intense for her to stay on that side of the bridge any longer.

Bixby hit the stone passage in stride a minute after Tipton and the lava had already risen to just below the base of the bridge and started to climb over the edges. Leaping for the other side, the river of magma swallowed the stone bridge as she too ducked into the woods without fear of the tigers.

She burst through the final valley and into the clearing where the plane had already started its engines and was making a turn at the end of the runway.

"BIXBY, HURRY!" Tipton shouted from under the engines roar. He was standing on the bottom step of the jet holding his hand out as the plane started to lurch ahead. "HURRY!"

Bixby, coursing with adrenaline, gauged the trajectory of the plane as it started to move down the runway for takeoff. With a leap, she grabbed Tipton's outstretched arm and swung up onto the last step with him and his 'Tickle Tart' underwear.

Looking back, the lava had also burned away most of the forest and was barreling down on the tarmac.

"For your t-shirt Tipton; it should have a picture of you right now with the caption 'It's Too Hot For Pants,'" she suggested as they stepped up into the plane.

"I don't hate it," he replied as she could see him imagining it.

As the stairs retracted and the hatch pulled itself closed, Tipton unlaunched and the plane rose through the clouds. Bixby was on to the next one... Bixby was on to the next one.

CHAPTER SIXTEEN
A-MAZING TURN OF EVENTS

"I am not sure how he has managed to obtain the world's most qualified persons to compete in each leg of the race..."

Lying flat on her back in the middle of the aisle way of the jet, Bixby listened to how each of her competitors had solved the last section of the puzzle. She was puzzling over how Greg was able to go through each physical challenge of the race nearly unscathed.

"I'm telling you, Bixby, the man that went in with Greg solved all but the hieroglyphic puzzle, climbed up himself to retrieve the gears, and waited to finish putting the last gear in place until everything else was solved. Like clockwork, the man made the final adjustment to the statues and once they were both back at the fourth gear's home, they slapped it in place, and the two of them were over the bridge as soon as it made its way out of the lava. Greg has had to do virtually zero work on these levels," Arthur insisted.

"What about the tigers?" she asked, hoping they had a bout with them at least.

"They made torches, so when the tigers approached, they swung the flames at the tigers. After a short standoff the cats simply gave up in fear of the flames. Greg and his partner moved like clockwork. They swung across the lava just like you, and on the way back they used the same flags that Tipton used as a dress as their return torches."

"What other things are we noticing about this level besides Greg's knack for bringing in the most qualified person into each challenge?" Bixby asked as she searched for a first-aid kit to nurse her wounds.

"Is it important to note that in some of these levels you have to solve it separately, but in the office building all of the teams had had to work in the same location?'" Marin asked, unsure of what other oddities there were in the Riddle that they could use as some sort of leverage.

"I think it is a valid point, but I'm not sure the connection yet," Bixby said, still frustrated at the immense imbalance of resources.

"What about Wesley?" she inquired next.

"He had relatively the same trouble as you, but his dad, the foreman, was able to bail him out of this one. I guess before being a top executive at Dragonthorp Inc., he was big into hunting, archaeology, and a triathlete. You did complete the task a hair faster than the Dagger family, but I do believe they still maintain a slight lead over you," Arthur said as he calculated all the completion times of each team's legs in the race.

"So then, how bad are we losing?" Bixby asked, scared of the answer.

"Behind Greg, you are being defeated by nearly thirty-five minutes. In accords to Master Dagger, you are in a two minute and forty second deficit," Arthur finished as Hucklebee tried to plug in a moment of Zen.

"It doesn't matter if you finish first or second, you simply can't finish third. Like the story of the bear."

"The bear?" Bixby questioned.

"Two guys are running furiously through the woods. An eight-hundred-pound man eating bear is hot on their trails. One guy is ripping off all his gear and extra clothes which, while wiggling about, causes him to fall behind. The other guy turns to him and says, 'Hurry up, man. If you keep wiggling about, we won't be able to outrun the bear!' To which the guy, who is now twenty pounds lighter without his gear starts running again and shouts, 'I don't have to outrun the bear, I just have to outrun you!'"

Pondering the deep meaning of his story Bixby realized that Hucklebee was right: to get to the last level she simply needed to outrun Greg *or* Wesley.

The Command Center was quiet for the next half an hour to let Bixby rest. Hemsley was back to his corner chair with sweaty palms which kept the attention of Harvey. Marin started to stretch in the event that she was the next contestant to be paired with Bixby. Pippa and Tipton sat discussing the dangers that each of them faced and how the other one felt as they watched them face the peril. Mr. Richards kept his presence close enough to keep them from making out.

Thump.

Bixby's body rose off the ground about an inch and then dropped back down to the deck. The plane had hit its first bout of turbulence. The seatbelt signs came on for the first time and the plane began to bank to its right. Bixby hurried to her seat and peeked out the window. She could see what the Riddle was trying to show her.

"Guys!" she shouted, making sure that everyone knew she needed their attention. The crew gathered again at the TV to see what she saw.

"Is that a maze?" Tipton asked, squinting at the tiny view from thirty thousand feet up.

"I think it is an obstacle maze, but you can see that only part of it is out in the open, and then it disappears from sight into those random structures."

"You didn't think that Cody was going to let you see the whole maze from the air so that you could take a picture and then dance your way through, did you?" Marin asked sarcastically.

"Touché," Bixby replied.

"Does anyone find it a little strange that there is a bullseye with Bixby's name written in the middle of it there at the top of the Maze?" Pippa observed. "Come to think of it… I don't see a landing strip anywhere either," she said, finishing her thought.

"Then it won't surprise you that it looks like something laying on Greg's bullseye already, and that looks like two people floating down to Wesley's spot," Tipton said, squinting at the screen, now sitting in his seat with a fresh pair of pants on.

Beep. Beep. Beep.

Bixby's eyes darted towards the cockpit as it started screeching and buzzing. The gauges that were normally steady were now spinning out of control. A cabinet flap fell open, and hanging from each of the two hooks was Bixby's next challenge.

"I feel like we have already done this one, Cody," she shouted through the cabin.

"Hemsley, you wanted to do an obstacle course race in real life!" she shouted. "This is as real as it gets!" Bixby hollered as she recalled his letter about wanting to run a similar type of race.

"Wait a sec..." he started.

"The plane is going to crash, and we need to bail out of it as soon as you launch in, so I really don't have much time to debate my teammate!" she urged as she started to strap on her rig. Now that she knew it wasn't as terrifying as she thought it would be, Bixby moved with a bit of confidence.

Harvey took Hemsley by the arm and escorted him out of the Command Center. He had no fear talking to Hemsley in front of Arthur because their systems already could read each other.

"I'm going to say this only once before I push you into that Launch Room. I don't know why you are here at Pinnacle Manor, or who put you here, but I do know that if your intentions in this race are anything other than to get Bixby to the next leg of it safely, you will unlaunch and I will be waiting right here for you," he said with a nasty scowl on his face. Choosing his words very carefully he spoke one last time. "I am a program which means I don't feel remorse or fear. If you hurt Bixby while in there, you hurt the team and a lot of people don't get back what it is they are fighting for. If you unlaunch and have sabotaged us, I will not hesitate to hurt you in unimaginable ways…"

Hemsley could only gulp as he stood there wide eyed and in terror.

"GET MOVING!" Harvey shouted as Hemsley turned and dashed into the launch room.

"Good show, ol' chap," Arthur said as the door closed, and he pushed the codes to launch Hemsley. "You would have made a fine dad."

Bixby stood at the plane's controls watching their altitude spiral downward as Hemsley appeared behind her clutching the passenger seat.

"Fancy meeting you here!" he shouted over the roaring of the engines as they plummeted.

Bixby looked up with a pair of goggles over her eyes and a neon blue pack strapped to her shoulders and around her legs. "You have about thirty seconds to put that pack on before I jump out of this plane without you!" she shouted back as she pointed to the rig hanging on the wall.

"I thought each level started with a riddle?" Hemsley said as he clumsily began to put the pack on his back. Bixby aided him, getting all of his straps secure. As she clicked the last clasp closed the rear hatch of the plane tore open, letting out a frightful howl of wind rushing through the cabin.

"There is," she said pointing to the plate that was set into the wall behind where the packs hung.

I can defy gravity for a moment,
But I return with a thump.
Not a hop or a skip.
What am I?

"A jump?" he asked, making sure he was right.

"There are only six thousand feet between us and the ground, so my best guess is that Cody made this one easy for a reason!" Bixby yelled, looking at the altimeter that had digital numbers quickly spinning backwards.

"What is it with you in this level and jumping from things with a parachute on your back?" he said, trying to make a joke in the heat of the moment.

A terrible screeching siren blared over the cockpit squawks as a message above the exit door flashed in bright red letters.

CLIP SHOOT HERE AND THEN ANSWER THE RIDDLE

"This may be my new hobby when this riddle is over," she said as he fumbled to put his goggles on.

Bixby didn't hesitate as she ran over to the open door, turned off her com, took the clip from the top of her pack, latched it to the bar above her, and dove out with all of her might, vanishing in an instant.

"I am not sure I signed up for this!" Hemsley shouted to nobody as he looked over his shoulder and the digital readout was now slightly above four thousand feet. He could see the forest quickly approaching the front of the plane.

There was no more time to think. "AHHHHAAAH!" he screamed as he too clipped in and then darted through the open door and almost immediately, he was yanked up with a jerk into the clear blue sky. At first the wind made his limbs flop in unnatural directions. It was such a violent tug that he was certain that every joint in his back had cracked like bubble wrap from the jolt.

The view from a few thousand feet above the earth should have been breathtaking to see, but all Hemsley could think about was not dying as he fumbled with his toggles. Bixby felt much more comfortable at the controls of the newer model of parachute. She laughed and giggled as she floated on the winds; mostly at Hemsley who was screaming in a high-pitched squeal as he scrambled to control his gliding.

Bixby hit the bullseye with fair accuracy landing just outside of the center mark. Hemsley however, made his way into the trees fifty yards away.

"I don't want to die!" he kept screaming as he tore at his latch.

"Calm down, I've got you, you big baby," she razed as she made her way to the branch right above him and yanked his harness loose from the tree.

The fall was only a few feet to the forest below, but Hemsley hit with a moderate crash.

"You gonna live?" she asked, jesting again.

"I am not supposed to be here," he started mumbling. Bixby, seeing that he was at a breaking point, turned her focus to making sure he didn't lose it before even starting the real challenge.

"It's okay, it's okay... It is totally normal to be scared," Bixby said, knowing that it had been a long time since she had entered the Riddle for the first time herself and almost forgot the sheer terror she had felt. She was well aware of the fears of being inside, but she had learned to control them.

"Bixby, I am not supposed to be in this Riddle," he said, now huddled in a ball at the base of the tree.

Bixby's level of concern had gone from very little to very high in a matter of moments. "What do you mean you are not supposed to be in this Riddle? You agreed to be part of the team," she stated clearly.

"Bixby, I really like you a lot," he began his plea. "Getting those letters has been the happiest I have been in a long time, but I didn't come to join your team as a guy who liked you... I was sent here to feed information to Dragonthorp Inc!" he shouted.

Bixby's heart shattered in that instant...

The mood had gone from fun loving to harsh in a blink of an eye. The beast inside had been released. Rage overtook her as her forearm pinned Hemsley's neck to the tree.

"Talk, or I let whatever is waiting for us inside this leg of the race take you to the end you deserve!" she said coldly as she looked deep into his terrified eyes.

"I can't or they said my family wouldn't be safe." He sniffled almost to the point of tears.

Bixby kept the pressure on his neck. "When we walk into that maze the cameras will turn on and the world and our team will hear and see everything. I am going to turn around and run in there in exactly one minute. If you have something to tell me before I go you have sixty-seconds, starting now."

In a frenzy of information, Hemsley started blurting, "They found me through my relationship with Pippa. They have been tracking her ever since she became part of the Cody Club. A man came to my house and said that unless I helped them break into your system or feed them information, they would hurt my family including Pippa. The man said all I had to do was offer my help and wear one of these contact lenses," he spouted as he slid the contact around in his eye.

"I put it in before I started talking to you in the tower at Shadow Deep. I figured it wouldn't hurt anybody, and everyone would be safe."

Bixby recognized the contact that stared right back into her eyes because it was the same one she was wearing to transmit information back to the Command Center. Marshall had stolen the blueprint for her a few months ago.

"Go on," she growled.

He continued. "Then you and I got close while writing the letters, and I really like you Bixby!" he babbled in a flustered tone. "But then when I got invited to the Manor and saw that you all had something to fight for, I started feeling really bad because I was spying on you instead of helping. I think Harvey already knew something was wrong because he wouldn't let me near the server room. Dragonthorp thinks you have a gigantic army of people working with you, so he has known every move you have been making from the beginning of Shadow Deep, because of the contact in *my* eye."

Bixby didn't blink as he kept pouring information out on her.

"Dragonthorp most likely knows you don't really have an army in the Command Center. He is very afraid of you winning the Riddle, Bixby. I didn't want to die in here and not be able to tell you I'm sorry. I couldn't decide between my family and you!" he eagerly rattled off. He was now an emotional wreck, which Bixby had never seen happen to a boy before. Her mind was reeling.

Her heart was already in pain so she might as well feed off this emotion. Putting the pieces of her heart back together would have to wait until much later.

"You're saying that Dragonthorp Inc. sees everything you see and if you take it out or hint that you have given away their secret, your whole family is in danger?"

"I purposely turned it off before I jumped out of the plane so that I didn't break the rules, but if they are recording this apart from the live stream… I'm done for," he lamented, crushed at the thought that he was stuck in a no-win situation.

"That's how they knew the Boss Riddle at the end of Level Two without going into the kitchen," Bixby said, connecting the dots.

"That's also how they knew Marin helped you," Hemsley said, knowing that if Marin found out, she would also kill him.

"And they broke her leg for it," Bixby concluded.

"Marshall isn't safe either. I was at dinner when he told everyone about the back doors he had created," Hemsley added, finishing every last detail he could imagine telling her.

She could see the brokenness in his eyes as she stared deep into them. He put up no resistance to the force pressing against his neck. Though her heart was hurting, she hoped that everyone at Pinnacle Manor would see that what he did was plain awful, but Bixby had been there before in Level One. She had said nasty things about those closest to her. The best way to help him help her was to redirect her anger away from him, and back onto the puzzle.

Bixby's mind when she was in attack mode worked a little different than when she was cool and collected.

"Good!" she said deviously. "You and I will have to talk about our relationship later. Right now, *you* have to pull yourself together and survive the next few hours. Luckily, I don't think the cameras start until we run past that start line," she said pointing to the literal word 'Start' carved into a stone archway.

"But, Bixby…" he tried to interrupt.

"Don't stop being Dragonthorp's spy, and your family will remain unhurt: business as usual. To the world, you and I are two people who are falling in love."

"Bixby, they are cheating, and I helped them, wait… you don't like me anymore?" he asked, feeling guilty and now a little heartbroken himself.

Bixby's expression went monotone and heartless. She could see that even Hemsley was unnerved by her voice.

"Hemsley, by being honest with me, you have helped me more than you can possibly know. I'm not really sure how I feel right now except really, *really* angry at Dragonthorp Inc., which is a very good thing for the both of us right now. So, without further delay, we have a Riddle to solve," she said, releasing her grip on him.

Certain that they had not actually started this leg of the race because of the obvious banner that said, 'Start' on the other side of the bullseye, Bixby reached up and turned her com device back on as she began to jog towards the maze.

Hemsley, knowing it was his best chance to appease everyone, fell in right behind her.

"Pippa, I need you to do something for me," Bixby said, hurriedly.

"Name it," she responded.

"It's time to release the Timmons Nation from their cage," Bixby replied. Up until now they had helped Bixby rebuild Pinnacle Manor, and supported the team financially through their streams, while her parents were missing.

With a mischievous chuckle Pippa started clacking away at her keyboard furiously, "What'd you have in mind, Bixby?"

"I don't think Dragonthorp Inc. is playing fair. Without destroying anything, I need the Timmons Nation to make contact with every employee working at Dragonthorp Inc. and…" Bixby paused to choose her words. "I need them to keep Dragonthorp Inc. digitally occupied for the rest of the riddle and find out what file they are trying to open."

"How occupied?" Pippa asked, making sure she didn't overdo it.

"Somewhere between major system breach and all out chaos," Bixby replied.

"Yeesss! That is what I'm talking about! I'm on it!" Pippa said, rejuvenated at her new task.

"Everyone focus on that, and I will see you all when we are done here," Bixby said while reaching up and once again silencing her earpiece before crossing the start line.

CHAPTER SEVENTEEN

KEEPING IT TOGETHER

It wasn't very long into the maze before Bixby noticed that every turn around a hedge led to one of two dead ends. Each of those dead ends had a riddle scribbled on the wall: one wall was easy, and the other was hard.

"Troll bridge puzzles," Bixby said as her gaze went back and forth between the two walls.

"I'm not sure what that means," Hemsley replied.

"If I am correct, the harder riddle will take more time to solve, but it would lead to an easier challenge on the other side of the wall. If we choose the easy riddle, the challenge on the other side would be harder."

Bixby didn't want to explain that the legend of the bridge troll was that if a traveler couldn't answer the riddle, they were severely punished for failing the challenge. She was certain that right now, she didn't need to unnerve Hemsley more than he already was.

Each puzzle wall she walked up to, she would tap on the stones. Hemsley assumed that she was seeing if anything alive on the other side of the wall would stir. Each time she did her tapping, she would pause as if she were listening for something, but no sound returned.

After visiting both wall options, and a quick count, Bixby chose the wall with a sequence of fifty-five bunnies carved into the rock standing in a row. Each bunny had a random one-digit number on its chest. Below was a ten-digit combination lock: each dial spun from zero to nine.

"How are we going to guess ten numbers correctly to get that passage open? There has to be trillions of different combinations. The slide puzzle looks like we could solve it quickly," Hemsley said, eyeing up the opposite wall which had the easier of the two riddles.

"This one is the Fibonacci sequence," Bixby said out loud. "That slide puzzle is solvable in six moves, making this the harder of the two." She pointed to the rock wall with a series of bunnies.

"I don't even know what a Fibonacci is?" Hemsley said nervous and confused.

"Leonardo Bonacci better known as Leonardo Fibonacci was the guy who brought a sequence of numbers from eastern civilization to the western civilization in the 19th century. It was said to be used on the premise of solving the problem of the growth rate in the rabbit population; hence the rabbits."

Bixby crouched down in the dirt and started to draw as she taught.

"The series of numbers that builds from each other. The first two numbers would be 0+1=1. Then he would add the last two numbers in the sequence together. 1+1=2. Again, he repeated the process. 1+2=3. As he kept going with 2+3=5 and so on, the numbers grow exponentially. The sequence is the same every time. 0,1,1,2,3,5,8,13,21,34,55,89, and so on."

"So, the first number is zero," he said as he went to the wall to roll the dial.

"No. Stop! The first bunny has a seven painted on its chest," she cautioned him.

"Bixby, just tell me what to do. I don't want to screw things up," Hemsley said, pulling his hand back from the dials and wiping his palms on his pants. Bixby knew he was trying to help and planned to use his anxiety to her favor.

"Let's think this out loud together," she urged.

"Okay, what do we know?" he replied.

"We know that there are ten numbers on the dial and there are fifty-five bunnies on the wall. Fifty-five is the eleventh number in the sequence. And seeing as in the Fibonacci sequence the number zero represents nothingness we will move to number one in the Fibonacci sequence and assume that the first number on the lock will be the number painted on the belly of the first rabbit," she instructed.

"That makes sense also because he only gave us one number, which means the next number would be seven also, and we would know how to start the sequence to get all ten numbers," he said proudly.

Hemsley quickly spun the dial for the first two numbers to be seven, and then fourteen, followed by twenty-one and thirty-five.

"It is a substitution cypher mixed with the Fibonacci sequence," he said out loud as he worked.

"I am certain that is how this Riddle is solved," Bixby confirmed.

When the final number was in place, the stone wall behind them creaked and moaned as the slide puzzle that was there disappeared into the thick foliage. It was now a solid part of the maze, and no longer a possible passageway. After it had completed its transformation, the wall with the Fibonacci sequence on it slid open revealing the physical challenge that went with the mental.

"I thought you said your theory was that the harder the puzzle was the easier the challenge?" Hemsley said, looking at a series of steppingstones. These were not just any steppingstones. To move from one to the next they would have to time their move between razor sharp pendulums and guillotines that would slice them in half without slowing down their own momentum.

"If my theory was right, try to imagine the challenge on the other side of the wall of the easy slide puzzle," she retorted.

A shiver of terror shot up his spine as his whole body let out a shake.

"Worse than not getting chopped up?" he asked, following Bixby's lead onto the first steppingstone.

"They are moving so slow, Hemsley. Keep up and try not to die," she replied as she bounded to the next stone.

The duo bobbed and weaved from stone to stone as they timed the rising and falling of the guillotine chops, and the back and forth swinging of the pendulums. Once on the other side Hemsley let out a sigh of relief. "That wasn't so bad. I mean the chance of death was there, but I'm okay," he said, double-checking to make sure all of his appendages were still intact.

Bixby shot him a small glance letting him know that his humor would normally be accepted, but with all the things that had happened in the last hour, she was having none of it.

Bixby continued her tapping on each of the puzzles before attempting to solve one or the other. Each passage opened into similar difficult, yet manageable tasks. Solving a Bongard problem instead of a substitution cypher led the pair into an archery range where they had to shoot moving targets in succession in order to open the final door. If they missed a target or hit them out of order the targets reset. Next choice was a play on words puzzle or Sudoku. She could see that the Sudoku could be solved rather easily, so she turned her attention to the play on words puzzle.

A British man wakes up, has his breakfast, gets into the left side of his car behind the steering wheel, and looked at his appointment book. He has two morning appointments, one in Gloucester at 9am and Bristol at 11am. After an hour stop for a spot of tea and a few crumpets, he can make it to Coventry to his 1pm appointment. From there he will just make his 2:30 appointment in Warwick. After each hour-long meeting he will be home in time to have a 4pm dinner in East Greenwich. How does he make it to each one of his appointments on time?

"That's easy, he gets in his car, goes to his private jet, and flies to each of those British towns," Hemsley said.

"Nooo!" Bixby started to interrupt his thoughts.

As the final word rolled off of his tongue both him and Bixby fell to the ground in tremendous pain. The surge they felt through their body ceased as they lay on the ground. Looking up at the puzzles on the wall, the riddle rumbled closed, and the Sudoku was the only option left.

"I'm sorry!" was the first thing Hemsley could shout when the outpouring of pain ceased. He realized his immature answer was what had caused the puzzle to shift out of play.

"He lives in Rhode Island," Bixby mumbled as she pushed herself off the ground, dusted off, and walked over to the Sudoku board to punch in the missing numbers. She had to keep reminding herself that she was not to give away the fact that he had betrayed the team originally. Every time he opened his mouth, it was a little harder to keep that leviathan bottled up.

"It was a play on word puzzle. The words in the puzzle and cities are made to sound like they are in England. They are most likely able to reach each city via jet if they were in England, but the riddle said he got in the car on the left side. In Great Britain the steering wheel of the car is on the right side.

"The only way he could have made it to all those cities is if they were fairly close together. The only state that is small enough to have five cities that are within driving distance and sound like colonial England is Rhode Island," she instructed as she put the last number in place and the rock wall transformed into an entrance to another part of the maze. What was on the other side of the wall confirmed Bixby's theory of 'the easier the puzzle, the harder the challenge'.

"Do those dogs look like they want to eat us?" Hemsley said as the lock on the gate started rotating to a sound of clicking similar to a clock winding.

"I'm not sure if I want to find out. Let's go!" she shouted, bolting to the wall that had a random series of bricks protruding from the side wall a few inches.

"Now what?" Hemsley said as they started to climb.

"We are going to climb this wall up to the ceiling and then like a set of monkey bars we are going to swing along the top just out of reach of the dogs. Once over that far wall we will have to reevaluate our options," she finished as the timer was up and the gate swung open and six grizzly dogs crashed through their steel confinement's exit.

The first dog to the wall was able to catch Hemsley, "He's got my shoelace!" he screamed.

"Sacrifice the shoe," Bixby shouted back as Hemsley violently flailed as the dog tugged back. His fingers were slipping from the bricks, and he realized he was going to be without one shoe for the rest of the race, or dog meat.

Bixby on the other hand didn't realize how important her shoulder was until she had to use it in every single challenge. Normally swinging across a set of high monkey bars wasn't really a challenge, but with her injured shoulder she had to take them slow and one at a time. She only slipped once, but because she was using both hands, she was able to recover quickly.

"Now what do we do?" Hemsley asked as they now stood on the wall's edge between the dog kennel and a pool of bubbling grey liquid.

"Now we each jump for one of those ropes and try to build up enough momentum to swing over to the landing that has 'exit' marked on the other side of it," Bixby said as she gauged how hard she was going to have to jump, and how bad it was going to hurt her arm again.

"What if I miss the rope?" Hemsley asked, looking down into the churning goo.

"Don't miss the rope," she replied before she catapulted herself off the ledge and with both hands, she firmly grabbed the rope. Her weight mixed with gravity gave her shoulder a tug. The pain was real, but so was the possibility of death if she couldn't bear it for a few more seconds. She shifted her weight now more on her good arm.

"Could you swing mine over to me?" he shouted with a logical request.

Wanting nothing more than to make him earn his rope, she hesitated for a moment, but she recalled them being a 'thing' to the world. Any good friend would help him out, so she pushed it over to him with her unhurt arm.

As he swung out to meet her, she instructed, "Now we have to slide down this rope and swing like you were on a swing set. Once you feel like you have a good enough trajectory you are going to let go of the rope and land on the platform."

"Try is a good word for what I am about to do," he said as Bixby had already started rocking herself back and forth on the rope.

Without much of a burden, Bixby was at the platform in a few seconds. Hemsley yet again was struggling with the challenge. After a minute or two of wiggling on the rope, he started to develop a bit of a swing. Another minute more and he shouted, "Here I come!"

Bixby could see that he didn't have as much momentum as needed to clear the ledge by much, so when he let go of his rope, he did land on his feet, but on the very edge of the boiling pool of goo. Bixby grabbed his shirt with both hands and yanked him to safety.

"You're going to need to do a lot of the obstacle races before I let you into another riddle with me," she said rubbing her shoulder. Her frustration was starting to boil over. Even Tipton wasn't this big of a weenie.

Over the next few hours the pair solved riddle after riddle which lead to more riddles. Upon finishing another challenge, Bixby started to wonder why this leg of the race seemed so long.

"Something is not right," Bixby said while turning circles in their new section of the riddle.

"What do you mean?" Hemsley asked, looking for the next chamber in the puzzle.

"The last three legs of this Rennen were a few hours long. When we jumped out of the plane it was morning according to the way the sun was rising, now the sun is way over there." She pointed at the setting ball of fire in the sky.

"Maybe because we are getting closer to the end, the legs of the race get longer," Hemsley proposed as a solution.

"It is a good thought, but I don't want to wait around to find out," Bixby said as she did her normal tapping on the puzzle walls and then instead of focusing her attention to the puzzles, she started looking at the walls around the sections of the puzzle.

"How many puzzles have we solved?" she asked as she sat down in the dirt and closed her eyes.

"Do you need to rest?" Hemsley said not sure what she was doing.

"SHH," she hushed him as she rubbed her temples. She was indeed tired, but if she slept, she would fall further behind Wesley and Greg.

"Count in your mind how many puzzles we have solved in this riddle and the next word out of your mouth should be a number."

Hemsley took a seat next to her and closed his eyes, counting and recalling.

"Twelve," he said as he continued to wonder what it was Bixby was doing. In front of her she drew a large box in the sand and broke it into twelve different boxes.

"Okay, the next thing I need you to recall is the order of the riddles that we solved. The first one was the Fibonacci sequence," she said aloud as she drew the letter 'M' in the sand.

"Wait, how did you get an M from Fibonacci sequence?" he questioned.

"No time to explain. What's next?" she demanded.

"Next was the Bongard, followed by the play on words that I messed up," he followed sheepishly.

Bixby scribbled more letters in the sand as they continued to rattle off the twelve riddles that were in their wake.

"Is it an anagram?" Hemsley asked, looking at the letters she had drawn in the dirt.

"No. It's the answer to the riddle. We just need to find out what to do with it."

M A T T E R

H O R N M A

"I am lost, Bixby. What is Matter Hornma?" he asked trying to figure out what she saw that he didn't.

"It's the last location that I get to travel to," she said, popping up from her seated position and started pulling down vines from the rest of the walls.

"I have really tried at this riddle thing, but we both know I am no good, so please help me to understand," Hemsley pleaded. He hated how bad he was at helping Bixby.

"Help me pull down these vines, and I will tell you," she bargained, knowing her shoulder needed a rest from all the work.

Springing into action, he worked quickly. Though he wasn't good at riddles, he was great at doing chores that Bixby asked him to do.

"I wasn't tapping on the walls. I was reciting the order of letters," she said as she yanked at another vine.

"What letters?" he asked, pausing his work.

She pointed to the new riddle wall in front of them. There were small carved letters in the lower right hand of the riddle: very easy to miss. My grandpa always taught me that if there is something odd in the puzzle that doesn't fit, it might be the actual riddle itself."

He had a few walls already cleared by the time Bixby had her first wall clean.

"So, you were respelling the words over and over in your head to make sure you didn't forget?"

"Correct," she said, frantically searching.

"What are we looking for?" he shouted from across the maze.

"We are looking for a grid similar to the one that I just wrote in the dirt.

Thirty minutes of tearing the walls of the maze apart lead to Hemsley finally getting to the solution first.

"Found it! But it only has ten boxes!" he shouted as Bixby ran over to where he was standing.

"We only need ten boxes," she said as she franticly scratched a letter in each box with a pebble she found on the ground.

MATTERHORN

"Who is Matterhorn?" Hemsley asked as the ground began to rumble and the walls began to shake.

"It's not a who. It's a what and we are going to need to start running again," Bixby said as the maze walls locked into place.

The previous dead end had shifted, leaving a single straight pathway that led out of the maze. On the other end of the tunnel was what looked to be a helicopter. In the distance they could hear very angry dogs as they looked at the tunnel that now had all their completed maze challenges laid out in front of them one right after another: ten in all. Only this time the dogs were coming from behind them.

"This obstacle course would have been a lot shorter if we would have figured this out on the third or fourth letter," Bixby said, disgruntled as she pushed out into the course.

Hemsley bounded through the guillotines and pendulums in step with Bixby.

"Those dogs won't follow us across the boiling hot goop!" he yelled, jumping this time to his own rope.

Over Hemsley's shoulder he could see stones rising out of the boiling water allowing the dogs to make their way across.

"What were you saying?" Bixby cried back from the landing.

"That's not fair!" Hemsley shouted, slamming down on his hip. He had overshot the mark completely missing his footing.

"Stop looking back and focus on what is ahead!" Bixby barked, knowing the dogs were breaking his concentration and slowing them down.

They bounded through fire, crawled over and under a series of laser beams, over a rope wall, and finally through a pressure lock system that when a person stepped on the wrong stone a series of darts shot out of the wall.

Bixby made her way through without a scratch. Hemsley on the other hand was nursing a blistered hand, rope burned thighs, and part of a dart sticking out of his right leg and two in his right arm.

The dogs were closing fast. There were only a few yards between the end of the tunnel and getting on the helicopter. Bixby helped Hemsley as he hobbled his way onto the landing pad where a large black Pave Hawk Search and Rescue helicopter had begun to turn its blades. She helped Hemsley up into the first seat, as she buckled him in. "How do you feel about completing your first obstacle race?" she asked, plopping down in the seat next to him.

He smiled at her sarcasm and shouted back over the thundering turbines, "I may scratch out of the one with my buddies."

Thunderous barking could be heard over the turbines as they warmed up. They both turned to see that the dogs had made it out of the maze and were headed straight for the helicopter. Bixby knew that as soon as she pulled the massive chopper door closed, Hemsley's time in the maze would end. The tinted windows gave Bixby her window of opportunity to unleash the leviathan. With her left hand, she yanked at the door's sliding handle. With the momentum of the turn, and with all of her might from Hemsley's blindside, Bixby swung with clenched fist striking his eye square in the socket. His head whipped back against the seat as he moaned in utter shock. The duo could hear the ravenous dogs bouncing off the side of the metallic door harmlessly as the chopper reached full flight capability.

"What was that for?" he reactively asked.

Hemsley had made choices that were best for him, but not for Bixby. She didn't want to imagine the weight he held. Before nearly taking his head off his shoulders she did take into account that he finished that leg of Level Three without unlaunching, ruining the entire riddle for her. But his stupid choices did light a fire in the depths of her soul that she never knew existed.

"I just chose a side for you!" she shouted over the screaming of the helicopter engines as she looked into his eye to make sure she had completely destroyed his eye piece.

"You and I can talk when I get back from the Matterhorn Mountains in the Swiss Alps, but until then tell Pippa to get the rest of your people to safety and don't make me regret it!"

She couldn't tell if his eyes were saying thank you, or starting to tear up in pain, but she was looking deep into them as he disappeared.

CHAPTER EIGHTEEN
UNINVITED SURPRISE

Everything was a mess again. Bixby's mind was now a twisted pile of factual wreckage. She was sulking again like in her room after she failed the frozen water climb. The blades of the helicopter would have been a nuisance if it were not for the noise cancelling headphones she was wearing. Nobody spoke to Bixby because she wouldn't allow them; her communication device was switched off.

There was no need to think about the Matterhorn because this level didn't allow for anyone to prepare for what came next. Bixby chose to ponder what pieces to Cody Dragonthorp's riddle she already had obtained.

"C'mon, Bixby. You can figure this out," she said to herself.

Her mind raced between Cody visiting his five manors before disappearing, a hundred million dollar offer, ten years of no clues, the business draft, the secret library, the Riddle, the details of each of the three levels so far, the prizes Cody offered each contestant; nothing made sense. But it was the image of Cody standing in the middle of the jumbo jet saying a nickname that only her grandpa called her that captured her focus.

"Spot," Cody said over and over in her mind. Grandpa kept showing up in the riddle from the very first level all the way up to the picture in the CEO's office.

"What is it about my grandpa that I need to know, Cody?" Bixby whispered to herself. "There has to be some sort of connection between everything."

The helicopter banked hard right which drew Bixby's attention out the window her head was previously resting upon.

In the distance she could see the massive whitecap mountains that she could only assume was her final destination. Bixby put her thoughts on hold as she switched back on her communication system. She needed to rally her team.

"How is everyone holding up?" she queried while watching the peaks start to grow in the foreground.

"Bixby! Everyone, she is back online!" Tipton shouted from the Command Center. "Bixby, how are you holding up?"

"I'm sore, tired, and my shoulder is killing me, but I'm alive," she said, trying her best to sound overly confident.

"Bixby!" shouted Pippa as she pushed aside one monitor and pulled another one in front of her. "What do you need? What can we do for you?" she asked, interlocking her fingers, and then pressed out, cracking every joint in her hands.

"How is the Timmons Nation faring?" Bixby inquired.

"That is a great question, Bixby," Pippa began. "At first Dragonthorp Inc. was practically in shambles. Every single project has been downloaded or at least exposed. We know everything. And that is when something strange happened."

"Gotta hurry up, Pippa," Bixby said as the mountain range hurriedly grew.

"Dragonthorp Inc. shut down and everyone there is only focused on protecting Dragonthorp Estates: it's a digital fortress," Pippa said with a huff. She sounded a bit defeated.

"They're protecting Dragonthorp Estates?" Bixby asked rhetorically, repeating Pippa's information before her mind was lost again into puzzle solving mode.

"That's what I said," Pippa replied.

"They *are* protecting Dragonthorp Estates," she said a third time as she was certain another puzzle piece had fallen into place.

"Pippa, I need you and the Timmons Nations to keep the pressure on. Do not let Dragonthorp Estates breathe even for a moment," Bixby insisted.

"Is there something we are looking for?" Harvey asked from the back of the room.

"I don't care what you find as long as at the end of this level they think they are being digitally attacked," Bixby said as she sat up in her chair and grasped the handle of the helicopter.

Marin burst into the Command Center decked out in her Holo-Riddle Suit and a scowl that meant she was ready for war. "You ready to do this, Bixby?" she barked. Bixby loved the energy. There was something about competing side by side with a beast like Marin that jacked her up as well.

"You, me, and this leg of the race with our old pals Greg and Wesley?" Bixby asked with a sense of animosity.

"Down a few minutes, but not out," Marin replied with a grin.

"Time for the underdogs to take the fight to them?" Bixby asked enthusiastically in return.

"Those two idiots aren't going to know what hit them," Marin replied as she pounded her fist into her palm.

Arthur was now shaking his head at their locker room banter.

"When you land, Bixby, I am going to need you to run into the tent as fast as you can so that we can get started on the data. I already have the specs on Matterhorn Mountain that the riddle is letting us see, and the current weather right now looks clear," Pippa said as she franticly looked over the potential strategies.

"Bixby, you do realize we are probably going to have to make the same climb that the athletes and scientists made before most of them were killed?" Marin asked as she finally introduced the elephant in the room.

"I was hoping it wasn't, but I didn't think any of us are dumb enough not to think that the Matterhorn isn't our final test," Bixby said softly as the helicopter descended and hovered over its final resting spot.

"Here we go!" Pippa said, urging Bixby along through the tension.

As the rails touched the asphalt Bixby cracked the latch and dashed for the rather large tent. This time there was no lock or riddle on the tent door. She assumed that everyone understood what needed to be done on this leg of the race. Bursting through the canvas flaps, Bixby stopped abruptly.

"Bixby Timmons! As I live and breathe!" shouted Greg in his newly formed sinister voice. Next to him stood the devil herself: Mad Maggie Murdock. Bixby reached over to the table next to her and grabbed what looked to be a pair of climbing axes. The one in her right hand she slammed pick first into the table, burring it deep into the grain. Holding the second one out she gestured to her opponents, challenging them to step closer to her.

"I dare you," Bixby said.

"Woah now, Bixby, I have her on a short leash," Greg said as he finished clipping a climbing pack with ropes and snowshoes to his back. "I know you are not stupid… there is a storm brewing on that mountain, and who better to take up with me than a survival expert?" Greg asked, gesturing to Maggie who was cleaning her nails with a hunting knife.

"Dogs bite, even on a leash," Bixby replied while staring right at Maggie.

Maggie's eyes narrowed without looking up. Bixby could tell that she was trying really hard not to respond.

"I'd love to stay and watch you two have it out, but there is a mountain I must climb," Greg said, pulling his last strap tight.

"Before you go, Greg, I'm curious, what are you going to do with that two percent company share if you solve Cody's riddle first?" Bixby inquired as she tapped the end of the pick on the table annoyingly.

The question startled Greg to a stop.

"Now that is a very curious question, Bixby. You said, 'if,' Timmons. I believe you meant to say 'when,'" he replied, deflecting her question.

"A hundred million dollars would be child's play if you win," Bixby said, strategically trying to get in his head.

"I hadn't even thought about it," he replied as he took a few more steps towards the tent exit.

"It would be a shame if all of Dragonthorp Inc. was worthless by the end of Cody's riddle," Bixby responded, certain that she knew his secrets now.

"Your team's little stunt on Dragonthorp Inc. was... unexpected, I will give you that. It even set me back a few minutes waiting for my partner to launch in, but it will not happen again."

"Lot harder to win when someone is turning your life upside-down, isn't it?" Bixby asked, poking the bear.

"It worked on you, didn't it?" Greg said with a hiss. His words pierced her deeply knowing that he was referring to her missing family and the heartache it created. "I would suggest that your friends stop dabbling in things they don't understand, or you will be responsible for their agony as well."

Bixby pulled the second axe from the table and her teeth clenched, ready to strike.

"There is no need for violence, Bixby. You and I will get our chance to battle it out in the final level together," he said with a grin as he turned for the door.

Bixby was confused at his boast.

"He's been dead weight from the beginning," Maggie said, slapping the back of Wesley's head as she went by him. He sat slumped down on a bench with two packs prepped and ready to go up the mountain. It was the first time Bixby had really taken inventory of him.

"See you in the next Level, Red," Greg shouted through the howling wind as he and Maggie disappeared out the door.

"What is he talking about, Wesley?" Bixby demanded as she still held firm to the ice pick with both hands.

"I was in first place until he pulled all of my outside resources."

"What does that mean?" Bixby asked for clarification sternly.

"I'm not going to make the climb, Timmons," he whispered in a barely audible tone.

"What do you mean he pulled your resources? You have everything you need right there," she insisted with a more clarifying question, pointing to his packs.

"Exactly what it sounds like, Bixby!" he shouted this time in anger. "He cut all communications to my team! He has my launch room guarded so that I can't unlaunch, and nobody is allowed into the secondary launch room to help me! I am literally stuck in this Level forever while you and him compete in the final round!"

Bixby was stunned at what she heard. That was a new low in the Riddle even for Dragonthorp Inc.

"By cutting you off, he guarantees that he makes it to the final round?" she repeated his lament.

"He knows everything about you, Bixby. None of us ever stood a chance," Wesley said.

Marin had spoken those exact same words to her one level ago, but this time it came from the person she had hoped *would* get stuck in the riddle. Facing the idea that it could really happen had the opposite effect, however, she felt... sad... for him. Bixby lowered the axes a little as she was now fully aware that Greg was the brain of team Dragonthorp and the person that needed to be eliminated in this level. Wesley spun around and flopped down on the bench with his back to Bixby and his head hung low to hide the tears welling in his eyes. Wesley must have not known about the Timmons Nation attack on Holo.

"I don't trust him, Bixby," Marin said over Bixby's earpiece.

"Neither do I, but if it is true, Wesley and I have to beat Greg," Bixby whispered back.

"Why? Just beat Greg in the next level," Tipton said.

"Trust me, Greg is the one we need to focus on," Bixby insisted.

"I think she is right," Marin agreed.

"Then what are you going to do?" Pippa asked.

"We should let him sit and rot," Tipton said, thinking about all the cruel things he had done to him and Bixby in school.

"Give me a moment to think," Bixby said as she raised one foot off the ground and thought. The group sat patiently as they watched her eyes inside her eyelids flash back and forth before a sneer pursed Bixby's lips. They knew Bixby had something, but she wasn't showing her cards just yet.

"Marin, I need you to launch in. Pippa?"

"Yes, Bixby?" she replied as she sat up in her chair.

"Can we put a call out to the Timmons Nation and see if anyone is willing to launch in with Wesley?" Bixby asked. "Make sure you ghost them in, and make sure to lock the system. Dragonthorp Inc. knows it is us that has them pinned down, don't be surprised if they start fighting back," Bixby said, knowing that even if Dragonthorp Inc. was watching they would have no idea what it meant when Bixby said to 'lock the system.'

"We could, but nobody is going to want to be his teammate, or risk their lives on that mountain," she replied as she started to type.

"Offer them some of Tipton's t-shirt money," Arthur said, trying to sweeten the pot.

"What t-shirt money?" Bixby inquired.

"Tipton is an internet sensation, and his t-shirt 'It's Too Hot For Pants' has a backorder of almost a million shirts," Pippa gloated.

Bixby chuckled a little, "How's Marshall dealing with that?"

"Marshall is doing just fine, thank you for asking," he snarked, answering for himself as he clomped through the Command Center's doors and sauntered his way over to the buffet.

"How's your head?" Bixby asked with a smile, thinking about how big of a weenie he was during their time together.

"My head and my bank account are growing more happier by the minute. They would both be better if Pippa hadn't got a copyright for the phrase 'It's Too Hot For Pants' and taken 75% of my profits, but free money isn't all bad," he said as he slapped together a sandwich.

"Yeah, he's still out of it. The real Marshall would be throwing a fit," Bixby commented as Marshall's eyebrows grimaced knowing she was right.

"Who knew there was a big softy inside of that posh exterior?" Pippa razzed more.

"Ahhh, I don't think you are going to have to give away my money," Tipton said, pointing to the screen.

Bixby rescanned the room and Marin, as expected, was standing behind the prep table. It was her partner that made her gasp.

"Mr. Richards?" Bixby questioned, shockingly.

"Grandpa!" Pippa shouted at the Holo-TV screen.

"I hope that is my pack already to go? I don't want to do any more work than I have to," Max Richards shouted in Wesley's direction.

Wesley spun around to see who was scolding him. "Who invited you in here, Father Time?"

"Father Time... That is a good one... I should unlaunch now and help you lose, but my launch room parameters are tied to yours now. Neither of us are unlaunching until I tap-dance my way up and down a man's mountain with you, sissy boy," Mr. Richards said, puffing his chest out in jest.

"Wait! *I*'ve gotta lug an old man up and down the mountain?" Wesley proclaimed horrifically as he realized that the gentleman was boasting their unity in the adventure.

"You've got a better plan there, chump?" Mr. Richards snarled back.

It took Wesley a second to process it in his mind... It was his only chance to get out alive. "No..." he huffed, realizing he was doomed.

"One rule, bucko," Mr. Richards said as he began to stroll over to the packs Wesley had already prepared.

"You're going to finish second or third in this round whether you like it or not. No funny business and we will get along just fine. And if I think you are going to do something stupid to hurt me or these girls, I will push you off the mountain myself," he finished.

"That was like three rules," Wesley said as he pushed a pack across the table.

"Don't be a smart aleck. I know ten ways to make you cry without touching you," Mr. Richards growled.

Wesley wasn't sure how to take the old man, nor was he sure he wanted to know.

"What is he doing here?" Bixby asked quietly, reaching the table where Marin still stood.

"Don't ask me, Bixby. Harvey and I planned on you and I taking a very large head start, and then once we were in the clear, the strategy was going to be to have Pippa ask the Timmons Nation for a volunteer. I thought Mr. Richards was prepping the launch room for me while Arthur finished cleaning up the bloody mess Hemsley made inside... how'd he get that shiner by the way?"

"Beats me," Bixby replied. Hemsley wouldn't tell if he knew what was good for him.

"Anyway, next thing I know, Arthur walks out with the mess and Mr. Richards walks right in and sends himself into the Riddle," Marin finished.

"And you let him!" Pippa shouted into their earpieces.

"Listen, Pippa..." Marin started with a sour tone.

"Pippa, we are going to do everything in our power to bring him home safe. You know I would die rather than let something happen to him, right?" Bixby asked, trying to move the conversation along and sound as sympathetic as she could.

"A lot of good it did for your family, Bixby," Pippa yelled as she dropped her keyboard on the ground and ran out of the Command Center. Tipton rushed after her.

"Great. We just lost our lead hacker," Marin said, frustrated.

Pippa's jab knocked the wind clean out of Bixby, as she rested her head against her locker and thought about her missing family for a moment. Maybe Pippa was right.

Marin quickly formulated a backup plan. "Marshall, can you work with Arthur to keep the pressure on Dragonthorp Estates with the Timmons Nation?"

"I got this," Marshall said, slipping into Pippa's chair.

"Hemsley and Harvey can monitor the security of Pinnacle?" Tipton asked, offering a solution.

Hemsley bashfully stepped forward from his hiding spot in the back corner of the room.

Bixby almost said no to the Hemsley part but hesitated, knowing that nobody but Hemsley and herself knew about how he weaseled his way onto the team.

"Saddle up, lover boy," Marin announced.

"Only if Bixby will allow me," Hemsley said almost immediately. "I'm sorry, Bixby... I'm really on your side now."

"Did you two have a lovers quarrel when you were in the game together?" Marin asked, confused.

"You don't want to know," Bixby replied to Marin.

"Really, Bixby, I won't sit down in this chair if you don't trust me. Do you trust me? I didn't mean to hurt..."

Before he decided to spill his guts, she interrupted, "Listen, Hemsley, get in the chair and get to work!" she barked.

"Ahhhh, I'll take that as a *maybe you trust me*, which is good enough for me right now," he said as he nestled in and started to peck away at the keyboard.

"Hemsley, before you join Harvey, we need details about this mountain. By details, I mean what is the best way to climb to the top?" Marin said as she started putting on a pair of snow pants.

"How do you know you have to climb it?" Hemsley questioned.

Sensing the tension between the two, Marin put her finger up to Bixby signaling that she would answer for her.

"Hemsley, your questions and my tolerance are not off to a good start, but to keep me from raising my voice I am going to point out the giant map hanging on the wall with a picture of the summit of the mountain. On that mountain is a flag with Bixby's name on it," Marin instructed through clinched teeth.

"Right. Sorry. I will get right on finding the best way up the mountain," Hemsley said, knowing he was not Bixby's favorite person, and now not Marin's.

"You really think we can get both of them up and down that mountain without any problems?" Marin asked. The girls looked at the two knuckleheads brooding with each other.

"We no longer have a choice," Bixby said as she yanked her locker open and started her prep.

Chapter Nineteen
Setting New Boundaries

Bixby and Marin took about fifteen minutes to gear up and made their way over to where Wesley and Mr. Richards were competing in a staring contest, though not by choice.

"What do you know about this climb?" Bixby demanded from Wesley.

"It's a mountain, Bixby. We climb up, grab our flag, and then we climb back down," he said while maintaining his gaze at the bushy eyebrows of Mr. Richards.

Tapping her climbing axe on the table, Marin rephrased the question, "We are not stupid, Wesley and maybe this is a shock to you, but whatever you and Greg are up to is not working on us. If I find out that you are keeping information from us..." The tapping got louder. "Do you know what it feels like to have four pins put into a broken leg?" Marin asked, reminding Wesley of the last time they had met on the balcony of Shadow Deep.

Wesley gulped realizing that it was him who was outnumbered in this level.

"Listen, all I know is Maggie is one of the best survivalists in the world, and that Greg trusts only her with his life. They have all the data on the storm that day, and if that storm does hit the mountain, those two will be just fine. I also know that their plan is to summit before you had the chance to get halfway up the mountain..." Wesley paused briefly. "...He said he would love to watch *us* freeze to death with the other hikers at fifteen thousand feet."

"Us?" Marin asked.

"That is when he told me I was cut off and that you would have to save me or that I would live a long life in Level Three."

"I liked Greg better in Level One when he was a bumbling oaf," Bixby said under her breath.

"Which way is he climbing the mountain?" Marin asked.

"You're asking me questions that I don't know," Wesley said frustrated at the inquisition that he was undertaking.

"I still think you're a liar," Marin barked before she was interrupted by Hemsley.

"I think I have the information you are looking for," he began. "The Snowenwood Rennen had its contestants scale the mountain from the Swiss side, which from the helicopter ride in is where you are all based. Therefore, the climb is going to be called the Hörnligrat. I am not totally sure if you are climbing it as it was in the 60's like the original Rennen, or if you are going to be doing it like modern day climbers.

"Does it make a difference?" Marin asked. Wesley knew she was communicating outside of the four people in the room but had no idea what they were saying.

"Well, yeah it makes a difference. In the 60's there were no cable cars that would take you up to Zermatt and no lines and anchors already attached to the side of the mountain. That, and Hörnli Hut where you spend the night wouldn't exist, which means you would sleep two nights outdoors. One night before you scaled the summit and descend back to the Hörnli Hut for the night, followed by the trek back to the tent you are in now," Hemsley completed.

"No cable car equals long trip got it," Bixby said as she clipped the chest strap of her backpack in place. "We need to get to work, Greg already has a big head start on us," she finished.

"You're not *really* trying to beat him, are you?" Wesley asked, shocked.

"Hold still," Bixby demanded of Wesley as she grew close, pushed the ice axe to his chin, and reached towards his face. Wesley knew exactly what she was doing. Bixby reach up into Wesley's eye and then the other one, snatching out the same communication devices that she too had in her eye. Rolling it between her fingers, she crushed each one.

"If I beat him, you beat him, Wesley... and you get to unlaunch," Bixby said sternly as she reached the tent exit.

"Hemsley, is all that information uploaded to my Mini Holo-Writer?"

"You have all the information I do," he concurred.

"Destroy all your com devices," Bixby instructed before she too reached into her own eye pulled out the com set as well as the one in her ear, threw them on the ground, and smashed them so that everyone could see that they were on their own.

Bixby yanked back the tent's canopy door as snow came whipping through the opening. Turning back to the group who was now in shock at Bixby's boldness to go after Greg, she shouted through the blustery snow, "I didn't come here to finish in second place!" she roared as she disappeared through the doorway.

The wind would have been bitter if it were not for the layers of clothes provided by the Riddle. There was no doubt which direction they were heading as the Matterhorn was breathtakingly beautiful, but also the bringer of anxiety for the four explorers.

"Where exactly are we going, Bixby?" Marin asked as she caught up with Bixby who was already trudging through the vacant streets of a quant Swiss town.

"On the helicopter ride in I saw the cable cars which means we are climbing it in present day fashion," Bixby said as she marched forward as sunlight peaked in and out of clouds.

"That's good news," Wesley said, falling in step.

Uncomfortable with having Wesley in her blind spot, she stopped to set a new rule.

"Mr. Richards, I would like you to lead the way followed by Wesley, Marin and then me. I will adjust it if we need to push the pace, but we are as strong and as fast as our weakest link," she instructed.

"Hey, let's get one thing straight, little lady, I am as strong as an ox and as tough as nails," Mr. Richards informed.

"I know that, but this is your chance to prove it to *him*," Bixby said, pointing to Wesley.

Everyone in the group realized that Bixby more so wanted to keep an eye on Wesley, but nobody argued—not even Wesley, which again made Bixby a little uneasy.

"Very well then... To the summit," he shouted as he put his hiking sticks into motion and made for the cable cars.

After passing empty business after empty downtown business, Marin slowed down to have a conversation with Bixby.

"What's on your mind, boss?" she started.

Bixby pondered a little bit before answering.

"Cody said that my reward had something to do with a greater riddle about my grandfather, and if I won, I would have the final pieces to some larger puzzle. That would mean I already have some of the pieces."

"So, what are they?" Marin asked a question in return.

"That is my problem, I have no idea. I'm not sure if they are the riddle, or the times I heard my grandpa's voice inside the riddle..."

"You heard your dead grandpa's voice while in the riddle?" Marin asked, cutting her off as she was hearing this for the first time.

"Remind me to tell you about it when we are done. So, what's on *your* mind?" Bixby asked, changing the subject.

"We both know this is a trap, right?" Marin asked.

"I think that's a given, Marin. But this entire level of the Riddle has me all turned around," Bixby admitted.

"We knew this was a Geo Race from the start," Marin whispered back.

"That is the best part of riddles and puzzles; there are so many different types to learn about. But Cody's prize and the three levels have me going back to 'What is it that I should *really* be looking for?'" Bixby replied.

"I can be your eyes and ears in here, but I'm afraid I am no help with the grandpa thing," Marin said.

"I need you to trust me if I do something that seems crazy," Bixby said, trying not to sound ominous.

"Does this involve when we catch up with Greg and Maggie?" Marin asked.

"I'm not sure yet, but if the moment comes, just know I am mostly in control," Bixby replied.

"If you keep dancing with the edge of sanity, Bixby, sooner or later you're going to fall off," Marin warned.

"I know, Marin. I'm doing the best I can. That's why I'm glad you're in here with me," Bixby said in return.

"Just remember that if we end up in a confrontation with Greg and Maddie, Wesley is a wild card… and their three versus our three is still very uneven. Maybe we should consider staying away from team Dragonthorp and cruising in at second place. We have a lock in the next round as long as we are not stupid about things," Marin suggested one last time.

"I have considered that, but my dad said we have to win each round, and if you think about it, from here on out he is right."

"Not following you, Bixby," Marin said, confused.

"We fell for the clueless surfer dude the first two levels. But we know he is the smarter and more resourceful of the two guys left in the riddle, he is the most dangerous one. Whatever trap they have planned, if I am ahead of them, they will need to catch up to me to spring it. If I am behind them, they both can work together to force me into last place," Bixby said, confident she knew more than she was letting Marin know.

"Whoever is in charge, you are facing Dragonthorp, Inc. the rest of the way through," Marin replied, knowing Bixby had a long road ahead if she wanted to solve Cody's riddle first.

"That's why I'm happy to have you and the Timmons Nation on my side," Bixby said with an elbow nudge of her partner.

"There it is!" shouted Mr. Richards as he started to jog towards an abandoned cable car lift under a sign that read *'Greatest View in the World.'*

"Here we go," Marin said as she started to jog after him.

"How do we get in?" Mr. Richards said as he reached the locked chain link fence outside of the attraction. Wesley reached the fence second and, without hesitation, jumped on the barrier and started to scale.

"No rules inside the riddle, Old Man Time! Cops aren't going to get you for trespassing," he yelled as he sat at the top.

"Except the ones you tattled to in the heist part of this level," Bixby replied, sarcastically.

"They *were* helpful, weren't they?" Wesley replied in an arrogant manner.

Mr. Richards reached up and caught Wesley's foot as he went to jump down into the powder below. Wesley came down with a thud in the fresh powder. "Oops!" he said to Wesley as he popped up out of the snowbank. Wesley knew he deserved that, so he didn't bother with a response while Bixby smiled from ear to ear while racing up the fence herself.

Once onto the platform the four competitors could see that there were three cable car tracks awaiting the teams. One was missing, leading the group to the conclusion that Greg and Maggie had indeed found their way here. The other two cable cars were each labeled with 'Bixby' and 'Wesley' respectively.

"See you at the top," Wesley shouted as he rushed for his car.

"Ooh, my hip," cried Mr. Richards.

"Seriously?" Wesley groaned, halting in his tracks, and returned to the group.

"How bad does it hurt?" Wesley inquired.

"Bad enough to keep you from running ahead," he replied with a grin.

Wesley knew he was in for a long trip. The pairs each entered their own cable cars and Bixby's first concern for the lack of actual word riddles was no longer a concern. On the panel board was the first riddle of this leg. Two coin-slots with an imprinted message above the slots.

THIS CABLE CAR REQUIRES A TOLL. IT WILL COST FIFTY-FIVE CENTS TO GO TO THE TOP AND BACK. I REQUIRE EXACT CHANGE, AND ONE OF THE COINS MUST NOT BE A NICKEL. IF YOU GUESS WRONG YOU WILL BE GIVEN A TWENTY MINUTE TIME DELAY.

Sliding the glass window open on the adjacent car, Wesley inquired in, "This riddle is impossible. The only way to have two coins adding up to fifty-five cents is a fifty-cent piece and a nickel, but it says that one of the coins can't be a nickel!"

"You really are one of the dumbest smart people I know," Bixby said, pulling out the change purse that was part of the supplies given back at the tent. She pulled out a fifty-cent piece and a nickel and slid them into their appropriate spots. As the coins hit the change pit the cable car hummed into action and off Bixby and Marin went.

Bixby leaned out her window and yelled down to the dumbfounded Wesley, "One of the coins *isn't* a nickel, it's a fifty-cent piece!"

Smacking himself on the forehead, Wesley rushed to the controls and followed Bixby's lead.

The cable car ride was slow which gave Marin and Bixby time to discuss hot topics like Hemsley, the larger meanings to the Riddle, guessing what Mr. Richards and Wesley would be talking about, and strategies. The conversation quickly faded to silence for a moment as soon as they jetted over a clearing and the mountain range of Matterhorn came into full view.

"I'm not going to lie, the views in each of these levels are astounding. I could get used to heights if each time I went up was as beautiful as this," Bixby said, making her way to the front window of the cable car.

Marin would have agreed if she could speak, but the raw magnitude of 15,000 feet of rock face and snow woven together was something that had her heart racing. After a stunning moment of reflection Marin was able to give her thoughts.

"You realize that those competitors in the 60's had to climb that without a lift or guidance?"

"Glad Cody is taking it easy on us," Bixby said jestingly.

"You know what I meant," Marin said with a laugh. It was the first time Bixby had seen Marin lighten up, but her face quickly washed over with concern.

"What is it now?" Bixby inquired.

"Do you think Mr. Richards is going to make it?"

"I think you need to worry about yourself. Mr. Richards thinks he can do this, and that is half of the battle," Bixby replied as she started to strap on her pack.

The cable car crept toward the pinnacle of its climb, and a large reflective sign read:

WELCOME TO YOUR STOP:
3,383 METERS ABOVE SEA LEVEL.

"But seriously, do you have a plan of action if we run into Greg and Maggie?" Marin asked finally as the car slowed as it approached its destination.

"I'm more of a 'think it up as I go' kind of girl, but you are more than welcome to put a plan together," Bixby said as she clipped her last buckle into place and the car slowed to a stop.

"You're making me nervous, Bixby," Marin said anxiously.

"These days, I make myself nervous sometimes," she replied as she stepped out of the car.

"Oh boy..." Marin whispered under her breath.

"How was your trip, Mr. Richards?" Bixby shouted from across the platform.

"It was great! I'm ten bucks richer!" he shouted back.

"What?" Bixby asked as the teams reunited.

"Father Time here is a swindler," Wesley said as he pushed past the group looking for the next clue.

"You do realize that money inside of a hologram is pretty much worthless?" Mr. Richards said to the even grouchier Wesley.

"Not the point, Old Man!" he hollered back.

Bixby could only assume Wesley lost a bet to pass the time up the mountain.

"Shall we?" Mr. Richards asked as he started to stroll down a deliberately carved cave walkway.

"Are you sure you know what way we are going?" Bixby inquired after him.

"If we are climbing that mountain, we should probably follow the path that says, 'To the Matterhorn,'" he replied, pointing to the snowy peaks rising through the clouds and tapping the snow off the sign as he went by it.

"Duh," Marin and Bixby said to each other in unison.

Once out in the open, Mr. Richards abruptly stopped and assessed his surroundings. First, he pulled off his mitten, licked his finger and held it up in the air. After putting his mitten back on, he grabbed a handful of snow and packed it into a tight snowball. Turning it once over in his hand he gave it a gentle toss over the side of an embankment, watching it intensely as it went over the edge. Lastly, he took several deep breaths in and slowly let them out. He was concentrating on the puffs of smoke that the frosty air created when he was exhaling.

"What are you doing now, Looney Bin?" Wesley inquired.

"Just getting our bearings, my boy," Mr. Richards proudly tallied back.

"So now that you have your... *our* bearings, can we start climbing the mountain?" he asked Mr. Richards who seemed much happier than his normal reserved self.

"And that is why I'm leading the way. To climb the mountain the quickest, we will need to go that way!" he shouted, pointing in the complete opposite direction of Matterhorn.

"I told you he was crazy... The mountain is that way, Grandpa," Wesley said, sounding like he had finally outsmarted Max Richards.

"Yes, the mountain *is* that way, but the snowmobiles that will help us get there quicker are *that* way," he replied as he shoved off towards several giant wooden sheds with a medical search-and-rescue cross painted in red on the side of it.

Kicking in the door and shattering the locked handle on the frame, Mr. Richards had exposed several bright green Snow Banshee snowmobiles.

"No cops inside the Riddle," Mr. Richards chuckled as he reached the slickest of the machines. "This one is mine!" he shouted as Wesley peered in after him. "Y'all find your own... And everyone has to wear a helmet!"

"How'd you know these were here?" Bixby questioned as Mr. Richards saddled up.

"While you kids were doing searches on how to get up the mountain, I was doing a little research on where the medical stations were in case of an emergency. I happened to stumble across an article on the equipment the search and rescue teams use up here," he finished as he roared the engine to life and revved the high pitch yelp of the engine.

Marin shrugged, knowing she had missed this detail.

"Ha, ha! Banshee! Get it?" Mr. Richards yelled over the screaming motor.

With pleasure, the trio of kids jumped on their very own snowmobiles and flipped the 'On' switch.

"Anyone notice that Greg and Maggie are on foot?" Marin asked, pointing out the path carved in the snow through the riven below them.

"Not sure how they missed snowmobiles, but I'm sure we would have too without Mr. Richards," Bixby said as she slipped her helmet on and brought her machine to life. "Time to catch up!" she shouted as she gave the throttle a pull which rocketed the sled out of the shed and onto the fresh powder.

The snowmobile ride was only fifteen minutes before they reached the first walking trail up the mountain, but it was energy they didn't have to burn walking like Greg and Maggie.

"Hide them behind this patch of trees and cover them with those fallen branches," Mr. Richards instructed, pointing to the hiding spot.

"Brilliant. With any luck we will already be ahead of Greg and Maggie by the time we get back here, but let's not take that chance," Marin replied.

As the group of travelers reached the threshold of the bridge fastened to the side of the cliff, a riddle was carved into the base of the rock.

"Solve the riddle, or risk the bridge collapsing under your feet as we climb?" Mr. Richards chuckled to his male counterpart.

"Riddle, right," Wesley replied as he gazed at the wall and read aloud. "Add two to eleven to get the answer one."

"My answer is most certainly not, 'Not possible,' because I don't want to get a burn on my arm like all the last time I said, 'Not possible' out loud even though it wasn't my final answer," Wesley said, rubbing his bicep.

Bixby and Marin knew that he must have received a burn when he asked Bixby about how to solve the cable car riddle.

"How is it possible that you made it through the other two levels?" Marin asked as she came to the answer's conclusion.

"He had Greg to do all of the work for him," Bixby proclaimed as she took snow in her fist, waited for some of it to melt, and used the water that dripped from her hand to write her answer on the rock face.

"That is not true, Bixby! What do you know?" Wesley shouted defensively. Bixby knew Wesley was a hothead, and a window had opened for her to see if she could push him into saying something stupid.

"What do I know?" Bixby raised her voice. "I know that in Level One Greg knew most of the answers to the Riddles without even trying while you were covered in burns. That either makes him really smart, which means he has no need for you as a teammate *Ooorrr* you were relaying the answers back to Greg to make sure he could keep up making him as weak and dumb as I originally thought... *ooorrr* he is the boss and you and Maggie are his flunkies. I'm pretty sure we now know the answer to *that* riddle already, now don't we?" Bixby said as she turned to stand face-to-face with Wesley.

"You can't prove any of that," he said, monotonal. He had unexpectedly calmed down and her window to get him to slip up and give her some unknown details had mostly closed.

"I know more than you think," Bixby said smugly, trying to keep her poker face on. She had no idea how much Wesley actually knew about her and the Timmons Nation.

"Bixby, you have no clue who you are dealing with," Wesley replied, shaking his head as she stood face to face with him.

"There is that phrase again. Why don't you tell me more about *who* I'm dealing with," she insisted.

She wasn't certain if he was talking about himself or Dragonthorp Inc., but deep in the recesses of his eyes she saw something that made her more and more confident that he was terrified instead of poised. It was in that moment that she knew what she was going to do when she met with Greg next.

"Nothing? Oh well, I'm sure I will find out soon," Bixby said, knowing that she was poking the wrong bear.

As Bixby finished writing her answer on the wall, next to the bridge appeared a safety cable anchored into the side of the cliff. That way if anyone was to slip or the bridge was to break, there was a second line of security.

"Cool," Mr. Richards said. "I always wondered what this extra buckle was for," he said nonchalantly as he handed Wesley a snowball so that he could write '1am or 1pm' on the rock face before clipping the shoulder clasp of his pack to the safety cable on the rock wall. Everyone followed suit and the group fell into Bixby's required formation.

"You going to tell me what that was all about?" Marin asked as the two again fell slightly behind the boys.

"Wesley has a knack for talking too much when he is mad, I'm just digging for a little info," Bixby replied.

"Care to clue me in on what you found out in that little exchange?" Marin asked.

"Remember when I asked you to trust me?" Bixby inquired of Marin.

"Everyone knows that that is the first question you ask before doing something stupid," Marin responded.

"If you trust me, just be ready to back me up because I'm absolutely going to do something stupid here really soon," Bixby replied.

"You do realize that I have saved your life twice now in these riddles?" Marin asked in return.

"Then I can't promise you won't need to do it again before this is all said and done," Bixby replied. "And I believe I saved you once."

"No, you didn't. Daryl did," Marin corrected.

"I gave you a place to stay?" Bixby asked, trying to get a little credit.

"Are you sure you want that to be your answer when you need me to save you again?" Marin said with a smirk.

"We'd better not let those two out of our sight," Bixby replied, trying to change the subject.

After an hour of climbing further up the mountain, the group exited a bridge as it opened to a rock shelf and a clearing. In the distance was a cabin with smoke billowing from the chimney as dusk dimly reflected off the speckles of fresh snow.

"Oh, I can't wait to warm myself by the fire," Wesley said over the wind gusts as he started to run for the cabin.

"Wesley! No, wait!" Bixby shouted after him as Marin took chase.

CHAPTER TWENTY
MASKS OFF

"What's happening?" Mr. Richards asked, confused at the sudden excitement.

"Greg and Maggie are in that cabin, and the last thing we want is for the three of them to become friends again," Bixby said as she followed Marin in the chase for Wesley.

As the three approached the cabin and within a few feet of tackling him, a whistle and a flash of darkness flew past their heads.

"Take cover!" Marin shouted as she turned from chasing Wesley to sliding across the frozen tundra behind a rock. Wesley had crumpled to the ground from the arrow narrowly missing his cheek. He franticly crawled back to safety with Marin.

"Aww, you missed!" came a cry from the crow's nest of the cabin.

"I think that was a pretty good shot on a moving target, with a crossbow, from fifty yards away," the distinct voice of Mad Maggie Murdock could be heard. Bixby couldn't see her because everyone had taken refuge behind the massive stone.

"Now, Bixby, I see that you have caught up to Maggie and me just before the sun went down. I believe a bravo is in order! However, I am going to need a bit of an edge going up the mountain tomorrow seeing as we are supposed to get a pretty bad storm and all!" Greg cried out over the wind.

"How about you come down here and you and I can settle this once and for all, Maggie!" Bixby shouted, ignoring Greg for the moment, and focusing on the one with the weapon. The beast within was ripping away at her insides to be let it out.

"Oh, Bixby, now why would we go and leave the comfort of this cozy cabin in order to play in the snow with you, an old man, the cripple, and my ex-partner?" Greg yelled back for Maggie.

"Do you always hide behind a girl, Greg?" Bixby tried to get under his skin a little.

"When she is as skilled as this one? Yes!" he replied, showing Bixby that her attempt at riling him up was useless. "Now if you will all excuse me, I will leave Maggie here to do what she does best. Oh, and if you try to push out towards the mountain before us, Maggie has permission to... let's just say she won't miss a second time. Good night, rejects!" he finished as he turned from the rail to go inside.

"Before you go to bed, tell me how old you are, Greg!" Bixby shouted as she stepped out from behind the rock that the foursome had taken shelter behind. Marin tried to grab her and pull her back, but Bixby waved her off without looking back. She was fully exposed to Maggie's weapon, but what would make most people afraid fueled Bixby's fury.

Bixby could see the question had stopped Greg in his tracks as Maggie was reloading the crossbow. Greg turned and put his hand on Maggie's shoulder signaling her to stop for a moment as he returned to the rail. For Bixby, this gesture put another piece of the puzzle in place.

"You have a lot of questions today, Bixby, and *that* one is a very interesting inquiry," Greg said with a sizzle in his voice.

"We started this riddle over two years ago, Greg," she reminded him. "How old are you?" she demanded.

He hesitated for a long time.

"You and I both know that I am the youngest competitor of the group," Greg replied, miffed, before releasing his hand from Maggie's shoulder. He turned and reached for the cabin door.

"The world is watching, Greg! Why don't you tell everyone how you were the only one to take advantage of the rules of Level One to alter your avatar, Greg! Or should I start calling you by your real name, Daemon Dragonthorp!" she screamed into the cold air.

He stopped with his hand clutching the cabin's door handle. She really disliked Wesley, but her real nemesis now had a name.

In his pause, she continued to yell out her conclusion. "Your birthday is February 29th which means even though you are old, because your birthday is technically every four years, you're young enough to compete."

His head bowed at the accusations.

"How's the digital mining expeditions going at Dragonthorp Inc.? Did you find out how much Cody knows about whatever it is you are trying to keep me from winning?" she continued.

Bixby knew she was throwing big cards on the table, but he had not taken her bait yet, so she kept at it.

"You didn't break into Pinnacle Manor to steal Harvey; you did it because you knew that if security was triggered, everyone inside would be protected at all costs. You tried to have me disqualified by forcing me to unlaunch during the security breach. Only the owner of Pinnacle Manor's sister house, Dragonthorp Estates, would know about that feature. None of the rest of the mansions have it, and when you circled the wagons around your house, you gave yourself away! How does it feel knowing that there is an army knocking at your front door right now and there is nothing you can do to stop it?"

He bit, knowing his plans were being unraveled to the entire world that was watching.

Bixby was ready to reveal that she knew about the eyepieces that he had used to cheat so far in the Riddle, but before she could blurt it out, he turned back to face his accuser.

"I thought for sure we hadn't left our homes for Level Two," Daemon shouted back.

Everyone besides Maggie was in utter shock at the unmasking of Daemon.

"I didn't think you had it in you to use my own tactics against me, but you're right, if you get in, I unlaunch," Daemon replied. "You're a tougher opponent than I thought, Timmons!"

"You didn't unlaunch me, but you *did* take my family from me!" she screamed with tears in her eyes now.

"I lost my only family long before Cody went missing, Bixby! You will get used to it eventually!" he replied coldly.

She didn't know what he meant, but she didn't let up her bold front. "No matter where I finish, Daemon, I promise that I will bury you and Dragonthorp Inc. when it is all said and done!"

The leviathan was roaring from within her.

"Tell that to my brother, Bixby! He can end this whole thing any time he wants!" he shouted back, anger painted across his face. Before she could say anymore out loud, he turned, grabbed the door handle, stormed inside, and slammed the wooden door behind him.

Maggie raised the bow and released another arrow to remind Bixby of her mission. Bixby leaned to her left slightly as it ripped the shoulder of her puffy jacket. Bixby was unphased as she never stopped glaring into Maggie's eyes. Bixby could tell that the gesture of fearlessness rattled Maggie enough that she fumbled with the next arrow.

"You don't have the guts, Maggie!" Bixby said before slowly strolling back to the rockface where the others stood in stunned silence.

The last light was fading behind a smaller mountain range as Maggie began to pull the string of the crossbow tight to load another arrow to keep the four opponents put.

"You're insane!" Wesley shouted as Marin immediately checked the hole in her coat to make sure she wasn't injured.

"There's blood," she said as she inspected the jacket.

"It's just a scratch," Bixby said pulling her arm away and put her ice pick up to Wesley's neck.

"How much of this did you know?" Bixby asked Wesley.

"N-nothing, I swear," he said with a gulp.

"I'm not afraid of you anymore," she said with laser eyes searing deep into his. "You'd better pick a side," she whispered in his ear as she drew close. The coldness in her voice was broken only by the sound of shoveling as she released the pressure from his neck.

"What's your plan?" Bixby asked Mr. Richards who was already working on something.

"We're going to sleep outside," he replied.

"Great! We are going to freeze to death out here," Wesley moaned as he took off his pack and nestled himself next to the rock wall and pulled his collar up as high over his face as far as he could. Everyone could tell her words had gotten to him.

"Get up and help or you *will* sleep out here in the cold," Mr. Richards responded earnestly.

"What are you gonna do, Old Man? Build us a house with a nice warm fireplace?" Wesley said bitterly.

"No, you fool, we are building a snow cave to save our lives, but if that sounds like too much work, then enjoy being a popsicle," he replied as he started piling snow up against a rock wall.

"What do you need us to do?" Bixby asked, knowing that she needed a distraction to continue thinking about her next moves.

"Get your shovels out and pile as much snow up against that wall as possible. Every ten minutes or so we will all go and pack it down. After we are done with that, we will carve out a small tunnel that we can all sleep in. Our body heat will keep the tunnel warm overnight."

"That is pretty brilliant," Marin said as she pulled out her compact shovel.

"While you do that, I'll build a trap that will let us know if Maggie decides to come and pay us a visit," he instructed as

Bixby and Wesley grabbed their shovels, turned on their headlamps, and started digging.

As predicted the snow cave took them about an hour to create. Mr. Richards was the last one in and packed the doorway closed with snow to retain their heat. He had created several small holes in the structure to let oxygen circulate into the cave.

"This is cozy," Wesley immediately complained about the living quarters.

Mr. Richards reached over to open the snowbank that was the door, "No wait... what I mean to say is how magnificent it is that we are going to survive here for the night!"

"That's better," Mr. Richards said as he pushed his way between Wesley and Bixby. "Teammates should sleep next to each other," he said trying to keep the teenaged boy from sleeping too close to his newly appointed granddaughters.

He then reached over to Wesley's coat in the dark and latched his safety harness clip to him.

"You afraid the monsters are going to come in here and get me?" Wesley snarked.

"We don't want you running off on us now do we?" Mr. Richards mumbled to Wesley as everyone settled in.

Wesley simply huffed.

"Sleep tight. Don't let the frostbite bite," Mr. Richards said, flicking off his headlamp.

Bixby's lamp was the last one lit. Her heart had not stopped racing. She had played almost every card she had, and in doing so, she declared war not only Daemon and his company, but an entire way of life for everyone on the planet. All she knew was that that from here on out, her foot could never come off the pedal, and nobody could see her crack. She pushed up over Mr.

Richards so that she could look Wesley dead in the eyes and said, "Monsters are already in here, Wesley." And then she reached up, turned off her light, and vanished into the darkness.

CHAPTER TWENTY-ONE
ASCENT

Bitter cold air ripped through the snow cave as Mr. Richards kicked a large hole in the roof of the structure while the rest of the team was sleeping.

"What is it?" Wesley shouted as he sat up, smacking his head on the ceiling of the cave.

Marin and Bixby were up and defensive but had their whereabouts enough not to make the same mistake as Wesley.

"Ah, that gets 'em every time," Mr. Richards chuckled as he stood up and started climbing out of the snow cave.

"What is wrong with you, Old Man?" he could hear Wesley bark after him.

"What time is it?" Bixby asked as she climbed out second.

"Ahh, I'd say roughly 3:30 am," he whispered back looking at the moon.

"Did he say 3:30?" Wesley grumbled from inside the cave where he was still holding his head.

"Yep," Bixby confirmed.

"Why are we up so early?" Marin asked as she started to climb out of the igloo and rolled out onto the fresh coat of powder that must have come down overnight.

"First, Marin St. James you will need to take several of these," Mr. Richards instructed as he handed Marin some medication for her headache.

"How did you know I had a headache?" Marin inquired surprisingly.

"One in four people suffer from altitude sickness above 8,000 feet. The first signs are struggling to breathe which I noticed after your chase with Wesley there—you should have easily caught him,"

"No, she couldn't," Wesley said as he popped his head out of the snowbank like a meerkat.

Both girls turned and simultaneously said, "Shut up, Wesley,"

His hands went up in the air immediately at the threat, "Okay!"

"Anyway, as I was saying, Marin I am sorry, but you were having severe trouble sleeping last night. You need to stay hydrated and keep down a lot of water. If you start throwing up, we could be in a lot of trouble, so don't push it. If you want, we can meet you back here on our way back through?" Mr. Richards offered.

"Not going to happen," she said as she grabbed the pills and gulped them down.

"Why are we up so early then?" Bixby brought the conversation back to the climb.

"According to my watch thingy here..."

"Mini Holo-Writer?" Bixby corrected.

"Whatever... according to it, the climb is going to take at least five hours to the top, let's say only a few more to get back down, and then the full descent back to the city will get us there just before dark. If we leave in the next hour, we can make some pretty good time," he said pointing at his wrist.

"He is right, there isn't a cloud in the sky. The more time we have in good weather, the better the chances we must at least make it back to here if the storm is really supposed to come," Marin confirmed tactically.

"Great, I'll set up the coffee, and you all prep the climb," Mr. Richards said pulling out a small burner and some instant coffee packs from his pack.

After the group had a meager breakfast and some warm coffee in them, they quickly cleaned up and prepared to make it to the mountain base.

"Still kind of dark to be hiking," Wesley said as he took his last sip of coffee. They stood in snow that was now shin deep.

"There are no lights on in the cabin, and it looks like Maggie is still in the crow's nest: how do we know she won't shoot us when we leave from behind this rock?" Marin asked, peaking around the protective barrier.

"Well, we have already fallen behind Greg and Maggie so we should do the best we can to keep up," he said.

"How do you figure? I also checked the crow's nest right as we woke up and Maggie hadn't left," Bixby said, confirming Marin's assessment.

"Because we got duped. There is no more fire coming from the chimney, which means they lit one, put a scarecrow in the crow's nest and snuck out the back door while we were digging," Mr. Richards pointed out what everyone else is missing.

"So, how do we know how far ahead of us they are?" Bixby questioned chucking her cup of coffee aside and throwing on her pack.

"I'm not sure, but that headlamp on the side of the cliff tells us they are halfway to the summit," he again wisely pointed out.

"You're the most observant crazy old man I have ever met," Wesley declared through the frosty air.

Knowing that Wesley's comment was the closest thing he had ever come to giving someone a complement, he simply replied, "Thanks... I think?" before pushing out into the blistering air towards the mountain base.

"Bixby?" Mr. Richards cried from the front of the line twenty minutes later.

"What is it?" she yelled back over the wind that was starting to pick up.

"What goes around the world but stays in the corner?" he inquired.

After a few steps of hiking Bixby bellowed back, "A stamp! Why?"

The blowing snow had kept Bixby from seeing the riddle Mr. Richards inquired about written into the rockface they were approaching. Looking down at her footing Bixby ran directly in the back of Marin who was now looking up at an angle of their next challenge. A safety rope appeared at the sound of Bixby's answer.

"I guess your answer is correct," Mr. Richards proclaimed as a rock fell to the side and two safety harnesses were exposed.

"Why didn't you ask me? I would have said 'stamp,'" Wesley mumbled as another rock fell away and he too grabbed a helmet and climbing gear from its place.

"Big baby," Marin said under her breath as she was getting tired of his griping.

Once clipped onto the safety rail, the climb itself was difficult, but not extremely insane. To Bixby it felt more like they were crawling up the mountain on their hands and knees versus scaling the side of a rock face, which made the task a little more manageable. Every few hundred feet there was a landing where the group could rest before they had to answer another riddle to receive another safety line to attach themselves to.

"How's everyone doing?" Mr. Richards turned and called down from up ahead.

"Fine," Wesley replied followed by, "Okay," from Marin and then Bixby shouted, "LOOK OUT!" from the rear as she looked up at her teammates.

Returning their gaze to the cliffs above them a pile of snow barreled down the face towards them.

"LOCK YOUR HARNESS BREAK ON, PRESS YOUR BODIES AS CLOSE TO THE MOUNTAIN AS YOU POSSIBLY CAN, AND HOLD ON WITH ALL YOU HAVE!" Mr. Richards shouted as he was following his own instructions.

The snow and rock crushed down on the tandem team with the force of being pelted by sandbags. The weight of the powder punched each of them into the side of the cliffs repeatedly. Muffled grunts could be heard through the roar of the mini avalanche. It lasted only a few moments, but it was highly effective.

"Marin!" Bixby shouted as she pushed her way back through the snow and gasped for air.

"I'm here!" she cried back.

"You hurt?" Bixby asked as she could feel her shoulder pulsing with pain.

"I think I am good," Marin confirmed.

"Wesley! Mr. Richards!"

"Unfortunately, I am still here with you," Wesley said as he checked himself over for damage.

"Mr. Richards?" Bixby cried out not hearing a reply from him.

"Mr. Richards!" Marin followed up at the sound of a dull moan still under the cover of snow.

"I got you, Old Man!" screamed Wesley as he dashed up the small gap between them and began to dig. Marin was stuck in place as she realized her head had started to throb from either altitude sickness or a rock to the helmet. Either way, she was dizzy.

Upon assessment, Bixby could tell that her shoulder had popped out again during the avalanche. Not wanting to show weakness to the group, Bixby prepped for what was to come next. The pain was intense, but Bixby didn't make a peep as she grabbed an anchor and repeated the same pulling motion that Pippa did outside of the coffee shop last time her shoulder had to be reset.

"Let me get some more meds out of your pack for your head," Bixby said as she reached Marin. She had a slight cut on her forehead, and was noticeably trying to focus on Bixby, but was struggling.

"Help Mr. Richards... I'll be fine," she said, catching her breath. Bixby ignored her, pulled out the Ibuprofen, and gave Marin a few before putting a bandage over the wound. Bixby could now hear Wesley shouting.

"C'mon, Old Man, don't die on me! I need you!" he cried. Bixby turned and raced to cliff's edge where Wesley had dug him out from the snowbank.

"He isn't going to die!" Bixby yelled, punching Wesley in the arm as hard as she could for saying such an awful thing. She then started to tend to the gash on the side of Mr. Richards cheek. Wesley didn't dare retaliate while she was tending to him.

Bixby quickly packed the wound with snow to keep the swelling down as she pulled out some gauze from the med kit in her pack.

As Max Richards started to come around, he began to mumble, "C'mon kid, we can make it... Just keep going," he said.

"That's the spirit," Wesley said as he helped Bixby.

"Nothing we can do for the others," Mr. Richards groaned.

"Teammates until the end," Wesley replied not knowing what to make of his last statement and still grossed out about the blood.

"Dang it!" came a voice from a few yards away from the beaten foursome pinned to the side of the mountain.

"I thought for sure that avalanche would have at least knocked one of them off the side of the mountain," Maggie snickered as they slowly repelled down the rock face gawking at the wreckage.

Bixby instinctively grabbed a rock and with everything she had threw the softball sized geode at Daemon and Maggie hoping it would hit them both, but as she released the stone she grunted in pain. She had forgotten her shoulder was in no condition to be throwing anything. It successfully reached the two, but harmlessly passed between them.

Though her mind was screaming in pain, her mind reminded her to not show any weakness to her enemies.

"Offer still stands, Maggie: come on over here and show me how tough you are without a bow and arrow, or an avalanche," Bixby challenged.

"For now, watching you suffer is good enough for me, but I'm sure our day will come," Maggie replied.

Bixby knew she was right, there was nothing to gain by answering Bixby's call.

"I was hoping for a little more blood," Daemon said, sounding disappointed. "And Wesley, you look pitiful. Anyway, see you at the bottom!" Daemon said with a wave of his hand.

"I'm going to cut your ropes!" Wesley shouted as he jumped to his feet. Bixby quickly latched on to his jacket and pulled him back.

"We already have two people hurt: I can't carry everyone down this mountain," she said in his ear quietly.

"You need to worry more about how you're going to survive the storm that is coming, Wesley," Daemon smirked. "Let's go Maggie; looks like the weather is changing," he said as they quickly disappeared.

Wesley, for the first time in the games, gave a look of true disgust for his old ally. Bixby had never seen him filled with anger at anyone other than her or Marin. Maybe he was on their side after all. Either way it didn't matter because they had to get up the mountain with two crippled partners.

"Listen, you and I can go ahead and get the flags at the summit. These two can rest up and recover for a bit. We will be back here in less than an hour, and we can all return together," he suggested.

"Not going to happen, Wesley!" Marin shouted from below.

"Why not?" he inquired.

"Because the rules say we must complete the race as a team. If you get the flag without your teammate, you will be disqualified," Marin informed as she finished gathering herself together. "I can make it up the last few hundred yards, but you are going to have to carry him the rest of the way," Marin informed Wesley.

"We get both of you to the ridgeline of the summit and then Bixby and I cross the vein to get the flags ourselves. If both teams do the same thing, Cody can't disqualify us both," Wesley proposed.

Bixby looked back at Marin and Mr. Richards as they both nodded in agreement.

Wesley unlatched Mr. Richards harness break and draped the old man's arm over his shoulders. He linked their hitches together and said, "Let's do this," before letting out a grunt and pushing forward.

Bixby and Marin kept pace, astounded by Wesley's newfound determination.

Out of breath and completely gassed by the last one hundred yards, Wesley crumbled to the snow packed ground as they reached the landing before the summit. The competitors could see that on the very edge of the tip of the mountain stood a metal cross with two golden flags on either side of it, waving in the wind.

"Why a cross?" Wesley asked as he pushed up to make the last climb.

"It's for all those who have died trying to make it here," Mr. Richards said somberly. Everyone paused a moment to remember that the Snowenwood Rennen had claimed so many lives. That cross was for those racers who had not made it to this point. But for those in Cody's race, they needed to continue on.

"You two rest here for a moment while we go get our flags," Bixby directed Marin and Mr. Richards as she dropped her pack from her shoulders. In a gesture of kindness, Bixby shouldered Wesley, clipped together their harnesses and together made their way to the top.

"If I didn't despise you so much, this could be a pretty cool moment," Bixby said in a low enough tone that only Wesley could hear as they reached the cross, overlooking hundreds of miles of hand painted wonder by the Almighty Himself.

"I could push you off the mountain right now if I wanted to," he said in tone unlike any he had ever used with her: jokingly.

"We are clipped together, and who would you have to look down on?" Bixby replied.

"Touché Timmons," he said as the two stood taking in the view above the clouds for a moment together. They were standing at heaven's gates above the world. But as always in the Riddle, the moments of awe never lasted very long.

"This leg of level three hasn't been all that bad, huh?" Wesley asked harmlessly.

Bixby's mind raced over the past two years, while feelings of disgust for his very presence came flooding back. Her face soured, and her eyebrows furrowed. If he was going to do some stupid, like help her beat Greg, he needed to get a few things straight.

"What? What did I say?" he questioned as she started to walk away.

Bixby yanked on the cord that joined them together to get him to move back down the mountain pass. He held his ground and didn't move until she answered him. Bixby turned and met his confused eyes.

"I have been burned, bludgeoned, left for dead, threatened with my life multiple times, dislocated my shoulder twice in this level alone, my family is missing, my house was gutted, I've been betrayed, my friend was beaten to a bloody pulp, I have had an avalanche dropped on me, and you have the nerve to say this hasn't been so bad!"

"I'm sorry, Bixby!" Wesley said, attempting to offer an olive branch of peace.

"Sorry? Sorry... that boat sailed a long time ago Wesley! The only reason you are sorry is because it didn't happen to you. You will turn on us the first chance you have if it means being in Daemon's shadow again," Bixby scolded into the wind that kept their conversation between the two of them.

"You really don't understand, do you?" Wesley said in a broken tone.

"Understand what? What could you possibly say to make me understand why you were a part of making everyone around me suffer?" Bixby shouted as she started to turn and walk away, again.

"You're doing it for the same reason I am..." he said boldly.

Bixby stopped but didn't turn around. She was giving Wesley only a moment to explain himself.

"At first, I wanted the one hundred million dollars because me and my family would no longer have to work for the tyrant Daemon Dragonthorp..."

Bixby turned her head to listen more closely but didn't give him the satisfaction of showing interest by turning completely around.

"My dad works seventy to eighty-hour work weeks, my sister and I spend every waking moment in our launch rooms pushing up our scores so that we can get the best jobs, and we never see each other as a family. With that kind of money, we didn't need Dragonthorp Inc. anymore, but then Cody announced each of our prizes and it changed everything."

"You need to make sense quickly Wesley, because I am losing interest," Bixby interjected, trying to speed things up.

"If I were to win the two percent share in Dragonthorp Inc., we would be a controlling partner in the company. Cody has fifty-one percent of the shares in the company, and Daemon has forty-nine. Their dad set the company up that way as a failsafe to keep Daemon from taking the business in a direction that would be harmful to Cody's inventions and other people. Their dad, Whitaker Dragonthorp, knew Cody would only do what was best for the company so he made him the final decision maker on all matters of business."

Bixby interjected, "By offering two of his shares to you, Daemon and Cody would own the exact, non-majority share in the company. You would have a third and deciding vote in all decision making."

"My family would no longer be a servant to Dragonthorp Inc., we would practically run that place. That would be worth way more than a hundred million dollars. But if Daemon wins…"

"…if Daemon wins, all of Holo is essentially his," Bixby concluded as she stood like a statue; cold from the bitter wind of nearly fifteen-thousand-foot picturesque summit, but also because she now had a picture the real stakes for which they were competing.

"Everyone in your beloved Snagleyville and on Holo-Basic would be crushed under Daemon. He would make the whole platform pay-to-play," Wesley said.

"You'd crush us to," Bixby replied.

"A day ago, you would be right. But after what Daemon did today and what you are doing to help me, I'm not so sure I would side with Daemon ever again," Wesley replied.

Wesley had just proven himself useful and maybe even an ally, but she couldn't let him know that just yet. Bixby had an epiphany on how to get information from Wesley, but to get it she needed to stop yelling and start listening. That might just be more difficult than everything she had already faced in level three, but if she was going to get him to try and help her eliminate Greg, she had to hope he was telling the truth.

"We have to go… now!" Mr. Richards cried out through the crisp air as he propped himself up on his knees.

"What do you mean?" Marin asked as Wesley and Bixby rushed back to his side.

Mr. Richards took off his glove again and licked his finger, "The wind is gone… that's very bad," he said as he wrestled to his feet.

He was right; moments earlier the wind was whipping up and over the crest. Almost instantaneously the wind had stopped completely.

"Repelling ropes appeared at the cliffs edge after you and Wesley claimed your flags," Marin informed. "Mr. Richards and I are already hooked in."

"How do you all know so much about this?" Wesley inquired.

"A long story for another day," Bixby replied as she helped him put on his harness just like Harvey's high ropes training course taught her.

"Be safe, but please move as quick as you can. This storm is going to start with brutal wind, and then snow like you have never seen before. Go!" Mr. Richards shouted as he started peddling down the mountain.

CHAPTER TWENTY-TWO
FULL SEND

There were a few slips and bumps on the way down, but with the impending doom of a mountaintop blizzard descending upon them, even Wesley had no time for complaints.

The climb to the top of the mountain had taken almost five hours, but the repel down the side took a little over one.

Mr. Richards took his usual lead as he trudged through the packed snow. The previous wind had erased the trail that led back to the cabin, so Bixby was assuming he was giving a guesstimation as to which direction they were going.

"What if Maggie and Daemon are held up in the cabin again to wait out the storm? A snow cave isn't going to save us, and we don't have enough food to last us very long up here?" Marin said, making their way through a small canyon.

"Nobody is staying on this mountain top tonight," Mr. Richards informed from the front of the line.

"Hey, Old Man, if this storm is as bad as they say it was, we may have to fight our way into that cabin to stay safe," Wesley interceded, trying to show that he was leaning more on the Timmons Nation side than the Dragonthorp Inc. side.

"There are two very good reasons why nobody is staying in that cabin tonight," Mr. Richards proclaimed has he kept marching.

"Care to share?" Marin asked as she was desperately trying to figure out his strategy.

"First of all, the storm that hit the mountain during the second Snowenwood Rennen dumped nearly ten feet of snow in a matter of hours. The roof on the cabin could be made of steel, but it wouldn't support the weight of that much snow—we would be crushed during the roof's cave-in," he said as they made their way around a boulder that would lead to the semi level rock field that lead down to the cabin.

"And the second reason?" Wesley asked, annoyed at Mr. Richards' suspenseful pauses.

"The second reason is because Daemon and Maggie made sure nobody was going to stay in that cabin tonight," he proclaimed.

"You must have been bashed harder than we thought," Wesley responded to the peculiar response.

Rounding the boulder, the cabin was in full view now... Mr. Richards was making much more sense than the teens gave him credit for up until then.

"Because they set it on fire," Bixby said, finishing Mr. Richards reasoning. "If we hurry, we may be able to salvage something that can help us," she shouted as they broke into a slight jog towards the inferno that was, up until an hour ago, the cabin.

Bixby and Wesley reached the blaze first. It was starting to smolder now. Bixby couldn't help but be reminded of the fire at Shadow Deep, and how the flames moved extremely fast and nearly leveling the castle in such a short time.

"Great!" Wesley screamed in frustration as he ripped his climbing helmet off and slammed it on the frozen tundra. "He's stamped our ticket to the morgue!" Wesley shouted some more.

"Grab what you can salvage!" Mr. Richards said as he reached the cabin third. "Anything large and metallic."

Marin finally reached the group as she immediately grabbed her knees and head with opposing hands.

"Marin, are you ok?" Bixby asked as she grabbed her arm to support her.

"All this running and climbing is making my head hurt more," she mumbled as she collapsed to the ground, and threw up.

"Mr. Richards!" Bixby cried over to the boys who were pulling metal sheets of the roof from the blaze, cautious not to burn themselves.

Realizing Marin was in serious trouble, and that her altitude sickness was advancing to a more dangerous stage, he grabbed Wesley's arm and two sheets of metal, proclaiming, "This will have to do!"

Wesley followed suit over to the girls huddled on the ground.

"You seem to know a lot about mountains. How are we getting her off this one?" Bixby asked. "She can't keep going and we need to move."

Wesley had already bent a curve on one end of a piece of metal and was working on a second sheet.

"When was the last time you girls have been sledding?" Mr. Richards asked with a smile. Bixby had no idea what the crazy genius was up too, but mountain rescue was not her specialty. He, however, seemed really comfortable up here, and Bixby was now becoming more comfortable with letting those who knew more than her lead, even if she was the team captain.

Wesley finished creating metal toboggans as Mr. Richards and Bixby helped load Marin onto one of the metal sleds. Using the climbing axe and some ripcord from the climbing backpacks Wesley and Bixby completed the third metal children's toy while Mr. Richards tended to Marin.

"We don't have several hours to climb down the bridge. Sleds are a little more dangerous, but it will cut a few hours of hiking down to a few minutes of very gnarly butt skiing. Let's get them over to the ledge next to the bridge," Mr. Richards instructed as he grabbed one of the empty sleds and began pulling.

"Did he just say, 'butt skiing?'" Wesley said. exasperated.

"Yep..." Bixby replied, just as astonished, grabbing the second piece of sheet metal.

"There is only three though," Bixby said.

"I will accompany Marin down the hill while you two go solo," Mr. Richards replied, grabbing one of the empty sleds.

"You forgot your sledding partner," Wesley shouted towards the crazy old man already answering his own question before he finished asking it.

"I'm sure a strapping young fellow like you can help a weak old man such as myself!" Mr. Richards called back as Bixby fell in line.

"Right... heavy lifting always goes to the super handsome strong guy," he grumbled, grabbing the makeshift sled's cord.

At the bridge's edge Mr. Richards had jammed his tobogganing the snow like a surfboard in sand when Wesley arrived with Marin.

"I will take Marin down with me and you follow me like a train. Count to ten after I push off and try and stay in my tracks. Whatever you do don't fall off the cliff," he said as he plopped down behind Marin on their sled, clipped himself to Marin's coat, and steadied himself on the edge.

"This isn't the way we came up! How do you know this path will lead back to where we started?" Wesley asked as thick snowflakes began to fall.

"Before all these fancy bridges and climbing gear, this was the pass to get to the top... I read that somewhere," Mr. Richards informed as he gave a hearty push over the edge.

"We are going to die, aren't we?" Wesley asked as he steadied his sled on the ledge and started to count to ten.

"I'm not lucky enough to have you die, but I *am* praying for a few broken bones," Bixby replied as she gave him a push over the brink with her boot.

Bixby had ten seconds of alone time to watch the majesty that was Matterhorn Mountain in the Swiss Alps as it began to fill with heavy water crystals. If it weren't for the fact that they were teaming together in the trillions to assassinate her, she would be more appreciative of their wonder.

"Surfs up," Bixby yelled as her battle cry down the mountain.

Beside the fact that there were absolutely no guardrails to keep her from flying off the edge to a sudden stop at the bottom, Bixby started to giggle as she bumbled down the rocky slope. A few times she was going fast enough to catch some serious airtime. If it wasn't for the sharp jolt to her spinal cord caused by metal on stone landing, Bixby would have liked to run into a few more aerials. By the looks of the tracks, Wesley was handling the mountain fairly well, but Bixby could tell that more than a few times Mr. Richards and Marin came dangerously close to the dead man's edge. The clouds had now surpassed the sun, and the snow was so thick it was like a curtain of fog and shadow had fallen on them in a matter of minutes. Bixby was having trouble seeing ahead of her. She knew she had to be approaching the bottom but how would she know what dangers lay ahead? Her next problem was the grade of the hill had become significantly steeper which meant there was no slowing down.

Through the wind and the snow pelting Bixby in the face now, she went to put her hands down in an effort to control her speed. From below her she could hear an exclamation, "DO NOT SLOW DOWN! GET AS MUCH SPEED AS YOU CAN!"

It was Mr. Richards, who was approximately twenty seconds ahead of her, yelling at the top of his lungs. Bixby was uncomfortable with how fast she was going, but the deep well that was Mr. Richards had not failed them yet. Bixby gritted her teeth, clinched the ropes as hard as she could and ducked her head behind the curve at the front of the sled; she was blindly out of control.

Bixby had wished for another aerial, and it was presently granted in a big way. Speeding down the slope and into a bit of a clearing, Bixby saw exactly why she needed to pick up speed. There was no turning back now as she could make out Wesley and Marin sprawled out on the snow, and Mr. Richards screaming for her to 'go for it.' Bixby recalled the first time the four of them reached the rope bridge on the way up the mountain. There was a deep crevasse below her the first fifteen feet or so. She was now barreling towards that void on a makeshift sled unable to stop even if she wanted to.

She had felt this feeling of suspended animation before in Level One when she sat in a slingshot that propelled her across a fracture in the in the hollowed-out mountain pass. She landed on a gooey bed of glow worms. This landing was nowhere near as soft as back then. Bixby hit the icepack with a crushing force that knocked the wind out of her as she glided another thirty feet across the densely compressed snow.

"Everyone okay?" Mr. Richards asked as he limped around and checked on everyone.

"You forgot to mention the gigantic hole at the end!" shouted Wesley as he gawked at the crack in his climbing helmet.

"You would have chickened out if I added that detail," he said, hobbling over to Bixby.

"I think you win for 'Furthest Jump,'" he joked as he did a once over of her. Everything seemed to still function even though it felt like she had been punched in the whole body by a dump truck.

"Give me a moment," Bixby stammered, trying to collect herself.

"You only get a minute while I load Marin on my Banshee," he said as he finished his check.

"Your leg," Bixby said noticing his limp.

"Not as bad as it could have been. Next time I won't try to catch Marin out of the air: lesson learned," he jeered as he disappeared through the snow.

The sound of a Banshee firing up could be heard over the roar of the wind. Bixby knew it was time to move and started making her way towards the headlight.

"Looks like they didn't find our toys," Wesley said, excited that the snow mobiles were still in play. He turned over the engine and fell in line behind Mr. Richards who was still helping Marin along. Bixby quickly followed.

She rushed to stay close enough to see Wesley's taillight which meant she nearly rear ended him on a few occasions when he slowed. Though the ride back to the lift was a little slower than before, the snow mobiles made up for some of the deficit they were in behind Greg and Maggie.

Wesley's Banshee flashed its brake lights. Bixby knew that it meant that they were stopping. Pulling alongside the other two machines they cut their engines so that they could hear each other. It was difficult as the moaning of the cable cars struggling to stay on the line bellowed through the gusty darkness.

"They took the cable cars!" Bixby yelled.

"How do you know?" Wesley inquired.

"I see faint tracks in the snow going down the tunnel, but no tracks down the hill. And one of the three cable cars are missing," she said, reciting the obvious.

"I can't tell how far ahead of us they are, but if there are tracks in this storm, it isn't very far," Mr. Richards replied and then placed his scarf back over his face. Bixby's looked at him and her mind unintentionally started doing puzzle solving of a puzzle she didn't know she needed to solve, Bixby's mind flashed back to the picture from the CEO's office, but before she could get started, Wesley shouted, "There is no way you will get me on those cable cars. This wind would knock it from its rails with no problem."

"I concur," the old man hollered back.

"The ski slopes!" Bixby pointed. "On our way up there were tons of ski slopes down to the bottom! We may not come out at where the cable cars started, but I am sure we can find our way back to the tent once we get down!"

"Do you know how to follow the skiing flags?" Mr. Richards inquired.

"No clue! There were no simulations on going down ski slopes!" she shouted back.

"There was, but I may not have uploaded those for you," Mr. Richards replied.

Bixby shot him a glance. She could tell that he had made a Freudian slip, but before she could call him out on it, Wesley shouted over them both.

"I do!" Wesley interjected.

"Then you lead my boy!" Mr. Richards directed, trying to avoid the conversation.

Before Bixby could complain about letting Wesley be the leader, her fellow competitor stomped his throttle and tore off into the storm.

Wesley was pushing the pace harder than Bixby was comfortable with, but to keep from getting lost she held hard on the throttle. The snow was now stinging her face like razor sharp blades. There was nothing in their packs to save them from the torment of the piercing blizzard's teeth. The end was near, but she had no clue how she was going to finish the race. Normally, she was aware of where everyone was coming down to the finish line. This time she was aiding an enemy; allowing him to take the lead ahead of her, and the other one was somewhere in the shadows of the storm.

The lights of the city were faint as the three Banshees cruised over the final ridge and down a beginner's level slope.

Seeing the village below Wesley turned off his headlight and opened up his throttle all the way as his rig screamed ahead of the pack. The brief hesitation that both Bixby and Mr. Richards had in chasing him was enough to let Wesley slip into the storm. At first Bixby wanted to chase after him but she looked over and Mr. Richards was still right there. Even if Wesley did find the tent first, he couldn't finish without his teammate. That insurance policy made Bixby's heart settle down as they continued to navigate the harsh weather. As the two snow mobiles reached the main lodge, they slowed to a stop in order to get their bearings.

"The lift is over that way!" Mr. Richards pointed up the vacant street.

"Are you sure?" Bixby asked as her mind whirled trying to get situated.

"Yes, because we crossed in front of the bagel shop on our way down to the cable cars," he reminded her.

"Right, so we go down that street two blocks, then left and it should be the last house at the end of the cul-de-sac," Bixby recalled.

"Right," he replied as he signaled for her to go before him.

"We do it together!" Bixby shouted over the wind. "Don't stop for Wesley. Drive that machine right up the stairs and into the front door!"

Mr. Richards nodded, knowing the instructions.

Bixby wound up the engine and punched the gas as her machine screamed down the narrow streets. The snow was deep, and the streetlights didn't help the masking blindness that the gusts were causing. Bixby followed her directions and hit every mark as her machine sprinted towards the front door.

Twenty yards from the door, Bixby heard the crash through the roar of the storm. She yanked on her brakes and slid her Banshee to a halt. Wesley was pushing himself up from the pavement as Mr. Richards and Marin lay limp on the ground. From the wreckage it looked as if Wesley had driven his snow mobile right into the tail end of Mr. Richard's Banshee. Jumping from her machine, she raced over and tried to help Marin first, but from the confines of the doorway next to her, a dark figured issued a boot-to-face maneuver that left Bixby flat on her back with a bloody nose.

"Now, now Maggie! We don't want her unconscious when she watches the four of us eliminate her from the Riddle, now do we?" Daemon barked as he made his way over to Mr. Richards. Through the double vision she had, Bixby could see that he had shed the 'Greg' avatar and the familiar face of Daemon Dragonthorp was now apparent to everyone.

No weakness, Bixby thought.

"Is that all you got, Maggie? Cheap shots?" Bixby shouted over the wind, pinching her nose while still on her hands and knees. Maggie just smiled before she kicked Bixby full force in the gut, ripping the air out of Bixby's lungs and maybe even breaking a rib.

"That oughta shut you up," Maggie replied.

"Look at this, the original Level One Riddle gang is all here!" Daemon jested. "Except this one addition," he chuckled as he snapped his fingers over the back of Mr. Richards head. Up until now Daemon knew nothing about who ended up launching in with Wesley.

"Let's see who our friend Wesley got to launch in with him," Daemon said, nudging Mr. Richards in the ribs with his foot. When he didn't budge, Daemon pushed him over with his boot. "Now *there* is a surprise! Hello, old friend," he said with a twist of his head. Mr. Richards was a loyal long-time employee of Dragonthorp Inc., and Bixby could tell Daemon was surprised he was *in* the level with Wesley since abandoning his position with Dragonthorp Inc. "Tsk, tsk, tsk. Wakey, wakey, good Mr. Richards. We have to get you and your partner, Wesley, safely to the tent," he continued.

By now Marin was crawling her way to the front door even though it was a long distance off.

Knowing Bixby was not going anywhere, Maggie easily caught up to Marin and placed her foot heavily down on the leg she had once destroyed. Marin's pain was familiar as Maggie spoke, "Didn't get enough of me last time I see."

The interchange caught Daemon's ear.

"Marin! You don't think I would let you and Bixby beat me and my good friend Wesley, do you? Maggie, see to it that Mr. Richards makes it to the exit before our friends here... because if you were to try and race us through that door you will have to explain to poor Pippa how her grandpa slipped and fell on Maggie's climbing axe," Daemon shouted over the wind.

Maggie returned to Daemon's side, reached down, and grabbed Mr. Richards around his neck, firmly pressing the sharp tip of the ice axe up against his back. "Walk, Grandpa!" she instructed.

Bixby's face was horrified as her vision returned to normal, but certain that Maggie would oblige his command. Bixby's body went as numb as it did in the ice-cold waters the day she had first given up. She sat in the snow paralyzed as her face was covered in hopelessness.

"Let's go, Wesley!" Daemon shouted at the battered boy, yanking him up by the collar.

"I'm sorry, Bixby. I had to do it for my family… it was the only way," he said sincerely as he stumbled while being pulled by the neck towards the cabin.

Bixby watched the four of them make their way to the cabin door while she shuffled to Marin's side.

Bixby put her arm under Marin to pull her from the snowbank before turning to see the foursome arrive at the deck of the Swiss bungalow.

"I'm still in awe that they were too dumb to fall for our little hoax," Daemon jabbed, standing at the ingress of the tent talking to Maggie.

"And they were stupid enough to let Wesley get on a Banshee by himself," Maggie chuckled as they backed themselves to the double wide cabin doors.

"And by the way, Bixby, you should be receiving your evection notice from Pinnacle Manor here shortly," Daemon finished with a laugh as he drank in the anguish that was now painted freshly on Bixby's face. Then he and Maggie simultaneously pulled the tattered old and young man through the tent door after themselves.

Bixby wasn't mad at Wesley for picking his family's wellbeing over her. Knowing Hemsley did the same thing had made her number than anything to other people's selfish choices.

She was also grateful for the choices of the people who were now fully on her side. Bixby had been waiting for this moment for a long time.

"Now!" Bixby shouted as Marin launched up with a hidden burst of energy that quickly overcame her as she hobbled up the stairs.

"After you," Marin said as she pushed Bixby through the threshold first.

Once inside the tent, the six contestants quickly gazed around at each other only a moment before Bixby caught Max Richard's eyes beaming.

"I knew you two had figured it out," the old Dragonthorp Inc. riddle writer moaned through the wreckage of his beat-up body.

Confused at their wide faced grin, Daemon started to realize it was *him* who had been duped but couldn't figure out how. "Wait! No!" he lamented.

"It's too bad that *you* two were too dumb to fall for *his* little hoax," Bixby replied with confidence.

"Mr. Richards stole my launch room before I could go in with Bixby," Marin taunted. "I had to launch in as the guest."

"Hold on, if the old man was Bixby's teammate and Marin came in the door last..." Wesley said in response to her boast.

"I had to do it for my family, Wesley," Bixby responded to him.

"On the plus side, you get to safely unlaunch," Marin added to the conversations with Wesley, knowing she had helped one of the people she despised the most. But she also knew it was the right thing to do.

Daemon's face went from joy to the same look of affliction that was previously on Bixby's face.

"Are you afraid of monsters, Daemon?" Bixby asked coldly.

The furious eyes of the true villain of Cody's Riddle met gazes with the leviathan that was roaring from inside of Bixby. She had exposed his secret and drawn the battle lines in doing so.

As the level began to unlaunch their partners first, Daemon gave Bixby one final riddle, "Your Grandpa thought he was just as brave."

Chapter Twenty-Three
The Memories and a Map

The door to Bixby's launch room nearly came unhinged as she exited. The team had been dispersed among the launch rooms to help anyone in need of medical attention.

"Move!" she shouted as she hip-checked everyone out of her path on her approach to Mr. Richard's Launch Room. Arthur stood at the door finishing his shutdown sequence. Bixby pulled the Holo-Writer from the wall, yanked the latch, entered the room, and locked the hatch closed behind her.

"What did he mean?" Bixby insisted as the energy continued to surge in her veins.

"I'm not sure," Mr. Richards said as he groaned to a stand.

"Please, don't lie to me! What did he mean!" Bixby shouted.

"I don't know what he meant by that!"

"Then how do you explain this!" Bixby shouted, pulling up the livestream footage from inside the Snowenwood Industries CEO office on the Holo-Writer. She knew the exact moment she flashed the picture around hoping the live stream would capture her with it so that she could come back to it once she unlaunched.

The old man stood there with tears in his eyes at the sight of the memory. He paused for a long time, gaining his composure.

"You were never supposed to see that picture, Bixby."

"And now I have, so you need to explain why you're in the picture, how you knew which training simulations to load that would help me get ready for the Rennen, and how you showed up in the Rennen knowing how to climb the mountain. Start talking!" Bixby shouted in anger now.

Another long pause moved through the room.

"I'm not even sure how Cody found a copy of it."

"Let's begin with who is the last person in this picture? I recognized you when you pulled your mask up over your mouth on the mountain and I would recognize my grandpa's eyes anywhere. Who is he?" Bixby asked sternly, pointing to the third gentleman.

She could tell that he was all out of options other than to answer.

"Whitaker Dragonthorp," he replied under his breath confirming Bixby's suspicions.

"Cody said if I win everything that he would tell me the last piece I need to know about my grandfather. You're a riddle maker, what pieces do I already have?" Bixby asked, knowing he had at least some of the answers she needed. He sat back down, laid his head gently against the wall, closed his eyes, and she could see he had vanished inside his head to recall the memories.

"I met your grandfather at a masquerade dinner party thrown by random invite. It was an amazing Phantom Ball. My wife and I had no status in the community so we figured it was a joke, but we went anyway because it would be fun," he began.

"Like Level Two?" Bixby asked, trying to connect the dots.

Mr. Richards nodded as he continued, "Within moments of arriving to the party, a man bumped into me. I spilled my drink all down the front of my only white shirt. I was both certain that it was an accident, but I was also mortified. The man quickly ushered me to one of the upper rooms where he rifled through the closet to find me a new shirt," Max said before chuckling. "I insisted I would just go home for the night, but he would not have no for an answer. Upon finding not only a shirt, but an entire suit that fit me, he left me to change out of my dirty clothes. I had never seen a suit as fantastic as the one he had given me. Once back at the party he took me and my wife from guest to guest introducing me. I felt like royalty."

"Who was the man?" Bixby asked, before Mr. Richards gave out another chuckle.

"Your grandpa was not only *the* most intelligent man I had ever met, but he also had amazing street smarts. He was a sponge and people were drawn to him like a magnet." Mr. Richards began to tell the story some more. "It wasn't until later that he revealed to me that he had no idea at the time whose suit it was he gave to me that night, only that it was my size and that I was in need of it."

"That sounds like grandpa," Bixby interjected.

"Either way, he moved through the party like he knew everyone, and I believed he did. He even found time to play with the children, though it was looked down upon. But it was when he paid a kid ten bucks to build him a fish tank that I was hooked on knowing deeply who this man was and why he chose me to follow him about the party."

"It was Grandpa who paid Cody ten bucks for the fish tank?" Bixby inquired. She recalled Tipton's endless knowledge of Cody Dragonthorp.

Mr. Richards nodded and said, "Later your grandfather had Cody convert the old water clock fish tank into the digital one you have sitting on your nightstand currently."

Bixby wanted to race out of the room with that knowledge and hug her new prized possession, but she needed the whole story first.

"Is that piece one?" Bixby asked.

"I believe so," he replied before a pause and then he continued.

"Those acts of kindness to the strange kid were noticed by Cody's father. They began regular conversations from that day forward, and your grandfather invited me along on every encounter because they liked the fact that I was into puzzles, riddles, and brain teasers. Whit had endless financial resources and connections, and your grandfather... your grandfather was the charm. He was the one with all the crazy ideas," Mr. Richards boasted.

"Then explain the picture," she insisted.

Max Richards shirked at her presenting it to him again.

"Bixby, I could write a book series about the adventures your grandfather took Whit and I on. He had a new wild idea every month, but that picture was the last time the three of us were really good friends. The idea for Holo was only supposed to be a silly video game where you launched in, solved some fun riddles, do some obstacles, and beat some of your friends to the end."

"Like in Level One," Bixby interjected.

"Not *like* Level One, it *was* Level One. Cody must have found our plans and actually completed the vision the three of us started so many years ago."

"So, Level One was your game, Level Two was how you all met."

"Precisely," Mr. Richards replied.

"But then why the Rennen for Level Three?" Bixby asked.

Before he could move on, Bixby's mind raced back to the prize Cody had promised. *I should at least know three of the four pieces to the puzzle about my grandfather*, she thought.

Mr. Richards continued, "Your Grandpa had the itch to create a digital Geo Race for our second virtual world. None of us had ever done a Geo Race before so how were we going to create a virtual one? Your Grandpa picked the biggest and hairiest one he could find so that we could make it even better virtually."

"The Snowenwood Rennen," Bixby said, making the connection.

"We didn't care about winning the race, we simply wanted to experience it. So, your grandfather convinced Snowenwood that we were potential sponsors for the race and wanted to watch what was happening up close. Adam Snowenwood fell over himself to give us access to the course in hopes that

Whitaker Dragonthorp would introduce him to people who could fund the future races.”

“If you knew what Cody was trying to tell me, why didn’t you say something?” Bixby asked sternly, knowing that Mr. Richards had kept the truth from her for some reason.

“Bixby, when you found your way into Level One, I thought it was cute that Cody had brought your grandfather’s game to life. I thought it even more honorable that he was telling our story through Level Two. Frankly, both would have been more fun if everyone in the riddles were not trying to kill each other,” he said, shaking his head.

He did have a point.

“It wasn’t until you said Snowenwood Rennen that I freaked out. Nobody was supposed to know about our connection with the Rennen.”

“But that doesn’t explain why you didn’t say anything,” Bixby replied.

“First, you need to know that the three of us agreed to tell nobody after what happened to the climbers, Bixby. If I tell you the real truth about what happened during the original Snowenwood Rennen in 1963, you may understand my hesitancy to divulge what I know,” Mr. Richards said sadly.

“You were on the mountain when the storm hit?” Bixby asked.

“All three of us were, Bixby,” Mr. Richards replied.

“This picture was from the *real* Snowenwood Rennen?” she inquired, adding to her long list of questions.

“I called your grandfather ‘Kid’ even though he was older than me.” Mr. Richards chuckled again.

"That's why you didn't make sense after you got hit in the head. You thought you were back on the mountain with my grandfather," Bixby said, making the connection.

"I didn't think anyone had caught that in my confused state."

"It's also why you knew so much about the mountain and how to climb it?"

Mr. Richards only nodded his head in acknowledgment. "When the storm hit, Whitaker wanted to keep going, but your grandfather insisted we go back."

"Grandpa was the one who saved everyone who made it off the mountain?" Bixby asked.

"The snow let out not one, but two avalanches before a rock smacked Whit in the head and knocked him out cold. Each wave of ice swept climber after climber away. Your Grandfather used the limp body slung over his shoulder to convince several other people to turn back until after the storm, but they all hid behind their rocks thinking they were protected.

"They froze to death on the side of that mountain," Bixby said with a chill in her voice and up her spine.

"Yes. The ones who were not buried by the second larger avalanche were stuck on the mountain only to freeze," Mr. Richard said.

"But that doesn't explain why you kept it a secret. It wasn't your fault," Bixby replied still missing one vital piece of information.

"The Snowenwood Rennen changed your grandfather. He spent the rest of his life finding people who wanted to give back to the world around them, and swore them into a secret society of do-gooders," Mr. Richards said with a smile as he looked off into the distance as if to recall something exciting.

"You've been at Pinnacle for a long time, why didn't you tell me any of this?" Bixby asked again. He had not yet answered to her satisfaction.

"They call it a *secret* society for a reason," he replied.

"Okay, you survived together, then started a *secret* society, then why did you fall apart?" Bixby asked for more detail.

His demeaner was completely deflated.

"Whit wasn't invited to join the society," Mr. Richards replied.

"Why not?" Bixby asked, shocked. She couldn't imagine Grandpa excluding anyone.

"From the beginning knew I was only there to keep record of our adventures. I loved being part of it all and was the first to sign up to help do good, but Whit and your grandfather were true best friends. They competed in everything. When we came back, Whit threw himself into bring Holo fully online. His only goal was to make it as realistic as possible and make a gazillion dollars- but he didn't see the destruction firsthand as your grandfather and I did. So, he wanted nothing to do with giving any of the money away. He scolded your grandfather for even thinking about donating money to people ahead of creating a global empire."

"So, Grandpa started the secret society behind Whit's back?" Bixby asked, hoping there was a better answer.

"Secrets are a cancer amongst friends," he replied confirming her hunch.

Bixby paused at such great wisdom.

"Your grandfather spent every waking moment and every dime he had on Holo or his secret society. In fact, it was your grandfather who in the chaos of the fallout of the last Rennen who convinced Adam Snowenwood to give him the ledger of participants who lost their lives. Your grandfather promised to bring comfort to all the families affected by the Rennen," Mr. Richards said with a smile.

"Did he?" Bixby asked.

"Adam and your grandfather both did," he said with a chuckle. "That felt good to finally say out loud," he added.

"What do you mean? Adam Snowenwood was tried for his crimes," Bixby asked.

"He was tried for his crimes, but a secret society needed a pretty big secret to keep being a good society," Mr. Richards replied.

"Grandpa broke him out!" she shouted in disbelief.

"He may have had a hand in helping him and that ledger disappear," Mr. Richards replied with a smile.

"My head is spinning. You do realize how crazy this all sounds? You all invented Holo, survived an international catastrophe, broke Adam Snowenwood out of jail, started a secret society to do good behind the back of Whitaker Dragonthorp, and somehow, we are all chasing after answers to some sort of riddle two generations later," Bixby said, exasperated at the insanity of it all.

"None of this would be a problem if it were not for the rumored treasure map your grandpa supposedly left before he died," Mr. Richards replied before slapping his hand over his mouth as if he had just let out the biggest secret in the world.

"WHAT!" Bixby cried out.

"Well, I guess you should know about that too," he replied, disappointed in himself.

"Yes! Yes, I should!" she replied.

"Your grandpa agreed to hand leadership over to Whit's boys who were coming of age and very savvy in their respective fields as long as your dad was able to freely work on his crazy inventions in the development department."

"That is certainly my dad," Bixby replied as the pain of missing him came back.

"Whit poured into the business side of Holo with Daemon, and your grandfather worked with Cody on the development side," he said.

"Grandpa is why Cody made Holo free for people who didn't have money to afford the fancy stuff," Bixby replied with another ping of pride to be a Timmons.

"The problem with being so close to Cody is that Cody may have figured out about the society and accidently told his brother about it, which made its way back to Whit," Mr. Richard said.

"So, what happened?" Bixby asked.

"Whitaker Dragonthorp went after your grandfather with all the rage and money he had," he answered.

"What does that mean?" Bixby asked.

"It means that one day Whitaker Dragonthorp chased after your grandfather, and neither of them came back," Mr. Richards answered back. "The last thing that anyone heard from either of them was a Holo message to everyone in the secret society, Adam Snowenwood, Cody, and Daemon Dragonthorp that had one simple sentence: 'Three clues left beind: X marks the Spot,' with the 'X' and the 'S' in Spot capitalized."

"What do you think that means?" Bixby continued her borage of questions. She was certain that Spot was in reference to her nickname, and she had an X intentionally in her name as a reference to a pirate's famous method of burying treasure.

"Nobody knows, All I know is that Cody is certainly going to great lengths to tell everyone something," Mr. Richards replied.

"Whatever it is, I'm sorry to announce that *Daemon* has gone to great length to make sure *you* never find out," Harvey said from behind Bixby. He had ghosted himself into the launch room.

Bixby turned sharply and asked, "What do you mean?"

"Daemon has shut down Holo."

Bixby's face scrunched in confusion.

"No Holo, no Level Four," Mr. Richards said.

"No Level Four, no answers," Harvey replied.

Knowing that Grandpa made her an expert at treasure hunting, she replied, "I wouldn't be so sure of that."

Acknowledgements

It is with a humble heart and great reverence that I say thank you to the teachers who have put their trust in me to be part of the classroom. It could have been the read aloud you did with your students, classroom visits, writing clubs, career days, book fairs, or anything in between. It is you that I stand up and clap with great enthusiasm. You are the heroes!

I would also like to thank the small bookstores that have taken Bixby on as part of their regular display of authors. It is so hard to be seen as a debut series, but you believe in us, and I love each of your support!

The Waild Family, Mrs. Witmer, Mrs. Roberts, Mrs. Hirneisen, Mr. Hoffman, Wee Scott Book Store, Waynesboro School District, Greencastle School District and many more! Thank You!

About the Author

Dwight D. Karkan is a man of puzzles, and he loves the challenge of a good riddle! Currently, his favorite puzzles and riddles are being a parent, husband, and youth pastor. Dwight knows we are all designed as a beautiful combination of awesomeness, uniqueness, passion, gifts, and talents, and the only way to get a little closer to discovering the answer of who we are is by engaging each other with love.

In 2019, Dwight's daughter Selah was diagnosed with Leukemia which has been their family's biggest puzzle yet! His hope for Bixby Timmons is not only to bring a light to students who want to do bigger things than they think they are capable, but also to help families who have been through a similar struggle. If you would like to know more about how Bixby is helping those in need, join our team on our Facebook Group "Bixby Timmons Series" or his website www.dwightkarkan.com.

ABOUT THE PUBLISHER

Tiny Fox Press LLC
11782 Little River Way
Parrish, FL 34219

www.tinyfoxpress.com